A Heart of Steel

part one

...when young love is
never to be forgotten...

by

Katherine Kobey

A Heart of Steel

part one

...when young love is never to be forgotten...

by

Katherine Kobey

Published by Cardinal Rules Press
ISBN-13: 978-1523869374
ISBN-10: 1523869372

Book cover design - Gina McCullough (www.GinaMDesign.com)
Author photograph - Brittany Sturdivant (www.lovebephotography.com)
Edited and formatted by Marley Gibson

Cardinal Rules
PRESS

Dedication

To Jack...
My Inspiration

Acknowledgments

My sincere appreciation for everyone's support throughout my writing journey...

To my dear friend, confidant, and partner in crime, Egla-Nora Richie. Her love, support, advice, and encouragement to pursue my dream of transforming my thoughts into words have been the inspiration for the trilogy of "A Heart of Steel." I'm thankful for our many hours spent on the road in search of the perfect setting and story. The fun we had imagining the characters, the situations they found themselves in, and the tears and emotions in pulling it all together. We plotted it together for the ultimate story. Thank you, Egla, my dear friend.

To my family, Celia, Michael, Evan, and Rachal, whom I love with all my heart, for their patience during the many times they endured my moments of struggles as I found my way in this new craft. Their cheers along the way have touched my heart. I love you all.

Thank you to my wonderful editor, Marley Gibson, of Cardinal Rules Press. Our finding each other was a case of serendipity stepping in and taking control. Everything about our journey; the fun and quirky comments, her ability to bring out the emotions in me, for her insights in helping me develop the characters along the way, for all the edits and revisions... all of which were great, by the way. For teaching me about "Ice Water Tea," and too many other things to mention. You are my great motivator.

Jossie A. Valles Vargus of the Village Coffee Shop in Valley, Alabama, who introduced Egla and me to their special little town.

To Jeanette Mason, who shared her many memories of growing up in Valley, in the 60s and 70s, the "Carrousel," and the "Maid of Cotton" pageant.

A very special thank you to Ron and Leuveda Garner for being such great hosts during my two months of writing in their precious "Twin Palms" cottage. Their hospitality and gracious nature warmed my heart at a time when I had no idea what I was doing. They welcomed me with opened arms and also into their circle of friends; Kathy and Tom Trocheck, Peter and Barbara Hand, and Jim and Patricia Wann. You are all wonderful souls.

To my early morning gym buddy, Deborah Baker, for introducing me to Tuxedo Road in Buckhead and the "The Machine" in Tuscaloosa Alabama.

To Mr. Clifford Moncus, for taking the time to share his insights on the history of the Chambers County Judicial Building in Lafayette, Alabama, and allowing me a tour of the old courtroom, which happened to be exactly the way I envisioned it to be in the book.

To Derek Drennen of Kirk-Drennan Law (www.kirkdrennanlaw.com), for his insights on the criminal and courtroom proceedings.

Chapter One

Shelby Porter pulled her Mercedes into the narrow parking spot. Coming to a complete stop, she reached for the gearshift, paused for a split second, and slowly put the car into park. She leaned forward with her hands folded and rested them lightly on the soft leather steering wheel.

She glanced across the quaint and picturesque view of the tiny Langdale Cemetery overlooking the banks of the Chattahoochee River.

Shelby found she had always been drawn to this peaceful resting place many times throughout her life and most notably at a very early age.

She breathed in deeply and let out a small sigh of relief. "I'm here," she whispered softly.

Seconds later, she leaned back against the seat and stretched her aching neck and shoulders. She rolled her head from side to side, working out the kinks from her long drive to get here.

Shelby sat quietly, bundled in her warm cashmere-lined, hooded trench coat. Staring across at the many headstones, she noticed the variety of markers, much like the people they represented—some small, some tall, some new, and many that were old and decrepit, withstanding years of weathering. They all stood comforted and protected beneath a canopy of moss-filled, knotty oak trees. The trees had survived majestically, unwavering for over a hundred years. Ironically, this graveyard was a place of peace and tranquility for many families from the Shawmut, Langdale, Fairfax, and Riverview communities, also known to the locals as the four villages, located in eastern Alabama.

The drive had given her the opportunity to remember the years she'd spent coping with her life from within a prison of emotions, trapped inside her quelled feelings of sadness, guilt, fear, and lost love. Yet, all of those things were now exposed and raw because of the arduous nightmare she'd lived through.

Restless and stiff, she breathed another sigh of relief and gently rubbed her tired and irritated eyes. "Just a couple minutes of rest," she said.

And then, her thoughts quickly turned to Jack.

It had been months since she had seen him. It was the day she raced out of the coffee shop on her way into protective seclusion. She recalled his confused state of emotions. There was no time to explain. Especially in light of all she had endured and had yet to overcome.

She'd lived through the turmoil of two men with conflicting emotions churning within her. Shelby could no longer deny her feelings for either man... Jack... and her husband.

Her loneliness had now given way for a second chance at true and real love. It wouldn't be long now; Jack awaited her arrival home, which made her smile.

With her head tilted back against the leather of the headrest, she tapped her foot along with Bobby Vinton's 1968 hit record, "*Roses Are Red My Love*," as it began to play softly through the car stereo speakers. She smiled as she sang along to the lyrics. The music brought back memories of a very special time in her life; the day she took Jack's hand for the first time. The reminiscences were as vivid today as they were over 37 years ago. Her eyes fluttered closed as she returned to that time...

Jack was gently tugging and pulling her up the hill.

"Hurry, Shelby," Jack yelled at her.

It was a hot summer afternoon and the blistering sun was beating down on the concrete pavement that stretched across the Kissing Bridge, nearly burning the bottoms of their bare feet as they ran faster across the bridge and climbed up on the rail.

"Jump, Shelby, jump," Jack shouted.

"I can't, I'm scared, Jack," Shelby said in a whimper.

He reached out to her. "It'll be okay, Shelby. I promise I'll be right here." He seemed too strong, confident, and firm. "Take my hand, Shelby."

She shook her head. "No, Jack. It's just so far. I can't."

"Aww, Shelby you're just being chicken shit." Jack mocked her in a deep, manly voice, snickering at her fearful nature.

"No, I'm not Jack," she shouted back.

"You better go now," he wailed. "Here comes a truck, Shell."

Before she could blink, Jack went flying off the bridge like a bald eagle up into the wind. Without another thought, Shelby followed suit and found herself soaring through the air like a baby bird leaving the nest for the first time. Elation sparked through her limbs as she headed straight for the cold, rushing waters of the Chattahoochee River below and landed in a big splash.

She could hear Jack shouting excitedly when she came up to the surface, gasping for air, but pleased with her accomplishment.

"You did it, Shell, you did it! See I told you, it would be okay."

Delight and exhilaration rushed through her body as she began to swim toward Jack. A hurdle like that should have been unimaginable for a mere girl of her age. She had envisioned jumping so many times before, but she could never muster the courage. She knew in her heart, though, the only one who could get her to take the plunge was Jack.

Yep, Jack was the one—on many levels.

The song on the radio ended, snapping Shelby out of her reverie and back to the present.

Time had taken a toll on her over the years and now she was back in the place of her youth. She'd endured months of rehabilitation and therapy and was doing her best to emerge at the end of her challenges as a strong-spirited and self-confident woman. Returning to her childhood stomping grounds was going to help her finish walking the path to those goals.

She had to forgive herself for the many years of harboring guilt, for not pardoning easily, and for manipulating the people she loved. She only wanted to protect them from the truth of the many years of pain she endured as a result of her poor choices. Those were all now things of the past. She must confront her fears, and vow to herself that there would be no more secrets.

She flipped down the visor, checked her make-up, and wiped away flakes of mascara from under her eyes. Her feelings for Jack had been hidden in the depths of her heart for so long, yet she wouldn't do it any longer. Theirs was a love so unfathomably captivating that it had burned its mark deep in her soul for years. Now, after all this time, she longed for him to learn of her heart's desire to rekindle their love.

Shelby gazed at herself in the mirror knowing she had something to smile about today and forever. She gave herself a wink, in an attempt to imitate how Jack used to wink at her as she flipped the visor back up. She reached across the car seat, picked up a basket of pink and white flowers, opened the door, and stepped out.

Shuddering, she said out loud, "It's chilly," as she felt the brisk and steady February breezes blowing through the cemetery.

A faint mist of rain now joined with the wind that teased the huge oak trees surrounding the cemetery where her parents, Joel and Frances Harrelson, laid peacefully at rest.

Before reaching her destination, she had stopped for a quick lunch at Bush's Roadside Diner. The marquee in front of the restaurant with bright red flashing lights had read, "Valentine's Special, Fresh Cut Flowers." It caught her eye, and she couldn't help but stop in.

She knew how much her mom had loved flowers, so she couldn't resist the chance to buy such a beautiful bouquet of carnations. Shelby, like her mother, inherited a love of gardening and found solitude and peace of her own when retreating to her oasis. She often referred to herself as an aspiring horticulturist when friends would marvel over her green thumb creations. She always gave thanks though to God, for His masterpiece of art revealing itself each time she finished a floral arrangement. She believed her talent for creating was all part of His beautiful display of hope and purpose for her life.

On this rainy and chilly Valentine's Day, Shelby shivered from the cold air hissing through the trees. She wrapped her long trench coat tightly around her, pulling the hood up over her head to circumvent the misty rain.

She cautiously stepped across the cemetery, avoiding the small puddles of water now gathered in the low areas of the narrow path, as she carried her basket of flowers.

Shelby approached the double marble headstone marked *Frances B. Harrelson, 1938-1994*, and *Joel R. Harrelson, 1937-2004*. Beneath their names was scripted, 1 Corinthians 13:4-8, recalling one of Frances' favorite Bible verses. One that defined the essence of true love:

"Love is patient, love is kind. It does not envy, it does not boast, it is not proud. It is not rude and is not self-seeking, it is not easily angered, it keeps no record of wrongs. Love does not delight in evil, but rejoices with the truth. It always protects and always trusts, always hopes, always perseveres. Love never fails."

"Happy Valentine's Day, Mom and Dad. I miss you both so much," Shelby said, as she leaned down and placed the bamboo-weaved basket of flowers at the head of their graves. Carnations had been Frances's favorite and she had spent many years growing them. She loved exhibiting them at the Callaway Gardens Flower Show every spring in Pine Mountain, Georgia.

Remembering the fun-filled day trips to Pine Mountain, Shelby laughed at how they would load up the station wagon with five-gallon buckets of water, placing dozens of carnations of every color in each container for safekeeping on the drive.

Frances would tell Shelby, "Make sure you put towels around the bottom of the cans, so the water won't spill and wet the carpet." Obediently, Shelby would tuck the many clothes around all the pails, just as her mom instructed her. It was Frances's meticulous way of caring for her beautiful flowers that made her a veteran Blue Ribbon prizewinner many times. Similarly, and almost as if passed down through the DNA, Shelby also found gardening to be a peaceful, comforting safe haven from the challenges of her life.

It had been a few years since Shelby had visited her parents' grave, for reasons she was ashamed to admit. Even though she only lived a short distance away in Columbus, Georgia. Shelby shrugged as she fussed with the flowers while trying to gulp down her feelings of the painful turmoil of her life.

Today, though, was different and she *needed* to come home. It was necessary for her to heal from all the pain and finally be free from the regrets. It was even more than that. She also needed to ask her parents' forgiveness for the selfish mistakes that had ultimately flung her—unknowingly—into a life of torment.

Only now was she ready to face the one thing that drove her away many years ago.

"Heartbreak," she said in a whispered breath.

Kneeling on the cold, hard, and wet ground, next to Frances's grave, she began to weep as the tears gently rolled down her cheeks.

The wind blew wildly around her as if embracing her sadness. Even though her shoulder-length brown hair was twisted up in a clip—easy for traveling—strays brushed against her cheeks and eyes as she bowed her head in shame. An admission poured forth from her.

"Jack broke my heart, Mom," she said through a sob. "He was the love of my life and everything in the world to me from the very moment I laid my eyes on him the beginning of our junior high school year. I can't forget the glow of his deep, dark brown eyes, and his messy, shaggy brown hair."

Wiping away tears from her cheeks, she continued. "And his adorable smile melted my heart when he caught my attention that first day of school."

Like all young girls in the 1970s, Shelby knew there were boundaries when it came to boys. Jack was every girl's dream but deep down in her heart, she knew he wasn't quite the young man her parents had hoped she would fall in love with and spend the rest of her life with.

"I just wish you had both known Jack the way I did," she said to the headstone.

She glanced up at the cloudy sky as if addressing her parents in a heavenly way, as well. Then, she turned her eyes back to the marker that bore their names and continued.

"Jack had so many delightful qualities," she said as she began to paint a picture of him. Shelby was unable to resist smiling at the memory of his funny little quirks as the vision of his face shone in her mind. "Jack was tall and handsome and he loved playing football all through high school. He was as strong as a rock and exhibited a killer muscular physique in those days."

She remembered how handsome, virile, and sexy he was even back then before he'd fully become a man.

"He was sweet and kindhearted," Shelby said. "He gave me the nickname, Tootie, which he called me all the time. He would always reach down and pick the purple flowers that grew wild around the community and hand them to me, saying, 'Here you go, Tootie.'"

Lost in memories of the past, Shelby kept on.

"He was funny and silly and would say, 'Tootie, there's a bumble bee on your butt, let me get him before he stings you.' I would just giggle and say, 'No, Jack, you can't.' Playful? Yes, he was, Mom and Dad."

"Jack was a dreamer like me. I remember he would play in the sand, making roads with the side of his hand while sitting on the bank of the river. He would pile the sand into hills along the road and say, 'That's our road, Tootie.' I would ask him where we were going and he'd just smile and wink at me, saying 'Wherever we want to go, Shell.'"

She continued. "Jack was an adventurer and he so loved trains. He and his friends, Walter and Hank, would spend hours exploring the rails that ran through town. They would pick up remnants and trinkets the trains had long left behind. And then, the explorer would give his treasures to me, so proud of his findings."

"We would sit for hours on the sandbags at the river and he would tell me about all the old railroad stories his grandfather, an engineer in his time, shared with him. Jack's favorite stories were the ones about the hobos jumping the trains as they passed through on the Chattahoochee Valley Rails," she explained.

"Jack had a bad-ass attitude sometimes. If he didn't like you, well, he just didn't give a damn," she relayed to her parents with a grin. "There were very few people that Jack didn't like, though."

Shelby paused for a split second as if to anticipate the unasked question from her mother even though she wasn't there. Instead, Shelby prompted herself.

"A saint? Jack? Oh no, not by any stretch of the imagination," she said with a laugh. "He got caught smoking out behind the school by Mrs. Crawford, but she just scolded him about how bad smoking was for you and let him be."

Then, she added, "Walter's alcoholic uncle, Ernie, was the perfect one to grab them a six-pack of beer for a fee of two dollars," she described with a knowing nod. "They would hide out in the bushes behind the old shelter at the boat ramp and get drunk as a coot. Of course, Jack's dad, Sheriff Emerson, would catch them later puking out their guts. He would shake his head, throw them in the back of the squad car, and haul them all home."

She laughed at the memory of such foolish and fun-loving kids. Ones who would one day grow into adults with so much sorrow and burdens to shoulder. Shelby sighed and said, "Yet, he was a very simple guy, living each day to the fullest. Mostly, he was committed to me and I know he loved me with all his heart."

Shelby reached up and softly smoothed the stray hair away from her face as she watched the leaves blowing fiercely across the cemetery.

"This was the Jack I knew, Mom and Dad, and I loved him dearly," she claimed. "Even though, many years later, I know he had innocently become entangled in a web he couldn't get himself out of."

A familiar ache pressed hard against her breastbone at the memory of Jack's betrayal. She'd spent years trying to tamp down the pain caused by such immature behavior. Still, she spoke to her parents. "I have to admit, I'm so ashamed of my unforgiving, self-centered attitude back then because you both had taught me to be kind and compassionate to others and always forgive quickly."

Something she hadn't done at that time.

"Jack tried so hard to reach out to me, to-to-to explain..." Shelby sipped in air hard now, trying very much to control her tears. "I refused and ignored him and actually pushed him away. I had lost the capacity to fully feel his love for me. I was devastated and heartbroken the night I found him..."

She gulped hard, unable to complete the sentence. The details didn't matter right now. She just wanted her parents to know how she felt.

"I know both of you only wanted the best for me. You encouraged me to let it be, so wanting to be the good daughter and honor your wishes, I gave up on Jack, thinking you both were probably right and moving on was best for me." Shelby brushed away another tear, this one a bit more forcefully. "I never stopped loving Jack, even though I tried so hard."

She reached out her hand and traced the letters of her father's name to have more of a connection with him as she spoke. "Daddy, I remember you told me you blamed yourself and mom for all the years of pain I endured, but, please know that everything was my decision and I have accepted that." She continued drawing around the granite lettering. "It's been a struggle, but learning how to forgive has actually set me free. Now, I have to focus on a second chance with Jack."

She switched her weight from one leg to the other as she continued to kneel quietly by her parents as a whiff of air rustled the leaves. The moss swayed in the trees to the tune of the winds circulating around. It was like watching and listening to an orchestrated and choreographed dance of nature.

She dabbed away the tears and closed her eyes, and slowly began to feel the presence of Frances and Joel and the gentle sensation of peace. She imagined their hands reaching down and, ever so softly, scooping her up into their loving arms.

It was late afternoon and the clouds made it feel like dusk and Shelby gradually stood and stretched both of her legs, cramped from kneeling on the ground. She reached for the lapels on her coat and tucked them tightly around her neck.

She was about to leave, but turned and said, "Please know, Mom and Dad, how much you both still mean to me and I love you with all my heart. I should have stayed and given Jack a chance to explain. Maybe things would have been different. He was the love of my life and everything I could have ever wanted and needed. I always believed we would spend our lives together. We would get married, be the first to give ourselves to each other, and we would have children... living right here in town with the two of you."

Shelby bit her lip as she finished. "You know the Cinderella story, find your Prince Charming, and live happily ever after," she said to herself. "I had lots of dreams, but none of them excluded Jack. You remember Gina, my best friend. Well, she and I would come up with some of the silliest fantasies." Shelby smiled remembering Gina, who was now in the same realm as her beloved parents. "My heart and soul were right here with Jack all along and it has taken me many years of pain to realize it. You see, I now understand that you only have one heart and you can only give it to one person. I gave mine to Jack."

Her heart was a gift to Jack wrapped with love, tied in a bow, and sealed with a kiss so long ago.

"Now, I have a second chance, and I intend to make it work this time," she said forcefully. "My being away has given me a renewed appreciation for life. I'm on my way to see Jack now," she said with confidence. "He has to know how much he means to me and my desire to spend the rest of my life with him. I hope he will feel the same way."

Butterflies fluttered in her stomach as Shelby left her parents' graves and returned to her car. She exited the cemetery and turned onto Highway 29 heading north. Shame spiraled over her when she considered how she suppressed the wonderful memories of growing up in this beautiful town, but her retreat at Tybee Island, Georgia, had given her a renewed appreciation for the little things in life.

Returning to Valley brought the feeling of opening a time capsule that had been buried many years ago. Driving through the familiar streets, she absorbed the scenery like a sponge soaking up an emotional spill.

Slowly, she passed over Moore's Creek and saw the Langdale Textile Mill. The mill was Jack's first job right after graduating from high school, so, of course, the building reminded her of him.

The traffic light turned red and Shelby brought her car to a stop. In anticipation of her return, she waited eagerly for the light to turn green; tapping her hands on the steering wheel and minutes later, she rounded the corner and drove down 23rd Drive heading into the Shawmut community.

"Jack is waiting."

Thousands of goosebumps suddenly hijacked her small, thin body as a big chill ran down her spine. Shivering from the excitement, Shelby slowed her car as she pulled into the overgrown and dimly lit driveway of her parents' home.

She quickly searched the long, covered porch for Jack and immediately saw him spring from the old high-back rocker.

She gasped at the sight of him, seeing his tall, thin, and muscular body, as he crossed the porch to the worn steps.

Excitement rushed through her body and her heart throbbed out of control. She switched the ignition off and fumbled at the car door handle as she tried to open it. Her nerves had her trembling as she threw open the door and without another thought dashed across the lawn and up the staircase. Shelby noticed his pace was quick and he suddenly moved toward her with both arms out.

Finding her voice was almost an exercise in futility, but she managed to move her lips.

"Jack," she whispered quietly.

A beautiful smile spread across his aged, yet still handsome face. "My Tootie," he said as he scooped her up and into his arms.

Her pulse pounded and they each hesitated for an instant as their lips met. The passion of his kiss melted her heart and swept her back in time over twenty-five years to their last reunion. She felt his fingertips on her chin and she opened her eyes to see him staring down at her apparently overwhelmed by her presence.

It was a feeling so familiar to them both.

A feeling that reminded her of a day so long ago.

The day they first met...

Chapter Two

The summer heat had finally made way for the cool breezy days of September 1968 and the promise of a new season was just around the corner.

While Shelby enjoyed her lazy days of summer, there were never any dull moments in her life. Often, she spent them sleeping in late when her parents didn't have chores for her early in the morning.

She would talk for hours on the phone with her best friend, Gina. Many times, you could find Shelby swinging under the big oak tree that draped the charming corner lot on 23rd Drive. If she wasn't in the mood for swinging, then she was skipping up and down the azalea-lined sidewalk, singing and dancing to her transistor radio.

The highlight of most hot and humid summer days and her favorite pastime was swimming and tubing down the cool swift waters of the Chattahoochee River with her friends.

Shelby was awake earlier than usual this September morning. Her heart was empty knowing Gina was in heaven now and wouldn't be going to school with her ever again. Losing her best friend over the summer in a swimming accident had shattered her world and she was having difficulty accepting that Gina was gone. Everything was going to be different now. The loss of Gina had left Shelby with a complete sense of emptiness in her heart and she couldn't imagine what Mary, Gina's twin sister, was feeling. Shelby and Mary had been friends, but nothing like her friendship with Gina. Her heart ached for Mary, knowing her loss was much greater than her own was.

"Oh gosh," she said in a whimper. The only thing left were the many memories they'd shared.

Today marked Shelby's first day of junior high school and a totally new adventure that was laced with bittersweet feelings. Her nerves felt like a bowl of jellybeans bouncing around in the pit of her stomach, setting off a wave of fretful jitters. She was confused with excitement and anxiousness. She wondered if she would find a new friend, like Gina, and if her classmates would be nice to her. She knew Mary would be there even if she didn't know anyone else. She hadn't seen Mary since the funeral, and because they had never been real close she wasn't sure what to expect when she did see her.

She would get to meet a lot of new people since it was the only junior high school in the area and served all the villages of Valley. The up and coming sixth graders would gather this morning in recognition of their successful completion of elementary school and the realization that junior high was a new beginning for them all.

"Wow," Shelby exclaimed. "I'm a sixth grader now." She stretched her legs and arms out in the air. "I can do this," she said, rolling over to check the time on her alarm clock. "Good I can lay here for just a few more minutes," she sighed.

With the perky personality of a poodle, every day was a bright and sunny day in Shelby's life and she was convinced this morning was going to be a fresh new start for her.

Shelby had loved elementary school and all of her teachers, but now, the last thing she wanted was to be treated like a kindergartner. She wasn't sure how she was supposed to act in junior high, but she was confident she would figure it out.

Her thoughts now turned to Gina again as she lay snuggled in her bed, the memories of their friendship flashing back. They were best friends since the first grade and were inseparable. They would squeal and run when the ugly boys would chase them around the playground.

She remembered the time Gina came to spend the weekend with her, just a few weeks before she died. Shelby's parents had gone out for dinner that Friday evening. Once they were sure her folks were gone, she and Gina cracked up at the thought of making a prank phone call, which they had learned from one of the boys in their fifth-grade class.

Gina picked up the phone and handed it to Shelby. "Here, you go first Shelby. All you have to do is dial the number and when they answer, ask them if they have Prince Albert in a can."

"No, you go first, Gina. I'm too scared," Shelby said, and with a swish of her hand brushed the telephone away.

"Oh, Shelby, you're just a 'fraidy cat," Gina said, throwing her hand in the air.

"No, I'm not, Gina," Shelby protested.

"Okay, I'll go first and then you have to promise to do one, too," she insisted. Gina reached for the handset and slowly dialed the number they had randomly chosen from the white pages.

The phone rang on the other end and a male voice answered. "Hello?"

In a disguised and deep voice, Gina said nervously. "Hello, do you have Prince Albert in a can?"

The voice on the other end of the call said, "Yes, I do."

Gina burst into laughter and cried out, "Well, you better let him out!" Then, she slammed the receiver down on the table. Both Gina and Shelby erupted in a silly high-pitched chuckle as they fell back onto the sofa, with both arms and legs kicking in excitement.

Just then, the back door opened and Shelby's dad, Joel, entered the room returning to retrieve his forgotten wallet. He asked, "What's so funny and what are you girls up to?"

Shelby struggled for an answer. "Oh, nothing, Daddy. We were just laughing and playing."

"Are you sure, Shelby?" he asked and turned to eyeball Gina. Gina was terrified and managed a phony smile.

Upon his departure, Gina was afraid they would be in trouble, so she made up an excuse saying she wasn't feeling well, her stomach was upset, and she needed to go home. Shelby laughed out loud at the incident when Gina's dad came to pick her up later that evening.

People would often refer to them as the Bobbsey Twins who snickered all the time when they were together and they made plans many times to dress alike the next day for school.

Shelby hugged her pillow now and rolled over on her side as she continued remembering her friend. There would be no more goofy times or tomfoolery.

Shelby was terribly heartbroken and the reality of Gina being gone had been hard for her to accept. She was grief-stricken the day they buried Gina in the Langdale Cemetery. Shelby cried out for her not to leave her when they began to lower the casket slowly into the ground.

Shelby clung tightly to her mom's embrace then broke down crying uncontrollably as they left the cemetery.

Shaken by the memory and still lying in her bed, Shelby softly said, "I'm going to miss you, Gina." Sniffling, she rolled over to catch another glance at the clock.

She noticed the time. "Oh man, I'm late," she said.

Shelby threw off the covers and hurdled out of bed, full of energy and excitement now. She grabbed her transistor radio and turned it on. She had it sitting on the edge of the nightstand with its antenna extended toward the window for the best reception possible. She loved having music playing softly in the background in the mornings while getting dressed for school.

Billboard's 1967 summer hit, "*Ode to Billy Joe,*" sounded out, so Shelby quickly reached over and turned the tiny knob to full volume to hear one of her favorite songs.

Shelby danced around her bedroom, fluffing her wispy, long brown hair while watching herself in the mirror. She held the brush as if it were a microphone and used it to belt out the lyrics along with Bobbie Gentry.

Not only was today an exciting time for Shelby, but she was looking forward to celebrating her eleventh birthday in just two days. Overwhelmed with anticipation, Shelby captured one last peek in the mirror, making sure everything was in proper order. She smiled to herself and whispered, "Here we go, Gina."

A loud voice shouted out to her from the kitchen. "Shelby, hurry up or you're going to miss the bus, sweetie," warned her mother, Frances. Rising early each morning, Frances buzzed around the kitchen preparing breakfast and packing lunches for her family.

"I'm coming, Mom," Shelby called back as she raced down the staircase.

Skipping into the kitchen, she threw her book bag on top of the counter; just missing the small glass of fresh squeezed orange juice her mother had waiting for her. Shelby was a bit of a clumsy child, always spilling and knocking things over and frustrating her dad, Joel. It only took small gestures, like batting her eyes at him to win back her dad's approval.

"So Shelby," her mom asked. "What would you like for your birthday?"

"Hmm... let me see." She thought hard as she tried to think of something she really wanted as she twisted her fingers through her hair. "Oh, I know, I really want a record player. Do you think Daddy would let me have one? Gina and I plan to..." the rest of the sentence died on the end of her tongue, unspoken. Then, she added, "I want to save my allowance and buy some records and practice singing." Shelby struggled to manage her emotions. Crushed by the words from her own mouth, she swallowed hard, drew a harsh breath in, and quickly released it.

She observed the look on her mother's face after her words spilled out and could almost sense that her mother was holding back tears as her own heart ached for Gina.

The next couple of days starting a new school without her best friend in tow were going to be very difficult for Shelby.

Frances reached down, kissed Shelby gently on the top of her head, and said, "Hurry now, Shelby, you don't want to miss the bus on your first day of school."

"Okay, Mom, but would you please ask Daddy if I could have a record player? Please, please?"

"Yes, I will, Shelby," Frances replied and nodded her head.

Shelby called out, "Thank you, Mom! I love you." And then, she darted out the door and bounced across the front lawn headed for the bus stop.

When the yellow vehicle finally arrived, Shelby moved inside swiftly to take a seat. In no time at all, she arrived at her new school home. Tentatively, Shelby stepped off the school bus. She looked around at the strange new place that was quite different from Shawmut Elementary School.

The area was filled with chaotic youngsters moving up and down the halls frantically trying to locate their classrooms. She was preoccupied and in awe of her new surroundings. Skittish, she searched the breezeway for a familiar face.

One thing she noticed instead was that all of the girls were dressed in hippie-like gaucho pants held in place by wrap belts. Their shirts were covered with vests and their heads were adorned with Indian style bands.

The glamor of growing up excited Shelby as she stood among the hustle, bustle, and chatter of words, ringing out loud in her ears. Shelby was amazed by all the commotion as she searched for someone to help her find her class. She noticed an old, gray-haired lady wearing big, black-rimmed glasses. She waved to everyone wandering the halls and guided them in the direction of their classrooms.

Shelby approached the woman and asked, "Can you tell me where to go? I'm in the sixth grade."

The teacher smiled warmly at her and said, "Why, my dear, I'm one of the sixth-grade teachers. If you will go down the breezeway and turn right, then you'll walk all the way to the last room. Check to see if your name is on the list, if it is, you can find a seat and I will be there shortly."

Shelby's brows lifted and her eyes widened as she noticed the woman's creepy voice, but even so, she seemed sweet and was really helpful.

She was eager to fit in with a cool group of people and finding someone like Gina was going to prove to be a very difficult task, but Shelby was hopeful and looked forward to developing friendships. And, of course, she had Mary. Maybe she would be the one to fill the void in her heart. She would have to see about that.

Just as the teacher had said, she found the appropriate classroom at the end of the hall, and, sure enough, her name was on the paper taped to the door. A long, green chalkboard covered the front of the room and maps of the world adorned the wall next to the entrance while the back of the room was filled with cubicles for the students to store their belongings throughout the day. The bank of windows on the opposite side of the room created the focal point and that's what caught Shelby's attention.

She danced her way through the maze of desks precisely positioned throughout the room. She spotted the perfect one for her on the far wall where all the windows opened to the bright sunshine. Staking her claim, she threw her purse on the desk, took a seat, turned, and peered out the window.

One of Shelby's strengths early in life was her ability to clearly, concisely, and confidently let people know exactly what she wanted. It was a personality trait she inherited from her dad. It was easy for her and she never had any difficulty deciding what she wanted and she was satisfied she could make it happen.

She never liked sitting in the front of the classroom because all the smart kids usually positioned themselves there. She was also definitely not someone to sit in the back because that was where all the dummies bunched up. However, the middle of the room was always a safe place, at least in her mind.

Breaking her focus from the outside, she glanced around the room, noticing how many students wore frowns on their faces. She beamed in their direction, recalling one of her mom's favorite quotes, "Smile at everyone, Shelby. They might be having a bad day."

Once again, Shelby faced the windows, as her thoughts quickly moved to Mary, who should be coming this morning, too. All of a sudden, three boisterous young boys entered the room, shouting out with loud voices and rattling everyone, particularly Shelby. Quickly reacting, she twisted her head to see what all the commotion was about. Great, they were in her class.

The boys approached, and Shelby was unnerved by such rambunctiousness. Being an only child, she'd never spent much time around boys and when she had, she thought they must have been born on another planet.

She was caught off guard by her emotional reaction of delight to one of the boy's cute smile. She didn't understand her unusual response to him. The boy kept his eyes fixated right on her, meeting her gaze. She wondered who he was and she was a bit shaken by his stare with a sensation that her heart might just pound right out of her chest. She dropped eye contact, as she didn't want to look back at him for fear that he might read the excitement in her expression. But as he and his friends came wildly into the room, he slid into the desk right behind her. She could feel his eyes on the back of her head.

She sat perfectly still, afraid to turn around. Then, she felt a light tapping on her left shoulder. She twitched a bit, startled at his forwardness. And then, he did it again.

"Hey, you, cat got your tongue?"

Her face heated up from embarrassment as she could sense others turning to check her out, as well. She swallowed hard, trying to find her voice.

"So, what's your name?" he asked.

Then, she quickly responded, "Shelby Harrelson."

The boy smiled at her. "Well, hey there, Shelby. I'm Jack. That ugly guy right there is Walter and the even uglier one is Hank."

Shelby laughed at Jack's introduction, but didn't really give a thought about the other two boys. Jack's dark brown eyes mesmerized her as they glistened with a sparkle. She was enchanted by his intensely low-pitched voice as he spoke to her. Oblivious to her surroundings, his presence alone captivated every fiber of her body.

Jack asked her, "Where are you from, Shelby?"

He grinned at her with his big smile. Shelby's face began to feel flushed, when she noticed many of her classmates had turned in her direction once again, anticipating her response.

She managed a strangled, "Shawmut."

Jack leaned closer to her. "Well, I hope you're one of the smart girls, Shelby, so you can help me with my homework." He looked over at his friends knowingly, nodded his head, and winked. They all began to crack up.

Shelby regained her composure and was intrigued by Jack's forwardness. She was eager to learn more about him. She lifted her chin in a display of confidence and asked, "So, Jack, where are you from?"

"Langdale," he replied with a bit of conceit. Jack was proud he was from Langdale; everyone knew it was the coolest place to live of all the villages. It seemed as though he wanted to provoke her a little more now as he fired out his next question before she had an opportunity to engage him.

"So, Shelby, do you like to fish?"

"Yes, Jack, I do," she exclaimed. "I caught many redbreasts over the summer with my dad down at the boat dock." She was surprised when this admission sparked a response of "whoa" from their classmates around the room.

Jack thought it was cool she liked to fish since the girls he knew had no desire to even go swimming in the river much less bait a pole. He turned to face her and caught her eyes peering at him. Shelby was someone he was going to get along with, he thought to himself.

She could sense his humbleness and accepted his wave of the white flag and she grinned in his direction. He was cute and she admired him for his sweet temperament.

They chatted several times throughout the day. She watched Jack during their lunch break when he sat across the room with his friends. It was obvious he was quite popular among the students. On a few occasions he looked in her direction and it made her blush, but she managed a smile and then turned away.

The school bell startled her as it rang out loudly and she clumsily dropped her notebook and scattered her papers across the floor. With a feeling of embarrassment, she scrambled to her knees as she quickly gathered her things.

Jack seemed to sense her anguish, leaned over, and said, "Let me help you, Shelby." He knelt on the floor and reached for her papers and his eyes rested directly on hers.

"Oh, thank you, Jack," she whispered.

"You're welcome," he replied. He extended his hand in a gesture to help her up from the floor. With a sigh of relief, she reached up and took his hand. His touch radiated with energy that sparked a ripple of goosebumps throughout her body.

He lifted her to her feet and she regained her balance. He motioned with a snap of his fingers. "Come on, Shelby, I'll walk you to the bus, try not to be upset, everything will be fine."

Shelby was surprised by his kindness and accepted his offer. Together, they walked side-by-side down the breezeway to the bus lane.

Her first day of junior high was pretty interesting and more than anything, she longed to share her feelings with Gina.

"Jack Emerson is his name," she whispered quietly, hoping Gina could hear her, on the bus ride home. She noticed Mary sitting across the aisle a few rows behind her staring out the window, and she could see the sadness in her eyes. Maybe tomorrow she would sit next to her, Shelby thought as her mind wandered back to Jack. She couldn't stop thinking about him. He was so cute and she liked him a lot.

Chapter Three

Jack seemed to enjoy sitting behind Shelby in class. His rowdy nature always got him into trouble throughout the year when he had a hankering for Shelby's attention.

He played with her long brown hair, especially when she wore it up in a ponytail. Of course, she did it on purpose, knowing he would tug at it. It had a mind of its own when it would bounce from side to side with her every move. She could tell he liked to play with it by the way he twisted it in his fingers.

Shelby never fretted over it because she liked it when Jack played with her hair. Of course, he had to be that quintessential sixth-grade boy and occasionally give her ponytail a quick snatch to catch her by surprise.

"Jack, stop," she said sharply.

Hiding her purse was another game Jack enjoyed, as well as playing jokes on her. He'd hide the bag and she'd become agitated, demanding he return it. He'd laugh and blame it on Hank.

Jack loved to ruffle Shelby's feathers, but she forgave him when he said, "You're kind of cute when you're irritated."

However, there were days throughout the school year when Shelby wasn't so forgiving of him. He could be a real butt at times. She felt like pinching his head off one Friday afternoon, right before the Thanksgiving holiday.

Shelby came home from school and her mom met her at the door with a glass of lemonade.

"How was school, dear?" her mom asked.

Shelby pouted as she took the drink. "Boys are so silly."

"At your age, yes," her mom said. "At all ages, really. Who's bothering you?"

"Jack Emerson," Shelby said and then took a sip of her lemonade. "He is such a dork. He steals my purse and hides it from me and then blames someone else and he is always hanging around with Hank and Walter."

"Boys will be boys," Mom said, busying herself in the kitchen. "That's why I'm glad I had my Shelby. Girls are so much easier."

Shelby nodded at her mom, but secretly, deep down in the pit of her stomach and her overly pounding heart, she really liked Jack a lot. She just didn't understand why he was so obnoxious.

"Oh, Shelby, you are young, sweet, and naïve," her mom said with a laugh. "Jack really has a crush on you. Don't you know that boys do the silliest things to get your attention? It's just their way of saying they like you."

"What?" Shelby exclaimed. "How can they like you when they're just dorks, all of them, even Walter and Hank?" she asked, frowning and a bit perplexed.

"It's true, Shelby. I promise that Jack likes you," Frances replied. "Watch the way he acts. You'll see what I mean, dear."

~~~

Back at school, Shelby opened her textbook and set her pencils on the desk next to her notebook. When Jack walked by, he playfully knocked her pencils off the desk.

"Pick them up, Jack," she demanded.

"Why?" he asked with a sly grin. Why did he have to be so cute?

"Because it's the polite thing to do," she said, trying to shame him.

Jack rolled his eyes, but he bent down and handed the pencils back to her. "There you go, Shelby. Don't be so clumsy next time," he said with a wink.

She started to say something smart, but remembered what her mother had told her. Had he just done that to flirt with her?

As the class got underway, Jack constantly poked her in the back to get her attention. She became irritated with him because he wouldn't leave her alone.

She spun in her seat and whispered to him. "I'm desperately trying to get all the notes on the blackboard for our test on Friday."

He just shrugged at her.

"Behave, Jack," she hissed out at him. She knew how important good grades were and how they would help her get into an excellent college one day. She wasn't going to slip behind on this test because of Jack, especially since the exam was right before the Christmas break.
~~~

Jack snorted when he heard their teacher excuse herself for a few minutes to take care of business in the principal's office. She instructed them to take their time getting all the notes off the board. With a quick cast of her eyes directly at Jack, she warned the class to be on their best behavior while she was gone.

The instant the teacher left the room for the principal's office, Jack gave Shelby a big poke in her side. Shelby squealed out her agitation with him now. She turned and caught a glimpse of a note in his hand. He motioned for her to take it.

She reached down, taking the note slowly and scanned the room to see if anyone noticed the exchange. Carefully, she slid it up into her book and calmly unfolded the paper.

Silently, she read his note....

Shelby, I like you, do you like me?
______ Yes ______ No
Check Yes or No
If it's yes, will you go with me?

It was her first Cinderella experience and Jack was the Prince who had just asked her to dance. "Oh my," she whispered. She was taken aback at the note while exploding inside with excitement. She paused and picked up her pencil, glancing over the room once again.

She checked *yes*.

Folding up the paper, she passed it back to Jack.

In a wink of an eye, Jack hollered out loud, like a crazy person and everyone in the room gaped at him. Shelby's cheeks flushed and she twisted around to see what he'd do next.

"Man, what's wrong with you?" Hank asked.

Jack smiled at her and answered his friend. "Not a thing. I'm the luckiest guy in the world."

~~~

The school year went by in a flash, it seemed, but Shelby couldn't have been happier because she and Jack had been going together now for six months.

As sixth graders, most boys and girls at the age of eleven and twelve were just learning how to treat the opposite gender, and often, their classmates teased them for being boyfriend and girlfriend.
~~~

Some of the girls in her class were even mean to Shelby, mostly because they were jealous that she had captured Jack's heart when so many of them couldn't.

It was the last day of school and Shelby was starting to anguish over how and when she and Jack would see each other over the summer. They sat quietly on the bench under the breezeway as they waited for their buses for the last ride home for the school year.

Shelby turned and looked into Jack's eyes. Then, she asked, "Jack, do you think we will get to see each other this summer?"

"I don't know, Shell. My mom says I have to help in the tobacco fields again this year."

"Oh," was all she replied.

"Do you ever go swimming at the Kissing Bridge?" he asked as he wound their fingers together. With his other hand, he reached up and brushed her hair back over her shoulder.

"Yes, I do. Mom or Dad usually take me and my cousins a couple of times a week after we do our chores," she answered with excitement.

"Great, Shell! Call me when you think you're going to be there and I'll get my dad to take me." Jack smiled at her as he squeezed her hand excitedly.

Shelby let out a contented sigh, knowing their romance didn't have to end. It would just shift gears.

~~~

The summer proved to be a very busy time for Shelby as she helped her mom prepare for the annual "Maid of Cotton" pageant coming up in the fall.

Frances played a big part in organizing the pageant every year while Shelby tagged along by her side and assisted when she could. Frances, a prim and proper woman, believed it was important for young girls to learn how to behave appropriately, so she taught classes on etiquette for many years.

It had been several weeks since school had dismissed for the summer and she was missing Jack, even though they had talked on the phone a couple of times. Shelby was always a bit afraid to call him for fear his mother or father would answer. But this late August morning her mom had agreed to take her swimming at the Kissing Bridge that afternoon and she was hoping Jack could come too.
~~~

She desperately wanted to see him. Without further hesitation, she picked up the phone and called him.

"Hello," the woman on the other end answered.

"This is Shelby Harrelson, is Jack there?"

"No, I'm sorry. He's still out in the field this morning," the woman said. "You're Jack's friend from school right?"

"Yes ma'am," Shelby replied shyly.

"Jack has talked about you several times."

"He has?" she asked wondering what he had told her.

"Yes, and I'm his mother Martha," she said kindly introducing herself. "Have you had a good summer? You know there's not much left of it and it won't be long and school will be beginning soon."

Shelby was feeling nervous now. His mother seemed nice. Don't say anything stupid she thought, after all, this is Jack's mother.

"I am. I'm helping my mom with the 'Maid of Cotton' pageant. She does it every year," Shelby told her.

"Well I bet that is fun, and you're enjoying it. Are you going to be in it?"

"No ma'am, you have to be sixteen to enter."

"Well, if you're anything like Jack describes you, then I bet you would win."

Shelby could feel the compliment stain her cheeks. It meant so much to her, especially coming from Jack's own mother. "Oh, thank you, Mrs. Emerson," Shelby replied.

"Do you know if he will be going swimming today at the Kissing Bridge?" Shelby asked as she twitched in her chair in anticipation of her answer.

"I don't see why not, Shelby. What time will you be there?"

Shelby looked at her watch. "Mom says about three o'clock."

"I will tell him you called as soon as he gets in."

"Thank you," Shelby replied, feeling jittery.

A few short hours later, Shelby stretched out on a quilt on the bank of the river and reminisced about her summer vacation, and how fast it had slipped away. She was excited to get their seventh-grade year started.

"Shelby! There you are," Jack yelled as he crossed the Kissing Bridge, startling her away from her thoughts.

"Hey, Jack," she said as she motioned for him to have a seat next to her on the quilt.

"Mom said you called," he replied, slowly taking a seat.

"I'm so glad school starts soon Jack," Shelby said lightly.

"Shelby, it sucks, doesn't it?" Jack peeked at her reaction.

"Oh, Jack, mind your mouth." She chuckled, thinking there was no hope for him.

"So, are you going to be one of those Maid of Cotton things?" he asked with a tad of sarcasm.

"I don't think so," she said decisively, as she rolled her eyes.

"Mom says you'd be a beautiful Maid just from talking to you. One day, Shell, you could be *my* maid. You know... cooking, cleaning, doing my laundry." He sneered, crisscrossing his legs.

"Jack, it's not a maid, like in cleaning up your house. It's a beauty pageant, dummy," she tried to explain.

"Shell, you could be both," he said with a laugh as he turned and dodged her arm as she slapped his shoulder.

"Jack, you're clueless!" she exclaimed. "And, yes, one day I'm going to be in the pageant," she said with a smirk.

They laughed together as the conversation turned back to the reality of school beginning soon. Jack reminded her that football practice started on Monday and he wouldn't get to see much of her before school began.

So, that was how it was. Jack spent most of the last few weeks of summer at football practice—after he'd worked in the tobacco fields, of course—and Shelby filled her time helping her mother with the upcoming pageant and pining away for lost time with Jack. She longed for the day they'd step back on to the ugly yellow bus and head into the classroom to be together again. Now, Shelby could only stoke her teen lust for her absentee boyfriend by reading romance novels Mary loaned her. And yes, it turned out that her heavenly friend Gina's twin sister had filled Shelby's yearning for a new best buddy.

Although Mary was similar to Gina and very dear to her, she would never actually replace Gina in Shelby's life. It was good to have a trusted pal, though. Besides hanging out with Mary, Shelby stayed awake at night reading her books, putting herself in the character's shoes, just waiting for that day she could go back to school and she and Jack would be together again. Where they belonged.

~~~

Shelby stepped off the bus for the new school year and once again joined the melee of students in the hustle and bustle of the breezeway. But this time, she felt right at home and knew exactly what to do. She scanned the area for Jack. He would be wearing
~~~

his number ten football jersey. She was so proud of him for landing the quarterback position on the junior varsity football team. He loved the sport so much and had worked hard to make the team—especially earning the quarterback position.

Whenever they spoke on the phone before school started, Shelby could see that Jack's ego soared. She had to keep him grounded even though she knew he was a great player and a promising prospect for the varsity high school football team in a couple of years. And, as sure as she knew it, as the school year and football season kicked into gear, Jack was the star and she was his biggest cheerleader, never missing any of the action.

It was after the Christmas holiday and the ringing in of the New Year was just an arm's reach away when Mary told her about a new movie playing at the theater.

"It's called *Love Story* and we just have to see it," Mary said excitedly over the phone.

"It sounds perfect," Shelby chimed back, as she thought of Jack and their own journey together.

"Okay, ask your mom if you can go Saturday afternoon. It's playing at the Langdale Theater."

"I haven't been to the movies by myself, Mary," she admitted. "But, I'm twelve now and just maybe my parents will let me do it. I'll ask and call you back."

Shelby couldn't believe it when her parents had no problem with her going to see the movie on her own with Mary. No argument, no begging. Just their blessing and the promise of a ride to the theater. Shelby had never felt so grown up.

Shelby was thrilled and called Mary to let her know she could go and would meet her there on Saturday at two o'clock.

Frances pulled the station wagon to a halt in front of the flight of stairs leading to the box office of the Langdale Theater. "Shelby, you have a good time and I'll be back for you later. Be careful and don't talk to strangers," she warned her daughter.

"I will, Mom. Thank you for letting me do this. I'll be careful and stay with Mary. I love you," she said as she reached across the seat and kissed her mom on the cheek. Shelby bailed out of the car and made a break for Mary who was standing in front of the theater. They waved at Frances as she drove away from the curb.

"Shelby, is Jack coming?" Mary inquired, eagerly.

"I don't know. He said he didn't care about seeing some stupid love story," she said with a frown. Had Jack come with her, they could have held hands in the dark and maybe even sneaked a kiss or two.

Purchasing their tickets at the box office for the first time was a new adventure for them, and the girls loved the idea. They knew it was just another milestone in their life. They snickered and entered the darkened auditorium with deep purple velvet seats that stretched across the theater. They chose seats in the back row beneath the balcony. The place was nearly filled to capacity in just a few short minutes. As the previews came on the screen, Shelby caught a glimpse of Jack searching the room. She could tell they caught his attention as they waved at him and he rushed to the back and settled into the seat next to Shelby.

Shelby was ecstatic and overwhelmed with joy when Jack sat down and she smiled in delight.

"Jack, I didn't think you wanted to see a stupid love story," she mocked, turning to Mary with a wink.

"Shelby, I wanted to make sure you and Mary were going to be okay since this is the first time you've been to the movies by yourself." He handed each one of them a bag of hot, buttery popcorn.

"Oh, Jack, I'm glad you changed your mind." Shelby smiled, looking at his face, as he watched the big screen.

Shelby and Mary wiped tears away from their cheeks as the movie ended. Jack turned his head to the wall and hid his face in an attempt to keep anyone from seeing his watery eyes. Shelby knew the movie had gotten to him.

"What an awesome love story," Shelby remarked. Everyone was silent as they slowly exited the theater. It was a movie so overwhelmingly emotional and one that they would never forget.

They crossed the theater lobby and went outside where they took a seat on the stairs.

Finally, breaking the silence, Jack jolted from the ground and started running the stairs as if he were at football practice.

Mary and Shelby watched as he made a complete fool of himself, grabbing them as he stretched his legs taking double steps in his sprint of the stairs, up and down he went.

Mary's mom drove up to the front of the theater and Mary sprinting down the stairs as she left Jack and Shelby alone.

Jack smiled at her and said, "Shelby, that was a really sad movie. Did you like it?"

"I had tears in my eyes, but it was good because he *really* loved her," Shelby replied.

"Yep, but it was too sad for me. I don't like it when people die," he said with a frown on his face.

"I know, Jack, it's really bad. I never told you about my best friend, Gina, Mary's twin sister." Shelby looked off into the distance for a brief second to gain strength to talk about Gina. She took a deep breath and pressed ahead. "She died a year ago and I miss her so much sometimes that it hurts."

He moved closer to her and wrapped his arm around her shoulder. "Wow, Shelby that's awful, what happened?"

She licked her lips and swallowed down hard, wishing that in doing so, she could make the words go away. "She drowned when her family was on vacation at the beach in Panama City." It was the first time she had ever told anyone about Gina's death, and she knew Mary never talked about it.

Jack's grip tightened on her and he said softly, "Oh, Shell..."

Shelby admitted, "I still can't believe she's gone."

"It's okay, Shelby. I had no idea," he said as he reached for her hand and held it tightly in his. "I'm so sorry, Shell."

She lifted her eyes to his. "It's okay, but please don't tell anyone."

Jack let out a somber sigh. "I won't. I promise." He paused for a moment and then said, "Thank you for telling me. I get it now and I'm here for you."

She snuggled into his embrace, just as Ali McGraw did with Ryan O'Neal, and everything was right.

Chapter Four

It was another hot and humid day in the late summer of 1972. Fourteen-year-old Shelby moved at a snail's pace and plopped down into the front seat of the station wagon lugging her overflowing tote bag tossed over her shoulder crammed full of her swimming gear.

Frances grinned and twisted her head at the sight of her daughter. "Shelby, do you think you have everything now?"

"I think so," she replied. "Wait, my purse!" She snatched the car door handle, flinging it open. She dashed for the front porch rocking chair where she'd left her pocketbook. She seized it and rushed back to the car. "Okay, Mom, I'm ready. Hurry, let's go."

Fifteen minutes later, Frances steered the station wagon down the gravel lane at the Kissing Bridge leading to the swimming area. Weeks of no rain had dust churning around in the air and Shelby was hesitant to open the car door.

Squinting to see through the dust, Shelby carefully glanced over the riverbank searching for Jack.

"Are you okay?" her mom asked.

"Yep," she replied, and opened the door. She flapped her hands in front of her face, coughing lightly from the still unsettled powder. She gathered her things and reached over to kiss her mom on the cheek.

"Okay, sweetie, I'll be back about dark, if that's good. I'm going to church to help with homecoming preparation. You be careful and have fun."

"I will, Mom," she said as she tugged on the heavy bag, climbed out of the car and made her way over to the grassy area near the sandbags on the bank of the Chattahoochee River.

Shelby found her perfect spot to set up camp. She shook out the quilt and then tossed it up in the air, letting it fall gently on the grass. She knelt down on the quilt, kicked off her flip-flops, and removed her tee shirt and shorts, revealing her new, pink bikini. Her dad had taken her shopping for it the other day and had been very concerned when he saw her model it.

"You're too young and innocent and you're developing too fast," Joel had said to her.

Shelby laughed at her dad. "Like I can stop myself from growing up, Dad."

He'd frowned at her and then smiled. "I don't have to like it."

A smile graced her face now at the memory, but she had to admit that the bikini did look pretty snazzy on her. Her breasts had filled in and her hips curved in the right places. She just hoped Jack took notice of her grown-up appearance.

She removed her things from her bag one at a time and meticulously placed them on the quilt. Grabbing her purse, Shelby searched for the breath mints she bought with her allowance. She opened the tiny package and tossed one into her mouth, wanting to make sure her breath was fresh when Jack arrived. She turned her transistor radio on to full volume, and repositioned it to eliminate the radio waves crackling over the speaker, and suddenly picked up "*It's Too Late*" by Carole King. She smiled and hummed along, as it was one of her favorites.

Lying back on the quilt, she rolled up her towel and placed it under her neck. The sun shone brightly in the sky, warming her skin and causing her to squint. She reached for her sunglasses and placed them on her face before relaxing with her Harlequin paperback while she awaited Jack's arrival.

Thirty minutes had gone by and the sweltering heat had Shelby sweating, so she sat up, crossed her legs, and wiped away the perspiration from her face and neck with her towel. Shelby stood up and walked over to the riverbank. She slowly climbed down and sat on the rigid sandbags. The coldness of the river had Shelby shivering when she put her feet into the liquid. She kicked the water up into the air as she gently splashed herself, creating chills that rushed over her body.

Shelby was startled out of her playfulness when she heard Jack shout out.

"Hey, Shell! Damn, Mom just dropped me off." He stumbled on the loose gravel as he scrambled across the dirt toward her. "I was afraid you wouldn't be here," he exclaimed, trying to catch his breath.

"Where have you been Jack... ass?" she said sarcastically. "I've been waiting for you."

"Damn, Shell," Jack replied.

"Jack, mind your mouth," she said teasing him, knowing it was his way of venting his frustration for being late.

"Granddaddy had us in the tobacco field all morning and then we had to help him load the truck and haul it down to the warehouse," Jack explained as he peeled his shoes off and tossed them aside.

Jack leaned over, extended his hand to touch Shelby's shoulder, and nonchalantly took a seat beside her on the sandbags.

Shelby was frazzled by Jack's innocent touch that sent waves of tiny goosebumps throughout her hot and sweaty body.

She slowly blinked her eyes as she felt his closeness, and she glanced down at his long tanned legs stretched out next to hers. Shelby was overwhelmed by the magnetism of his body as their legs touched lightly.

Continuing to explain his tardiness, Jack said, "Then, I had to wait for Mom to get back from town so she could bring me. I can't wait until next year when I get my driver's license."

"How exciting," she said as she turned to face him.

"I'll come pick you up and we can go to lots of places."

"Gosh, Jack, that would be so much fun!" she exclaimed, ecstatic over his response.

Jack noticed Shelby had begun to change, and he loved her sweet and funny personality, but that wasn't all he observed.

She was more than just a friend now and even though they had technically been boyfriend and girlfriend since the sixth grade, Jack's feelings for Shelby had begun to come alive. He knew in his heart that he loved her and wanted to spend every minute he could with her.

Jack watched Shelby as she rhythmically swung her feet in a circular motion to the tune of the cool rushing waters of the river. She slightly kicked her feet toward him and splashed him out of his thoughts.

Startled from the cold water, Jack smiled at her. "Hey, you!"

She frowned at the thoughts consuming her. "Jack, I hate that you have to work so hard in the fields. I know it's really hot out there," she said.

Jack reached over and took Shelby by the hand, gently squeezing. "It's okay, Shell. I don't mind it as long as I get to come see you when I'm finished."

Shelby let out a small sigh of relief as she smiled vibrantly at Jack. She returned his hand squeeze with one of her own that sent an electrical jolt up and down her arms. Even though she was hot in the summer heat, chills of excitement danced across her skin because of the close contact with Jack.

Jack let go of her hand and then slid into the river to cool off. He began splashing her in the face, as she roared with excitement when he reached up, grabbed her around the waist, and pulled her into the water as their bodies touched.

Frightened of the intimacy of his hips adjoining hers, she lightly pulled away from his embrace. She'd never been this close to Jack, or anyone for that matter, and it scared her for a brief spell. She was disappointed, though, when Jack eased his grip letting her go free.

He swam toward the pier, but called back to her. "Shell, come on, I want to show you what we found last week. I forgot to tell you Hank and I went tubing down the river and came upon this really cool place," he shouted out with excitement.

Still recovering from Jack's surprise embrace, Shelby was breathless and a bit startled by their intimate nuzzle. She smiled at Jack and hoped he didn't notice her resistance. She shook off her thoughts, breathed in deeply, and swam toward him.

"Come on, Shelby, I'll get you an inner tube." He climbed up on the pier, grabbed two inner tubes, and tossed one to her. He threw the other one into the water. Jack lunged in the air and then landed his butt right in the middle of the hole, creating a cannonball-like wave of water that landed right in Shelby's face. She laughed in delight while she wiped away the water.

She scrambled quickly, mounted her own float, and then followed in pursuit of Jack and his frantic maneuvering to the center of the river. The two of them were quickly swept away by the powerful current.

Jack gripped Shelby's hand and held it tightly against his inner tube as he steered her away from the bank. He tried to keep her from getting caught in the tree branches hanging over the river. She smiled as she felt his strong hand holding hers securely.

The river opened wide and they began floating freely along with the current. Shelby was captivated by the beauty of the unspoiled nature on the river and the picturesque view of the canopy of trees lined the water's edge; many of the tree's branches extended out into the river.

She was spooked by the sound of beavers flapping fearfully to catch their attention in an attempt to defend their territory, and she was surprised at their boldness.

Swiftly moving with the current down the river, Shelby had a sense of peace and there was no one in the world she would rather be with than Jack. He was very familiar with the waterway from his many trips up and down the river. She relaxed knowing she was in his care.

Around the bend, Shelby gasped at the breathtaking sight of a beautiful, white sandbar.

"Shelby squealed, "It's gorgeous!"

"It is, isn't it?" he replied.

She recalled the many times she and her dad had traveled the river and he often reminded her of how nature had a way of defining beauty. The sandbar was full of snowy white sand. She felt as if she had been picked up and dropped off on a deserted island in the Caribbean Ocean; somewhere she had never been before, but had seen pictures of in magazines.

With their feet kicking and hands splashing in the water, they maneuvered their way to the edge of the sandbar. Jack sprang from his float and snagged Shelby's hand, pulling her out of the inner tube.

"Welcome to paradise," he exclaimed.

She stumbled and he caught her fall. Their bodies crashed together, touching in sensitive places. Their eyes met in a gaze and Shelby looked intensely into the depths of his orbs. They just stood there holding each other, neither blinking, neither flinching. And then, Jack smiled at her and it took her breath away. She dazzled him with a grin of her own.

Playfully, Shelby began to swirl around like a child playing ring-around-the-rosy with her arms stretched out like the feathers of a free bird in the wind.

"Oh, Jack," she cried out. "This is wonderful."

Taking his hand in hers, they began to skip in a circle, around and around like small children. They kicked up the sand in the air as they went faster and faster.

It took only a few minutes before they both felt a little dizzy and they slowed down.

Shelby held firmly to Jack's hands and she tilted her face up to the sky, absorbing the sun's warm rays against her skin. She closed her eyes gently and smiled as she clutched his hands tighter.

Jack was nearly breathless, and for the first time, her rare beauty awakened his passion as it radiated from the sun shining brightly on her face.

He was overcome by his feelings and recognized now his love for her, completely absorbed in the magical moment. He had absolutely fallen in love with Shelby.

His eyes slowly moved over her beautiful body, wondering when she had gone from a girl to a woman. He pulled her gently to him and she lifted her head to look into his eyes. He knew she saw him staring at her body and she was okay with that. As he brought her closer, she uncontrollably succumbed to his embrace. He reached up and gently touched her lips with his fingers.

Shelby was ignited by a pulsating sense of surrender and before she could breathe another time, he leaned forward and kissed her lips tenderly, leaving her every nerve ending electrified.

"My Tootie," he whispered, holding her tightly in his arms.

~~~

Jack and Shelby were two peas in a pod. The magical bond they shared was a dazzling display of cheerful smiles, teasing, and fun times. They were best friends who were crazy in love.

Their liveliness fascinated their teachers and classmates alike. Jack's mischievous and charismatic temperament was always over-shadowed by Shelby's sweet and protective nature.

Just barely teenagers, Jack and Shelby continued their storybook romance, as many people called it, throughout their high school years.

In early October of their senior year, Shelby was waiting in the breezeway outside Jack's homeroom class. He appeared with a girl next to his side and introduced her.

"Hey, Shelby, this is Denise Davenport. She just moved here from Dothan," Jack said.

Shelby admitted that she was surprised at Jack for taking such an interest in her. There had been many girls that came to Valley over the years and he'd never even noticed them in the past. Then again, none of them had looked like Denise Davenport. She wore a pair of low cut hip hugger pants, revealing her lower midriff area, and her blonde hair hung past her shoulders in loose curls. From her quick overview of Denise and judging from Jack's reaction to her, Shelby knew that he wouldn't be the only one interested in helping this new girl feel at home in their school.

Shelby reached over, jerked Jack by the arm, and held him tightly in an attempt to stake her claim on him. Shelby's body language was all she needed to make sure Denise knew Jack belonged to her. She observed Denise's watchful eyes skimming
~~~

over her and gathering her own impression of Shelby in return.

Denise responded boldly, “Hey, Shelby. Nice to meet you. Jack’s been super-sweet to me since we met.”

“I’m sure he has,” Shelby said, glaring at him.

Jack didn’t get it, though. “Maybe you could show Denise around some, too,” Jack said, oblivious to the tension between the two girls.

Shelby reached under his arm and pinched his side. Jack jerked around and hollered, “Ouch!” Shelby just smiled and batted her eyes at Denise and said, “Okay, Jack. Sounds good. We have to go now.”

With a deliberate smirk, Denise said, “I’ll see you in history class, Jack. Save me a seat.”

Full of anger now, Shelby spun away with Jack on her heels.

“Shell, what the hell was that all about?” he asked.

“Oh, no you don’t, Jack... ass!” she exclaimed. “Don’t you be hanging around that girl. She’s no good, Jack.”

“Aww, you’re just jealous,” hc chimcd in and deliberately turned back at her, “See you later, Denise.” He knew he was adding fuel to the fire.

With an angry reply, Shelby reached up and slapped him on the back. “Don’t piss me off, Jack.”

After weeks of watching Denise throw herself into Jack’s line of sight and flirting mercilessly with him—much to his cluelessness that she was even doing it—Shelby needed someone to confide her feelings to. Her mother was the perfect person to listen.

“There’s a new girl named Denise who just moved here from Dothan, Mom. She doesn’t have many friends and, for some reason, she hates me. She’s always after Jack and desperate to get his attention, even knowing that he and I are together. I can’t be her friend and besides, she irritates me. It’s like she has something against me and I’ve never done anything to her.” She shook her head in dismay.

Frances imparted her opinion. “Shelby, I’m sure it must be hard for her moving like that and we don’t know her circumstances, so please just try to be kind and compassionate.”

“I know, Mom, it’s just so hard when she’s so mean to me and so obviously out for Jack’s attention or whatever else she can get from him,” Shelby replied.

“Shelby...” Frances said right before Shelby interrupted her.

"Denise stopped me in the hall the other day and told me I didn't deserve Jack and I better watch out," she said bitterly.

"She apparently has touched a nerve," Frances said.

Shelby cringed, though, when she heard her mother's voice tell her, "No relationship is without struggles, sweetie, and sometimes people come into our lives to teach us the importance of commitment. Maybe Denise is a blessing in disguise."

"I hope you're right," Shelby said.

As the months passed, Shelby heard her mom's words echoing in her ears, trying desperately to understand them. However, Denise's quest to win Jack's attention kept Shelby on her toes. Jack, who was absorbed in his own world of school, football, and guy things, was clueless and felt sorry for Denise.

"It's okay, Shell. Don't worry. All is well. You're my girl," Jack tried to soothe her apprehension.

"Don't *you* forget that," she said, hoping his words didn't come back to bite either one of them in the ass.

Chapter Five

On the eve of Valley High School's 1974 graduation ceremony, Shelby balanced cautiously as she climbed the steps of the bleachers towering over Ram Stadium.

The sun dipped low on the horizon as it began to cool down from a hot and humid May afternoon. She reached the top bleacher of the empty stadium, breathless and with a grateful sigh of relief. She quietly sat alone gazing over the football field as she began to reminisce.

She closed her eyes and could feel the excitement and loud roaring sounds ringing in her ears from the Rams' fans cheering on their favorite team. The stadium roared as Jack threw the football high into the air. She remembered it as if it was yesterday. It was a long toss and Hank leaped up with both arms extended. The ball landed effortlessly in his hands. The crowd thundered and Jack darted across the field filled with elation when he saw the referee's arms in the air signaling a touchdown. Valley High won the last game of the season in the fall of 1973, with Jack the hero.

Shelby was so proud of his accomplishments, even though it had been a struggle to keep him on a straight and narrow path; always living on the edge. He was the one who filled her heart with delight and she was grateful for the part he played in her world.

She reached up and touched the locket on the necklace Jack gave her for Christmas the year before; gently she twirled it around with her fingers.

She knew it was his expression of love for her. While it was a small trinket, its meaning was not only symbolic, but also realistic as it was his heart and he had given it to her. It was his love in the purest form and she could feel his arms surround her as she continued to rub the pendant.

She recalled he had helped her put it on the morning they'd opened their gifts. She was elated and loved it, and made a promise to him that she would never take it off.

Tomorrow would mark their first real-life milestone. One she now had bittersweet feelings about. It was the end of their childhood, the end of their innocence, but she had great hopes that they would share many more memories in the future.

Just the thought of leaving high school, her parents, and Jack for the next four years saddened her, but her desire to get her teaching degree so she could pursue her passion for educating children tugged heavily on her heart. She knew it was the natural path for her to take on her next life step.

Shelby sat proudly, and with her head tilted high, she glanced around the empty stadium once again, breathing in the remembrance of so many special memories.

She recalled how she watched Jack from the bleachers as he scrambled around the field on the days he had football practice. Periodically, between the coaches' calls, he would stop with a quick glance in her direction. Her heart would always flutter, but it never missed a beat when he paused and raised his hand for a thumbs up. It let her know that even though he was occupied with something he enjoyed so much—playing football—she was still never far from his thoughts. Shelby always returned a smile letting him know she was there watching. After practice, he would run up the bleachers all sweaty and stinking to snatch her up in a big bear hug, wiping her with all his nasty perspiration. She'd shiver in delight as she'd exclaim, "Eww, Jack!"

Sharing their high school years together had been amazing for Jack and Shelby. There were many pep rallies and parties, laughter, tears and cheers, friends, and riding the old school bus on their way to and from the football games. They talked, held hands, and she would cover for him whenever he went to grab a smoke. If she'd catch a whiff of beer on his breath, she would disguise it with mints she kept in her purse.

But, tomorrow symbolized a different era for them and she recognized she had to see this new age with a fresh vision for their future. Shelby found herself fretful over the unknown; she'd felt safe here with Jack. She had no idea how this next phase in their life would affect their relationship when she left for college in the fall. It would be the first time they would go their separate ways... at least for short periods of time.

She looked down at her watch and realized she was going to be late to meet Jack, but she wanted to reflect over the time she'd spent here at Valley High School. She was keenly aware that tomorrow evening she and Jack would share their last momentous walk on the football field.

The sun was setting now over the stadium and Shelby seized one last glance across the field. She stood and slowly stepped down the bleachers, excited for their achievements.

She brushed her hair away from her face as she reached the last bleacher and descended to the ground. She smiled, as she felt full of contentment, a breath of air filled her lungs and she quickly exhaled as she headed toward her car. She was ready to start the new journey into the next chapter of her life.

She hopped into her car and started it up. As she put the Volkswagen in gear, she tossed her hair over her shoulders and glanced into the rearview mirror at a place she held dear to her heart.

~~~

Graduation day had finally come and Shelby paced the sidewalk while she kept track of the time. Her nerves were beginning to unravel and sweat started to bead up on her forehead. She searched in her purse for a tissue, and gently dabbed away the perspiration trying to avoid messing up her makeup.

She was unnerved with Jack. "Where the hell is he?" she grumbled under her breath. She combed the parking lot for him. "He's late as usual." Walter and Hank were not there either, and she was sure they were responsible for his tardiness.

Shelby always tried to blame others for Jack's behavior, but deep down in her heart, she knew Jack was the kingpin leader and everyone else followed his command. There were times when she wished he weren't so free-spirited.

Everyone loved him despite his behavior. It had been that way for years now and Shelby wasn't optimistic he would change anytime soon. She had great expectations for Jack and his future. Many times she felt the need to shout at him. She dropped her head and shook it, as she smiled at the thought of him.

"Tootie!" Jack called from across the parking lot.

Shelby turned quickly to see him as he raced across the breezeway with Walter and Hank right on his heels.

"Get your ass over here, Jack. Where have you been? You are always making me wait," Shelby said, with intense firmness in her voice.
~~~

Jack reached to take her by the arm and with a silly grin on his face; he stumbled on the edge of the sidewalk.

In disgust, Shelby grasped him by the arm and swung him about to face her. "Oh Jack," as her words paused... *whoa,* she was taken aback by the strong whiff of his beer breath. "Have you been drinking? It's graduation, for heaven's sake," she continued to scold him in disbelief.

"Aww, Tootie, don't get your panties in a wad." He laughed sheepishly turning and winking at his friends.

"Jack, stand up straight," she said as she shook him by his shoulders and tugged at his clothes. She quickly turned to his friends and gave them a frown.

"Tootie, Uncle Ernie got us a cooler full of beer, and..."

"How many have you had?" she asked, stopping his words in their track. "You stink like beer."

"Aww, I'm okay," he said, trying to gain his composure.

"Damn it, Jack, you could have waited until after the ceremony."

Frantically, she searched her purse for a mint. Finding the last one in the package, she reached up and touched his lips. Jack opened his mouth like a puppy being given a treat by his master. She placed the mint into his mouth and leaned close to him. Gently, she kissed him on the lips and whispered, "I'll always take care of you, Jack."

With a twinkle in his eyes, he smiled and said, "I love you, Tootie." He professed boldly, "We have a cooler full of beer and we're going to celebrate right after the ceremony down at the Kissing Bridge, you'll have to come with us, Shell."

"It seems you've already started celebrating without me," she replied, looking at him in dismay.

Jack exclaimed with a slurred voice. "We've been out all day fishing and we just had to have one last beer on our way over and we caught a bunch of fish, too," he announced eagerly.

Shelby was annoyed at him now.

Brushing off the front of Jack's shirt and straightening his tie, Shelby boldly interceded. "If it's not smoking, it's fishing, and if it's not fishing, then it's drinking beer. You three better stop drinking, it's not good for you," Shelby said, cutting her eyes at Walter.

Walter grinned, threw his hands up in the air, and declared, "Hey, it ain't me, Shelby."

She took Jack's face in her hands firmly, demanding his attention one more time before the ceremony started.

"You are my best friend and we have made it this far. We *are* graduating, Jack," she said, still holding his face tightly to maintain his awareness.

Jack caught her eyes, and with a sincere tone of his voice, he said, "We made it, Shell. If it hadn't been for you by my side all these years, I don't think I could have done it. I know you're the one that made me do it."

He reached around her waist and pulled her close, holding her tightly in his arms. Shelby surrendered to his hug and held him closely; wishing time could just stand still.

Jack broke away, "Okay, ass." He reached down and pinched her on the rear end. "Shelby, there's the bumblebee again." Laughingly, he said, "Come on, let's do this."

Shelby flushed with embarrassment as she felt everyone watching them. She swatted his hands away and playfully slapped him on the back as he ducked from her swing. "Jack, don't do that," she said with a grin.

"Oh, wait. Come here just for a minute," Shelby said as she motioned him to have a seat on the concrete bench. "I know we only have a couple of minutes, but I brought my yearbook with me and I want you to write in it."

"Aww... Tootie," he said with a grin. He grabbed the pen, opened the book, and wrote:

> *Roses are red, my love, violets are blue, sugar is sweet, my love, but not as sweet as you.*
> *I love you, Tootie.*
> *Jack*

He closed the book and handed it over to Shelby. She opened it and read his note. Slowly, she shut the book and looked in his direction with a smile.

"Thank you, Jack, and I love you, too." Shelby reached over and kissed him on the cheek.

They were startled when Denise ran over to interrupt their quiet time to remind them it was time to line up. "Come on, Jack, you're right behind me. We have to hurry," she boldly announced.

Shelby squinted, cut her eyes at Denise, and shot a look toward her that could have burned holes in rocks. It was the one thing that irritated Shelby the most; in everything they did, Jack was always right behind Denise when it came to alphabetical order.

Jack, in a semi-drunk state, sprang from the bench and shuffled with his hands tightly in a fist and his arms moving in a motion of imitating a train, and took his place behind Denise.

"Toot, toot," he shouted out as he gave Denise a fun loving push forward. She radiated in delight over Jack's playfulness as she tilted her head and gave Shelby a smirk.

Shelby stomped away and took her place further down the line, several students behind the two of them.

Jack turned to face Shelby and with a giddy smile, blinking eyes and his innocent look, Shelby couldn't help but grin at his amazing silliness. She just hoped he could make it down the aisle, to his seat, and then up to the stage to get his diploma without falling flat on his face.

The music began to play over the loudspeaker and the announcer proudly introduced the 1974 graduating class of Valley High School. All one hundred and ten graduates paraded across the field toward the center of the stadium where everyone had a white folding chair awaiting their arrival.

Once they were all in place, the emcee motioned for them to take their seats. Shelby looked toward Jack and noticed his antsy and impatient behavior. He hated all the formalities of speeches and awards. Knowing he'd be feeling jittery, she gave him a smile and thumbs up to remind him that it wouldn't be long now.

The loudspeaker squeaked, as the music of Jim Croce's "*Time in a Bottle*" played out. Shelby closed her eyes as she sang along with the music. She wanted all of her wishes and dreams to come true, all tied up in a box full of memories and visions of how she would spend them with Jack. The music faded and she turned to see him staring at her.

It wasn't long after everyone had their walk across the stage, the ceremonial handshake, and receipt of the diplomas when the announcer instructed them to stand.

Jack scrambled without thinking and pushed his way through his classmates, to get to Shelby. He grabbed and hugged her as they reached for each other's tassel, and moved them to the opposite side of their caps.

"Ladies and gentlemen, friends and family, I present to you the 1974 Valley High School graduates," the announcer said.

Shelby and her classmates leaped for joy. Both she and Jack tossed their caps into the air in celebration of breaking with this stage of their life. Hugging each other tightly, they'd made it together.

Cheers erupted from the group of close friends as they bounced up and down, for their glorious achievement. Jack and Shelby had reached a milestone together, along with their high school friends, Mary and Justin, Walter and Sadie, and Hank and Wendy. Through the melee of the ceremony, caps lying on the ground, and the entanglement of sleeves from the robes a result of everyone hugging, Shelby could see Denise standing on the periphery watching everyone else.

Shelby felt a twitch of heartache as she caught a glimpse of Denise's sad expression as she turned and walked away still holding her cap.

Even though Shelby felt her heart reach out to her, the question remained; did Denise really think she would rush to her side to console her? Not a chance.

Chapter Six

The conversation at Sunday's dinner table had Shelby excited for Jack; he was starting his new job on Monday at the Langdale Textile Mill, a position secured by his mother.

Everyone knew the Textile Mill had been the driving force of the economy in Valley since the late 1800s, employing generations of families. The mills were gracious and they took a personal approach to caring for the people of Valley, welcoming everyone to their staff for years.

"Mrs. Emerson, I'm glad Jack will be working with you, maybe you can do something with him and hopefully keep him out of trouble." Shelby laughed as she talked to Jack's mother, searching his eyes for a bit of a comeback.

Mrs. Emerson tossed her head back and laughed. "Shelby, dear, I don't know if anyone can lasso this young man. We'll just have to wait and see. Maybe his dad can accomplish it for us."

Jack nodded, smiled, and continued to gnaw on his lunch. Fried chicken and mashed potatoes were his favorite meal and his mother was always catering to Jack's every whim.

Shelby commented, "He needs to grow up soon and start fending for himself."

Jack laughed out loud, turned, and glanced at her. "Nope, I like things just the way they are, Shelby. Mom takes good care of me." He added a wink at his mother for good measure.

As an only child, he had been fortunate having grown up with two loving parents. His father was the sheriff of Chambers County, and his mother worked at the mill. He'd had the necessities of life and nothing more, nothing less. "A simple life," Jack said.

Mrs. Emerson, a quiet and soft-spoken, God-fearing, southern lady, had an exemplary reputation in the community and

Jack often referred to her as an open book. To him, she was absolutely the perfect mother and he was proud of her.

His mom smiled at him from across the table; seemingly humbled at his remarks. She leaned over to Shelby and said, “You have to remember, dear, Jack is a miracle child.”

“I didn’t know that,” Shelby said, listening closely. “How so?”

Mrs. Emerson set her napkin down. “I came from a family of eight children, so I always wanted a big family of my own. But we struggled with two miscarriages before our Jack was born. The doctors weren’t even sure Jack would make it full term. So, you can image upon his birth, I claimed this boy to be a blessing and an angel from heaven.”

Shelby smiled hearing this story. “I had no idea.”

“I knew Jack would be my only child and that I would love him with all my heart,” Mrs. Emerson concluded. She reached over and ruffled her son’s hair. Jack just rolled his eyes and shoveled up another mouthful of potatoes.

Shelby couldn’t help but roll her eyes as she watched him. On the precipice of being a man, yet still just a little boy at heart sometimes. And, he was *her* angel, too.

“Yes, Shelby he’s my angel from heaven,” Mrs. Emerson proudly said.

Jack cast a glance up from his plate and gave Shelby a wink. “See, I told you I’m an angel, Tootie.”

Shelby raised both her hands in the air. “You never cease to amaze me,” she replied.

Jack had no desire for college, knowing he’d eventually step in and take the reins upon his father’s retirement as sheriff, a position held by the Emerson family for three generations.

Jack fully understood and respected his father’s position. Yet, he struggled with the untamed raging hormones that every young man experiences. He delighted in the rush of living on the edge, and many times, he found himself just short of a calamity. Jack often provoked his father’s authority and truly despised the façade of a “good boy” reputation.

But with Shelby’s watchful eyes scrutinizing his every move, she reminded him often of the day he would take his father’s position and the necessity to maintain his character.

Jack acknowledged his devious ways and accepted that Shelby was probably right, but his ego hungered for attention and he couldn’t seem to restrain himself at times. But in spite of it all,

Shelby did quite well in sustaining his stature, for the most part, he admitted.

Jack sat quietly observing Shelby and his mom cleaning the kitchen. "Those two ladies are my entire world," he whispered under his breath. He acknowledged how much they got along and it warmed his heart.

Jack had spent the last few weeks examining his own life and he anguished over Shelby's departure in the fall for college, knowing things would be different.

They had spent the last six years together and she meant everything to him. She was his best friend and he was going to miss her sweet smile and demanding ways—always telling him to behave and stay out of trouble.

He knew Shelby loved him, but he was beginning to feel insecure at times as he counted down the days until she left for college. He prayed often that their relationship would remain strong while she was away. He didn't know what he would do if he ever lost her.

A knife pierced his heart when he recalled Denise's agonizing words, during a conversation in history class just a few short months ago. She'd told him, "Jack, get a grip, man. You know she's going to leave you here, go off to some fancy college, and find someone else. She's beautiful and you know all the guys are going to be after her."

He had played Denise's words over and over in his mind and his heart ached as he confessed she might be right. Shelby was a vivacious, confident, and passionate young woman and he recalled the many times she shared her compassion for children and her dreams of one day becoming a schoolteacher.

Shelby noticed his gaze and loudly banged a wooden spoon on a metal pot she was drying. It startled his thoughts and he smiled at her.

"What's up?" she asked.

He just shrugged and smiled. Her heart melted at his sweet disposition.

Jack slipped back into his deep thoughts. He desperately wanted to marry Shelby, but he hadn't been able to muster up the courage to pop the question. Even though he loved her with all his heart and fearlessly wanted Shelby to be the one he spent the rest of his life with, he doubted he was good enough for her. She deserved so much more. Shelby would talk about the beautiful house they would have someday and, of course, lots of children. He often wondered how he could possibly give her those things being just a mere mill worker and the hope of someday being fortunate enough to land the sheriff's position.

He had considered going to college, for Shelby's sake, but he'd barely made it out of high school and there was no way he felt he would make it in college. He could only hope and pray she would return to him someday and that was all he had to hold on to. His love for her was deep and he was willing to let her go to pursue her educational dreams. After all, what could he possibly offer her?

"Nothing more than a simple life with a simple man," he resolved as he recalled another conversation with Denise. She smarted off to him that there was nothing simple about Shelby, that she expected the better things in life. Jack needed to be more realistic about his situation and not disappoint her if he couldn't follow through and he was sure he never wanted that to happen.

When the dinner dishes were cleaned away, Shelby and Jack moved out to the front porch to swing. She noticed how quiet he was, not quite himself. The breeze began to blow across the porch and the sky darkened as they sat together.

Worried she asked, "Are you okay?"

"Yep, Tootie, I am. I've been thinking about how things are going to be different now. Life just seemed less complicated when we were in high school," he said, nodding his head.

Shelby smiled. "Sure, it was, but we have to move on, grow up now, and everything is going to be wonderful. You'll see," she said, gazing into his eyes. She reached down and patted his leg comforting him.

"Shelby," Jack reached for her small, soft hands and took them gently into his. "Let's make a promise to see each other as much as we can this summer."

Sadness now plaguing his face, she rubbed his strong and muscular hands between hers and gently squeezed them to convince him all was going to be fine.

"I promise if you will, too."

"I promise, Tootie," Jack replied.

He reached his hand up and brushed away the stray hair from her face as he smiled. "Tootie, I love you with all my heart."

Within seconds, their embrace weaved their thoughts, hearts, and souls together like a piece of silk being strung into fibers that made up the fabric of their relationship.

Shelby felt his delicate touch and with a sigh, she whispered, "Jack, I love you."

Entangled in the emotions, she was worried about him. Was she doing the right thing by leaving him in the fall?

Suddenly, thunder roared across the sky, breaking their deep, intimate thoughts. Startled by the loud noise, they each screeched with laughter. The shower began to pound the ground as a flood of water fell from the sky. Shelby grabbed him by the hand and pulled. He resisted, though. "Oh no, Shelby," Jack pleaded even as he laughed.

"Come on, let's go play in the rain," she said eagerly.

He was keenly aware of how much Shelby loved dancing in the raindrops. If he could count the times they'd done this over the years, it would be hundreds, he was sure of it. Boys were typically the ones who loved to slosh around in the water and mud, slinging it all over girls.

But no, Shelby was a rare gem and delighted in the water falling from the sky. She often referred to it as God's liquid sunshine.

Jack gave in to her tug. Shelby pulled him out of the swing and they kicked off their shoes as they dashed barefoot down the steps and into the pouring rain. Jack held tightly to her hands while they lightheartedly splashed in the puddles of water. The droplets fell from the sky, down on their heads and over their faces as they danced in the rain.

He watched her every move; her childlike behavior fascinated him. Not many people their age were as playful as Shelby and it oftentimes sparked the child in him to come alive.

He was going to miss days like this when she left in the fall. But for now, he was extremely grateful and satisfied knowing that her heart belonged to him.

Even though he was not sure what tomorrow would bring, he had today, and that was what was most important to him.

~~~

It was barely five o'clock in the morning when Jack was startled by the loud alarm clock ringing on his bedside table. He had spent most of the night tossing and turning in anticipation of starting his new job.

Within the hour, he was up, showered, shaved, and out the door on his way to the mill.

The sky was dark, and the news reported severe storms for the day in Valley, but Jack wasn't particularly concerned as he looked up at the fast-moving clouds hovering low.
~~~

The weather report apparently had everyone in a bit of a tizzy this morning upon their arrival at work. The chatter about the storms moving across lower Alabama had all of the supervisors' attention.

Jack reported to the spinning room where his mother had just briefed all of the workers on the protocol for any bad weather. She made sure everyone knew to stay away from the spinners if the power went out, to be extra careful when the power came back on, and to keep their hands away from the gears.

"Jack, I'm glad you're here," his mother said, as she motioned for everyone to start up the machinery.

"Is everything okay, Mom?" he asked with a concerned look on his face.

"Yes, we have all these women in here and it gets scary when we hear about bad weather on the way. Our floor manager isn't here today, so I'll need you to take his place."

"What does the floor manager do?" he asked. This was his first day. What did he know about any sort of management?

"Oh, don't worry, son. You just have to walk the floors and make sure the ladies don't need anything," she instructed him with a smile.

Jack felt the excitement and confidence of his new found duties and quickly shot his mom a wink, and said, "Hey, I can do that."

"I know you can, dear." She turned on her heels and headed toward her small office.

It was right after their lunch break and the machines had just been fired up again for the rest of the afternoon's work. The loud sound of the mill's emergency alarms began to blast out an ear-piercing noise. Jack was terrified by the blare and ran back toward his mother's office when the electricity began to flicker. A loud, thunderous noise exploded throughout the mill; the lights and machinery went off leaving all the women frightened and panicking in the dark room.

"Jack, can you hear me?" his mother called out to him.

"Yes, Mom," he shouted back.

"Okay, I need you to make your way to the back corner and flip the main switch off," she hollered.

The lights began to flicker off and on, as did the big spinning machines. He saw everyone stand still as he made his way toward the back wall. The room instantly became pitch black leaving everyone in the dark. The sounds of frightened women moving around echoed in his ears as they could hear the rustling of the wind shaking the mill's roof. He walked cautiously as he got closer to the end of the row. Cries bellowed out from several of the women, but he remained focused on his journey to the main switch.

An enormous clap of thunder roared across the mill and the lights flashed on once again, causing the motors on the machines to restart. From behind him in the far corner of the room, Jack heard one of the women cry out in a loud, torturous, and blood-curdling scream.

"Ooh, God, please help me!" she wailed out, obviously in intense pain.

The room went black again, except for a small amount of light coming in from the window high in the top of the twenty-foot ceiling.

Jack, horrified by the clamor, stopped dead in his tracks. Around him, everyone began to panic as they, too, could hear her continued cry for help.

Jack turned toward the sound of the bawling, "Please be quiet!"

He tried to follow along in the darkness in the direction of the woman's whimpering. His mother seemed to be closer and he could see her making her way to the lady. One woman pulled a lighter from her apron and flicked it on to give him a small beacon to follow and help him make his way to his injured co-worker.

The lady's voice was shrill with pain as Jack reached her. With the help of the low, flickering light, he saw another woman find her way back to the main switch on the wall. She reached up and slammed it down with all of her might.

After a few minutes, the electricity flashed back on, and loud gasps filled the room as everyone caught a glimpse of the woman bent over the spinner with her arm caught in one of the gears. Blood was splattered everywhere.

Jack roared out, "Give me an apron. Hurry!"

People scrambled to remove their aprons and toss them toward him. He quickly tied one of them around the upper part of the woman's arm, close to her shoulder, to restrict the loss of blood through the laceration to her forearm.

"There, there, Mrs. Wilson. We're going to take care of you," his mother said in a calming voice. Martha wiped away blood from her face as she held her tightly in her arms comforting her.

Jack worked diligently to rescue her arm from the spinner. Taking his mother's lead, he, too, spoke in a low and peaceful tone.

"You're going to be just fine," he said to her. "God's going to make it all better real soon for you."

The woman glanced up at him with fear in her eyes and a look of hopelessness and stared at him as he continued to gently work the gears. Even in her immense pain, she smiled weakly and whispered, "You are a good man, Jack." She slowly closed her eyes and continued to moan.

In no time at all, Jack freed her arm from the machine and they gently moved her to the floor. As he held pressure on her laceration, he continued to speak softly to her until the ambulance arrived.

"We've got it," the paramedic said, moving in. "You did a great job."

Jack stood back as the medical personnel took over. His breathing was staggered and his adrenalin started to catch up with him. Distraught from the incident, his body trembled as he stood by in near shock and watched them wheel Mrs. Wilson away on the stretcher. He let out a long sigh as he turned away from the crowd. He ran his bloody fingers through his hair and wiped the sweat from his forehead with the sleeve of his shirt.

As the woman was taken out, her coworkers began shouting cheers for Jack. Everyone grabbed at him, slapping him on the back, and even hugging him, thanking him for everything he had done.

"You saved her from bleeding to death," one woman said to him.

Humbled by all of it, Jack chortled, "I guess I did."

The truth was, though, without even knowing it, Jack had been forced into adulthood his first day of work.

Chapter Seven

Shelby's love and compassion for people captivated her customers as she started work at Johnson's Grocery in early June. Familiarity with her customers was a strong point for her and she enjoyed talking to them when they returned weekly for their provisions.

Everyone, with the exception of a short, grumpy, old man named Mr. Forest, loved her sweet disposition.

Shelby smiled at the way Mr. Forest greeted people. He wore his hat backward most of the time, and he would drop his head, and with a tilt of his hat, would grumble, "Hello."

He was often found meandering the aisles of the grocery store, gathering a few things in his shopping cart, mostly coffee, milk, and bread. But, he was sure to return several times a week and it appeared there were only enough groceries for one person.

Shelby tried many times to get him to talk when he would come through the checkout line. She often wondered if he lived alone or if he had any family. She thought he was kind of cute in his own special and weird way and she had taken a liking to him and oftentimes found herself guarding him against underserved criticism by others.

Shelby's protective nature was stirred and surprised one afternoon when Mr. Forest came into the store with a tall, thin, blonde-haired, green-eyed young man. Shelby was intrigued by the young man's smile and stature. One would have to admit that he could've erupted right off the pages of a men's fashion magazine.

She nodded to Stella, the other cashier, to check him out. The young man waved in their direction when he caught a glimpse of their eyes. He acknowledged Shelby's presence with a casual nod of the head as he strutted past her and down the canned goods aisle. Her gaze followed him as he lingered alongside Mr. Forest.

Stella swung her shoulders and hips in a shimmy, "Well isn't he a Casanova with his cutesy little smirk."

"Shush..." Shelby whispered across at her. "He might hear us."

Curiosity was beginning to kill Shelby and she wondered exactly who this handsome young guy was.

"Okay, mind your manners, missy," Stella added, "Don't you go forgetting about Jack now, you hear?"

Shelby's faced blushed at the remark. "Oh no, he's the love of my life and I wouldn't ever risk our relationship and mess that up," she declared.

Mr. Handsome captured Shelby's undivided attention though when he startled her. "Can you tell me what aisle Prince Albert in the can is on? Are you familiar with it?" he asked as he grinned at her.

Shelby burst out laughing when she remembered the prank call she and Gina had made many years ago. "Are you serious or are you just making fun of me?" she asked with a sneer as she put her hand on her hip and looked him square in the eyes.

"Huh? Yes, I'm serious. My uncle wanted me to grab him a can," Mr. Handsome replied with uncertainty.

Shelby was completely caught off guard. "Oh... umm... okay, yes, it's on aisle two on the left top shelf." She pointed in the direction of his request.

He smiled and said, "Thank you." Then, he saluted her with his hand, turned on his heels in proper military form, and headed for aisle two.

She brushed off her silliness and, for a split second, she felt a wave of embarrassment sweep over her. She did, however, keep a watchful eye on him, recalling his words.

Shelby watched closely as the two of them entered her checkout line and placed their groceries on the counter. She reached over and flipped the conveyor belt switch causing the food to roll slowly in her direction.

"Hello, Mr. Forest, I see you have a shopping companion with you today. I hope y'all found everything okay," she inquired in a more-than-usual greeting.

"Yep, Miss Shelby, this is my nephew, Richard Porter," he grumbled as he pointed to his nephew.

She reached her hand out to Richard for a friendly handshake. “Hey there, I’m Shelby Harrelson.”

He reached for her small hand, reciprocating on the introduction. “As my uncle said, I’m Richard Porter.” He held her hand gently and a bit longer than just a usual shake.

Shelby pulled her hand away slightly and felt she was being sucked into his gaze. She tried to concentrate on verifying the prices for each item, but she couldn’t help but observe Richard’s look and wondered if he was flirting with her through his bright green eyes.

“It’s a pleasure to meet you,” he said as he finally let her hand go free and nodded his head at her.

Shelby proceeded to ring up the groceries as they chitchatted. “So, Richard where are you from?”

“Columbus, Georgia. I’m here for the summer to help Uncle Forest around the house some,” he remarked. “How about you?”

She lifted her eyes coyly. “Me? You mean where am I from? Here, obviously, since I’m at work,” she accented with a smirk.

“Well, sure,” Richard said, laughing. “I mean, like are you originally from here or visiting relatives?”

“I’m from here; grew up here. I just graduated from Valley High School a few weeks ago,” she explained as she began to bag the groceries.

“I just graduated too, from Columbus High School,” Richard said. He handed over a loaf of bread to her and their fingers tangled for a split second awkwardly as the food went into the paper sack. He pressed on, though. “I’m going to the University of Georgia in the fall,” he proudly announced.

“Really?” Shelby countered. “I’m going to the University of Alabama in Tuscaloosa. Roll Tide!”

“Go Dawgs!” he said with a laugh.

Shelby tossed her head back. “My friend, Mary, is going to Georgia, too,” she exclaimed.

“Well, maybe I’ll have an opportunity to meet her this summer.” Then, he asked, “You didn’t want to be a Bulldog?”

Shelby shook her head. “Bama’s got a great School of Education. I’m going to be a teacher,” she said proudly.

“How cool is that?” Richard said as he grabbed the bags of groceries. “Hopefully, I’ll see you around.”

“Yeah, that would be great,” she said with a smile. “Y’all come back.”

Richard lifted his hand and waved. “Great to meet you, Shelby.”

She saw Richard's eyes beaming at her as she turned away to her register to check out her next customer in line. "Hey, Mrs. Anderson," she said, although her attention was on the charming young man she'd just met.

"Why, Shelby, you rang in those potato chips twice," Mrs. Anderson scolded.

"Oh, so sorry," she said and then winced. She needed to demolish the thoughts of the man with the bright green eyes and concentrate on doing her work.

~~~

It had been a long day and Shelby removed her apron as she walked into the break room. She popped open a can of Coke and sat down to rest her legs. *He* slipped back into her thoughts, though. Her first collective ones of Richard were compelling. He was tall, handsome, had a cute smile, and his eyes, well, there was something about his eyes that she just couldn't explain. They had a twinkle in them and they made her smile at the mere way he looked at her.

"Wow," she whispered. She had never met anyone like him and she hated to admit it, but it made her heart race in a crazy beat. No one other than Jack had ever flirted with her or looked at her like Richard Porter had done today. She had to admit that it made her feel... special.

But then, Jack always made her feel special, too.

She beamed as a vision of Jack's sweet smile filled her thoughts and she couldn't wait to see how his day had been. He was whom she wanted and he was the love of her life. She wouldn't be swayed away by some stranger's beautiful eyes.

It was getting late and she knew she wouldn't get to see Jack tonight. She punched her time card and left the store, ditching thoughts of Richard behind as she rushed home to call Jack.

~~~

The weekend promised to be a relaxing time for Jack and Shelby as they lay next to each other on a quilt in their favorite spot at the Kissing Bridge. The transistor radio played soft music as they indulged in the hot summer sun.

"Jack, do you remember Mr. Forest I told you about?" Shelby inquired, as she sat up.

"Uh-huh," Jack responded, lying next to her with his eyes closed.

"Well, Mr. Forest's nephew came with him into the store the other day. He introduced us. I had no idea he had any relatives. I've never seen anyone with him, at least since I've been there," she explained. "He's our age and seems real nice, nothing like grumpy, old Mr. Forest."

Jack opened one eye and dipped his chin down to catch what Shelby was telling him with a little more interest. "What did you just say?" he asked.

Shelby repeated her statement about Richard while Jack took a more serious approach to what she was telling him. "Yeah, we talked some, while I rang up the groceries and he told me all about himself," she announced innocently and oblivious to Jack's inquisitive demeanor now that she had sparked his interest. "He's quite different from Mr. Forest, though. Stella thought he was handsome and smooth and called him a Casanova." She paused for a minute and contemplated. "Come to think of it, he looks a lot like his uncle. Even though he's grouchy, I think Mr. Forest is kind of cute," she confessed.

Jack cleared his throat as his interest deepened. "So, you think this guy is cute?" he asked.

Surprised with his curious interest all of a sudden, she responded by tilting her head back and cutting her eyes at him. "Yes, he's kind of cute, but so what? Just because someone is cute doesn't mean I have an interest in him. I'm sure there are pretty girls down at the mill, right? You know you are the love of my life." She reached down and kissed him on the top of his head. "I love you and you have nothing to worry over," she told him.

Jack looked up and smiled. "You're my Tootie and I love you, too." He fell back against the quilt on the ground and closed his eyes, as he replayed Shelby's words in his mind.

Jack felt jealous and wasn't sure he appreciated her boldness to confess how she felt about this Richard person. Denise's words once again haunted him and he was fearful she was right about Shelby leaving in the fall and what would happen once she was away from Valley at her new college campus.

He would just have to make sure that he stayed at the forefront of her mind until it was time for her to leave for college.

~~~
~~~

An annual tradition in Shawmut was the Fourth of July celebration on the circle. Jack and Shelby rarely had any extra time to spend with their friends, so they wanted to spend the Fourth celebrating with them, just like old times.

Shelby glanced around at their group of friends as they sat surrounding the concrete picnic table. Everyone was laughing and having a good time and it encouraged her to always keep friends close to her heart.

She was saddened for all the wonderful times they'd spent together over the years because most of them would be leaving in just a few short weeks to go to college, just like her. Their lives truly would be spread out far and wide from now on. She hoped they would all keep in close contact and promise to get together when everyone came home on the weekends and holidays.

Shelby was startled out of her thoughts as the voice of the emcee spoke loudly across the speakers welcoming everyone to the annual Fourth of July celebration. He announced the day's activities; square dancing by the Hoe Down Gang, the greased pig showdown, the dunking booth, and the donkey basketball game between the police department and the school staff. Then, later in the evening, the fireworks show at dusk. He reminded everyone of the refreshments for sale, like the delicious apple pies and ice-cold lemonade. He ended his announcements with the introduction of Dorothy Sheppard, the 1974 "Maid of Cotton" singing "*America the Beautiful.*"

Jack laughed, as he winked at Shelby and said. "Tootie, you missed out on being my maid."

Shelby happily smiled back.

The circular park was now filled with families and children running and playing, squealing, shouts of joy, dogs barking, and music filling the air as the Fourth of July celebration got underway.

Fascinated by all the people, Shelby observed everyone around the circle taking part in the festivities. Suddenly, she caught a glimpse of Richard Porter across the circle. He captured her attention with a rather friendly smile and motioned his hand in her direction. Caught off guard by his boldness, she quickly returned his gesture with a shaky wave and nonchalantly spun her head away, breaking his glare.

Jack noticed the exchange of the friendly gesture and quickly demanded an explanation. "Who's the guy, Shelby?" he questioned her with an irritated and angry look on his face.

The gang all listened as she calmly responded, "That's Richard Porter. He's the one I told you about the other day. You know, Mr. Forest's nephew," she explained.

Full of curiosity, everyone looked to get a glimpse of this new guy. Jack frowned as Richard Porter once again nodded in their direction and proudly displayed his charming smile.

"So, this is the guy you think is so cute?" Jack asked sarcastically and in an insensitive manner while he kept his eyes squarely on Richard.

"I can't believe you would say that," Shelby shouted as her eyes widened and gaped at Jack, annoyed by his remarks, given their conversation earlier in the week.

"It's true, Shelby, you told me you thought he was cute," Jack grumbled with a display of anger.

She fired back. "Damn it, you know what I meant by that."

"Hell yes, I do! It means you like his looks," he said in an escalated and irate tone of voice.

Sensitive to his insecurities, she tried to lessen the situation, wanting him to know it wasn't like that. "I told you—"

He interrupted in a shout that stopped her words. "I know exactly what you meant. Is this the way it's going to be? Are you going to be waving and smiling at other guys when you leave for college? Is that what I'm going to have to put up with?"

Shelby was speechless over Jack's behavior as she tried to control her feelings. This was not like Jack at all. He'd never been jealous a day since she'd known him. What had put these thoughts into his head?

When the gang turned to look at the young woman approaching Richard, Shelby realized it wasn't a *what* that put these thoughts into Jack's head, it was a *who*.

Everything died down as the group watched Denise Davenport; dressed in a flowing yellow sundress, approach Richard Porter carrying two beverage cups. She handed him one and leaned in provocatively to show just how friendly she could be.

"Well, there you go," Shelby quipped.

Then, she took a sigh of relief, when she saw Denise and Richard arm-in-arm, but she had to admit that she was confounded by how they'd come to know each other. Either way, it didn't matter and she was grateful to see them together.

Shelby latched back on to Jack and said, "Look, he's got eyes for Denise, not me. You have nothing to worry about."

Jack growled low, but let it go for now.

Everyone watched from afar as Denise and Richard exchanged friendly chatter and laughter. Eventually, Denise noticed people staring in their direction. She smiled and waved at everyone. Denise wrapped her arm around Richard and pulled him along with her. They cruised across the circle in the gang's direction.

Shelby was a bit frazzled and she hoped that seeing Denise and Richard together would alleviate some of Jack's anxiety.

As they got closer, Shelby was apprehensive and mindful of Jack's quick temper. She reached over and placed her arm through his in an attempt to restrain him from creating a scene. She felt resistance as he took a small step forward, breaking away from her embrace. She was taken aback by his behavior, but remained calm.

"Hey y'all, this is my new friend, Richard Porter," Denise said happily, as they approached the small group of friends. "He has relatives here in Valley and I'm showing him around. Hopefully, he will meet new friends while he's here," she added with excitement.

Folks shook hands and introduced themselves, but Jack hung back, not being as friendly. Shelby felt relieved that Jack's foolish behavior was unwarranted and reached under his arm and gave him a pinch, just to prove her point; he had no reason to doubt anything she had said about Richard. She just wished she'd never told him that she thought Richard was cute. Jack was going to hang that over her head forever.

Throughout the celebration, Jack kept his distance and kept a watchful eye on Richard as the rest of the gang exchanged friendly conversation with him. He doubted Richard's motives for their coincidental meeting and Jack grumbled under his breath.

"So, Richard, you play any sports in high school?" Hank inquired.

"I played on the golf team for the last several years and we won the state championship the last four years," he responded, proud of his accomplishment.

"Wow, that's pretty awesome," Denise, clamored.

"How about you, Hank?" Richard asked.

"Yeah, I didn't play golf, but all of us played football," he replied as he motioned his head in Jack's direction. "Jack was the quarterback and Walter and I were receivers. We didn't make it to State, but we did pretty good," Hank said with a laugh. "Jack was the hero, no doubt about it, unlike the rest of us," he said with a grin on his face.

Richard turned to face Jack, "Damn. Quarterback, huh? That's pretty impressive. I bet you got all the good-looking girls falling all over you," he said forwardly. "We never had anyone watching us play golf, just the coaches. Golfing isn't glamorous like football," he said with a knowing smirk.

Jack cut his eyes at Richard. "You got that right man. It has its perks. And, yes, I guess you could say I had a lot of girls falling for me." Jack stepped back, crossed his arms over his chest, and leaned against the picnic table as he tittered at the thought of all the girls falling for him.

Shelby wasn't happy as she watched while everyone seemed amused over the exchange of words between the two guys. It appeared they were enjoying the scene, but she was afraid they would only egg Jack on.

"Richard, how does your girlfriend feel about you playing golf?" Jack inquired.

Richard sneered at him. "Didn't have one then and don't have a girl now, so it really didn't matter. I preferred to play the field. I can have any girl I want without any type of commitment," he said. Then, he added, "I hear you and Shelby have been a thing for a long time. How's that going to work out when she leaves for college and you stay here?" Richard asked curiously.

Denise must have been sensing what Shelby was thinking—that the tension between these two was going to burst into something bad. Shelby watched as Denise stepped closer and took Richard by the arm. "Want to come get another hot dog with me?"

Richard stood his ground, though.

Jack's mood became visible as he uncrossed his arms and stepped forward. "We've been a thing for a long time, and you can bet your sweet ass it will be for a long time to come. Besides what goes on with us is none of your damn business." He took his index finger and poked Richard firmly in the chest as he emphasized his last two words.

Richard threw his hands up and said, "Hey man, I'm... I'm sorry. I didn't mean anything bad about it."

Denise quickly tugged on Richard's arm to steer him away from the others. "I really want that other hot dog," she said. "Come on with me, sugar." As they turned and walked away, Denise squealed, twisting her head to look back. "We'll talk to y'all later."

Shelby, now irritated with Jack and his insensitive behavior, pulled him aside as they walked away from the others. She began scolding him for his foolish attitude toward Richard. "What the hell is wrong with you?"

Jack, in return, lashed back at her in a tone of voice she had never heard from him before. "Listen, Shelby," he said. "I don't need you telling me how to behave. I've had enough of you always telling me what to do."

Shelby's hands flew to her mouth as she was shocked by his remarks. She remained speechless and reached for him in an attempt to comfort him, but he stepped back and away from her.

"Stop it, Shelby. I don't need you to take up for me."

The commotion had captured everyone's attention. Walter moved in and reached for Jack's arm to get him to calm down. Jack pulled away. The crowd grew larger and onlookers surrounded the group as Jack's nasty temper began to flare.

"I'm not some dumb kid," he said to her—to everyone. "I saved someone's life the other day. Why don't you give me some damn credit for having a little sense for once in your life, Shelby? I'm not eleven anymore!" His chest rose and fell quickly as he expelled the thought.

Shelby stood trembling as she faced Jack while the feelings of humiliation and confusion coated her. She quickly turned to run away. Unable to keep her balance, she stumbled to the ground. She fell on a bed of rocks and took a deep cut to her knee. She screeched out from the painful fall as blood gushed down her leg.

"Shell!" Jack said as he reached for her arm, but she retreated from him.

"Get away from me," she cried out.

"Shelby's hurt!" Wendy shouted.

Suddenly, Shelby was surrounded. She pressed her hand to her knee to stop the bleeding, but all it did was intensify the pain.

Jack scrambled to her side, but she shoved his hand aside immediately.

"I don't need you, Jack!"

"Shelby, wait, I'm sorry. Please let me help," Jack said in a plea of shame.

She managed to pick herself up from the ground and noticed all eyes were on her. She pushed her way through the crowd, and she shuffled across the circle and down 23rd Drive with a limp as the blood continued to flow freely from her open wound. She had no idea how she was walking while at the same time leaving a trail of deep red fluid on the ground behind. She just wanted to get away from Jack, from the celebration, from everything.

He stood alone, wonderstruck by what he had done. This was not like him to upset Shelby this way or at all. He cringed as the image of her face replayed in his mind and the look of horror in her eyes, filled with confusion and hurt, especially when he tried to comfort her. Heartbroken, he shook the figment out of his mind. He shoved his hands into his hair and slowly walked away with a feeling of complete remorse.

Reaching home, Shelby sat quietly alone with both feet in the tub. The bleeding had subsided from the laceration. She evaluated the depth of it only to find a small slit in the skin that had bled plenty.

A knock on the opened bathroom door startled her, and she heard her mother's voice.

"Shelby, dear are you okay? I heard what happened. May I come in?" her mom asked sympathetically.

"Sure," Shelby replied as she wiped away blood from the cut.

Frances slowly sat down on the side of the tub and put her arms around Shelby, kissing her gently on the top of her head. "How's your knee, is it okay?" Frances inquired.

Shelby looked into her mom's eyes. "It's good, just a small scrape on my kneecap. The bleeding looks worse than it is. It'll be okay." Then, she took a deep sip of breath and said, "Jack was so mean to me. I don't know what's wrong with him. He's been acting funny lately and I don't know what to do," she admitted.

"It's all a part of growing up, sweetie. I know he is going to miss you when you leave and sometimes that's really hard for guys. They think you don't want to be with them anymore. This happens a lot when young people graduate from high school and they begin to pursue their careers. It doesn't mean you don't ever want to be with someone, it only means that to get prepared for a life together you must both sacrifice your wants for a short time," Frances said with a smile.

"I wish Jack could understand," she said.

Frances took the washcloth from Shelby's hand and cleaned around the cut. Then, she dabbed the wound dry with a towel, spread a good amount of petroleum jelly over it, and covered it with a fresh Band-Aid. Frances smiled and said, "Now, let me kiss the hurt away."

Shelby smiled childlike in agreement and held her knee up for her mom's healing kiss.

As painful as the cut was, Jack's words were worse. An ache jabbed at her heart as she agonized over how he had treated her. Much like she'd been henpecking him all these years and he just couldn't take it anymore.

The phone in her bedroom rang and Frances stood. "I'll get it, dear," she said as she walked away.

"Oh, Jack," Shelby whispered. "How could something like this happen?"

"Shelby, it's Jack," Frances relayed as she returned to the bathroom.

"Oh, I just can't talk to him right now. Tell him I'm not home yet," she pleaded with her mom.

"You should talk to him. At least, let him know you are okay," she directed firmly.

"I'll call him later, Mom," she promised.

Right now, he was the last person she wanted to speak to. They both needed time and space to cool off.

Chapter Eight

Jack rubbed his eyes and squinted from the bright sun gleaming through the window over the head of his bed. He threw the sheet off his legs while he stretched them high into the air. He was beyond tired after a sleepless night, thinking about Shelby, and how angry he was with himself for being so jealous of that Richard guy.

Shelby had always been very open and honest with him about everything. He couldn't believe that now, of all times, he had doubted her love. All because some slick guy waved at her.

Way to go, Jack.

He had to stop being so fearful of her leaving for college; he had to believe all was going to be fine. He couldn't let anyone put unnecessary thoughts into his head when he and Shelby only had a short time remaining together.

He reached for the phone on the nightstand and dialed Shelby's number. His attempts to reach her the night before were unsuccessful and he wondered if Mrs. Harrelson had given Shelby his message to call him.

The sound of the phone rang in his ear, he waited, and it rang and rang again.

"Hello," Joel answered.

"Mr. Harrelson, this is Jack. Is Shelby there?"

"Hey, Jack. Hold on and let me check." Jack could hear muffling as if Mr. Harrelson had put his hand over the receiver. "She's in the bathroom right now; can I have her call you?" Joel asked.

"Yes, please," Jack said sadly.

He didn't want to hang up and held tightly to the phone, as he bumped it against his chin. He pleaded in silence for Shelby to call.

He dropped his head as he slowly placed the phone back down on the receiver. This wasn't like Shelby to not return his calls. He had to keep the faith and he was confident she would call him soon. At least, that was what he hoped. He had to convince himself that everything would be okay.

Jack rolled out of the bed in his blue and green boxers and scurried into the bathroom where he caught a glimpse of himself in the mirror, face-to-face with a bearded man, and slowly examined the two-day-old hair growth.

"Hmm... a beard and a bit longer hair maybe?" he said, hesitating as he viewed himself from side to side. "Nah... Shelby wouldn't approve, but a shower and shave ought to do it," he whispered and rubbed his face with both hands.

Jack sprinted out of the shower as the phone rang. He didn't even grab a towel as he padded over in his wet feet, scrambling to answer it. He believed it would be her. The water dripped from his body as he grabbed the handset. "Shelby," he called out.

"No, it's me, Walter. Hey, I wanted to check on you. Have you heard from Shelby?"

"No, man. I've called and called and she won't take my calls, either her mom or dad answer and they just tell me she will call me back," he replied brushing his wet hair back from his face.

"Damn, I'm sorry," Walter said sympathetically.

"Yeah, man. I'm okay." Although, he was anything but.

"You want to go fishing today?" Walter inquired.

"I don't know. I was hoping to see Shelby, but since she won't call me back, I don't know what to do," he said, hesitating.

"Oh, come on. Shelby loves you. She'll call you," Walter said trying to persuade him. "Come on out with me. It'll get things off your mind for a while."

"Hmm... okay, what time?"

"I'm heading to the boat dock now, come on when you can," Walter said.

Jack dried off, dressed, and slid into his shiny, new, 1965 Midnight Blue Metallic Ford Mustang, a graduation present from his mom and dad. The tires squealed noisily as he pulled out of the drive and headed straight for the boat dock.

As he drove, he was overwhelmed and hurt by what happened the day before and he considered maybe he wasn't entirely to blame. After all, Shelby was the one who'd pushed his buttons when she admitted Richard was cute. Surely, she could understand his insecurities when she said things like that to him.

Thoughts of her dissipated as he pulled up to the old shelter next to the boat dock and put the car in park. He glanced over the pier in search of Walter and noticed all the people lined up to launch their boats for a fun-filled day on the river.

Walter hollered at Jack and motioned him toward the boat. "We're ready," Walter shouted out eagerly.

"Uncle Ernie, got us a case of beer," Walter said, grinning as he pointed to the Styrofoam cooler stashed in the hub of the boat.

"Cool man," Jack cheered with a thumb up.

"Here, you drive," Walter, said as he tossed the key in his direction.

Jack caught it in his hand as it flew up and over his head. "Touchdown," he whooped and hopped into the boat.

"Thanks, man, I needed to get out this morning. It's driving me crazy that Shelby hasn't called me back. I need a distraction or two," he said his voice trailing off.

A cooling off period for the both of them would be in good order right now, he thought as he fired up the motor.

The sound of the boat engine roared in Jack's ears as he twisted the throttle, pulled away from the dock, and headed for the open waters of the Chattahoochee.

The sun shone bright and warm on his face as he lifted his head toward the sky. With one hand on the control, he reached up and ran his fingers through his hair as the wind blew gently on his face. Fresh air was exactly what he needed.

Once they reached their regular fishing hole, Walter popped open a cold one and pressed Jack on what was bothering him.

"Hey man, so what's going on with you?" Walter inquired as they sat quietly. They cast their lines into the overgrown slough of the river where the best redbreast and bass were all tucked away.

"I don't know. I guess I'm scared to death of losing Shelby. She's leaving for college soon," Jack admitted sadly.

"Aww, you know Shelby loves you and wouldn't do anything to jeopardize your relationship. She's a good lady."

"Yeah, I know," he said. His voice trailed off as he popped the top and quickly chug-a-lugged the can of beer, he grabbed out of the cooler. "I don't want to think about the future. It makes my head hurt. Let's just fish, man."

"You got it," Walter said and tipped his beer can at him.

The two of them sat for most of the afternoon, drinking and juiced up each time they caught another fish. Most were fatties; not many throwbacks at all.

Celebrating a successful day of fishing and a boat full of redbreast, Jack and Walter were feeling no pain from the generous cooler of beer. They packed up their fishing poles and headed in, happy with the day's catch. When they arrived back at the pier, Jack slid the boat up to the dock and brought it to a quick stop as he had so many times before. Walter grabbed the rope from the front of the boat and tossed it over the pylon, and secured it tightly to the pier.

"I hate to leave you, but I've got to be at work in an hour," Walter expounded as he climbed up onto the pier.

"It's good. I got it," Jack replied as he began to tidy up the boat.

"Thanks, Jack," Walter said apologetically, as he raced across the dock and to his truck.

Jack, inebriated and clumsy, opened the cooler and grabbed another can of beer, plopped down on the boat seat, and let his thoughts quickly return to Shelby. He waved his hand in the air in a toast to her beautiful face, when he was startled by a girl's voice.

His heart soared, at first, hoping Shelby had sought him out, but then, he saw the leggy blond and slumped a bit in disappointment. "Hey, Denise. What brings you out here?"

"Hey, Jack, how's it going?" Denise asked as she hopped off the pier and into the boat with him. She sat directly facing him. "You okay?" she asked sympathetically as she shifted her body closer and moved her hand playfully on his knee.

Jack twitched a bit at her touch, and then he responded, "Yep. Everything's great," and without another thought grabbed the side of the boat to steady his balance.

Denise grinned at his unsteadiness and noted, "You're pretty woozy, aren't you?"

"I'm good," he countered as he fell slightly backward against the boat laughing. He opened the cooler once again, took out another can of beer, and shoved it in her direction. "Here you go, have a cold one on me," he said with a hee-haw.

She watched him closely as she pulled the tab on the top of the can. Jack motioned for her to join his toast. Denise slowly raised her beer and their two cans clanked together. "What are we toasting to?" she inquired.

With his head tilted in the air, and his eyes slowly blinking, he said, "To Shelby."

Denise seemed to have something mischievous on her mind, he thought, as she smiled and raised her beer can again to his.

"Here's to Shelby." She took a deep sip and then asked, "Have you heard from her since the incident last night?"

"Hell no," he interrupted, his blood boiling now at the reminder. "She won't answer my phone calls. Piss on her, Denise. You're probably right. She's going to go off to college and find some rich dude and leave my ass here," he exclaimed as the alcohol-fueled his anger. Then again, she was his Shelby who loved him. "Maybe she won't. Maybe she'll just go off and—"

Denise smiled once again and moved closer to him. Then, she cut him off, interrupting his ramble. "Hey, Jack, take me for a ride, won't you?"

He nodded and with a sheepish grin said, "Hell yeah... sure... why not? Let's do it." He turned and jerked the rope on the motor as it fired up.

Denise scrambled to release the rope from the pylon and then hopped back into the boat.

If Shelby had her future all mapped out with her college life and all, Jack could throw caution to the wind and live it up some, too.

He throttled the boat up and sped away.

~~~

Shelby pressed her head against the window as she tucked her pillow up until it was comfortable under her sore knee to keep it elevated in an effort to avoid any further swelling from the laceration.

Her favorite place to be in the entire world was the small bay window bench in the corner of her bedroom where she viewed the outside world. A special spot where she could sit, read, play with her dolls, and dream. Mostly, though she could see Jack as he pulled up in front of her house over the years. She'd hoped to see him today, but he hadn't sought her out.

The more she mulled over what happened, the more hurt she became, but she had to admit she missed him and regretted her decision not to talk to him when her mom and dad had told her he called. She wanted to see him and not talk to him over the phone.

It was Friday, though, and they always promised to meet at the Kissing Bridge and she was sure he would be there just like every other time. They would kiss and make up. Everything would be okay. *They* would be okay. She couldn't wait to see him.
~~~

She had to apologize for her bad behavior and get everything back on track. She didn't want him jealous of someone she barely knew. She needed Jack to know how much she loved *him*.

His words from last night fell on her chest like a knife piercing her heart. She had no idea Jack hated her telling him what to do and she felt horrible for doing so all these years. It was in her nature to be a bit of a mother hen to him, nurturing and supporting him, nudging him in the right direction.

However, he had never let on that it bothered him and she vowed she would never do it ever again. She had to let him grow up and be the man he was meant to be. She understood that now and hated that it took such an intense—and public—argument for him to let her know.

"I promise, I'll never tell him what to do again," she whispered.

With a broken heart and all alone, she sat for what seemed like hours as she ached and longed for him. A vision of Jack popped into her mind; he was pulling his car up in front of her house. She bolted from her seat and raced down the stairs, her hands skimming the staircase handrail. She runs out the front door and wraps her arms around him holding tightly to the man she loves. Knowing all will be okay. She smiled as her flight of imagination slowly dissipated.

She could faintly hear the ticking as the second hand was slowly creeping around the face of the clock on the nightstand. Time was crawling today, she thought.

After a while, she just couldn't wait any longer. When she turned to check the time, she noticed it was still early.

She went over to her mirrored dresser and sat down on the bench. She freshened her makeup and put on her new "Precious Pink" lipstick. She looked into the mirror, puckered up, slid the smooth gloss and rubbed her lips together. She brushed through her long flowing hair and tossed it up into a twist.

Maybe she would wear the new sundress she had bought earlier in the week with pink and white stripes and tiny shoulder straps. "I need to look nice for Jack," she said with a smile. Even though he constantly told her, "You always look so pretty."

The dress curved along her body and accentuated her waist; the front dipped low giving way for a better view of her cleavage. She smiled and captured one last peek in the floor-length mirror in the corner of her room. She did look pretty and was glad she had decided to wear it.

She gathered her things, slipped on her cute Candies shoes, and slowly hobbled down the stairs into the kitchen where Frances was busy preparing supper.

"Shelby, we're having spaghetti tonight, are you going to be here? Wow, you look really cute, dear," Frances, exclaimed as she looked up from the stove.

"No, and thank you, Mom, for noticing. If Jack calls again, please tell him I've gone to the Kissing Bridge and I'll see him there," she said somberly as she limped down the steps leading outside. She closed the door to the red Bug and threw her things onto the seat and slowly backed out of the drive.

Shelby carefully, but quickly drove through town to their special place. She parked her car and then shuffled across the pebble-lined drive of the Kissing Bridge. She knew she was a bit early, but she wanted to be waiting when Jack got there.

She had no reason to believe he wouldn't come. They had promised each other on Fridays, for sure, that they would meet after work. However, she had to admit today there were grown up type challenges she wasn't looking forward to dealing with. It was days like this she wished she were back in junior high.

She was so hurt by the episode; she just couldn't bring herself to take his calls, she needed to see him face-to-face instead. She knew he had the day off because the mills always closed for a few days the week of the Fourth of July.

Her knee throbbed with irritating pain, but it was nothing compared to the torment her heartfelt from the incident. She longed to see his face and touch him, and no phone call could take the place of his presence. She wanted to know if he really felt that way about her telling him how to act all the time. Why had he become so angry with her?

They had always had open communication about everything. There was nothing she couldn't tell him, even the silly comment about Richard. She understood now that Jack was insecure about their relationship and he needed to be comforted and confident of her love for him. Always.

She sat alone on the sand bags and gazed at the ripples of water as they danced along the top of the river. She could feel the heart charm touching her neck and she caressed it softly between her fingertips. She had Jack's heart right in the palm of her hand.

She opened her purse and removed her transistor radio. She stretched out the antenna and turned the volume up as Simon and Garfunkel's "*Bridge Over Troubled Waters*" played out.

She sat quietly and swayed to the rhythm of the music. They had never had a blow up like this before and she knew a lot of it stemmed from Jack having some anxiety over her leaving in the fall. Of course, their relationship was going to change some, but it didn't have to end. They could make it work.

She wasn't going to give up on him. He had to know that she would never want him to be anything more than himself—who he was—and that her love for him was absolute, strong, and went to the depths of her soul. No other guy would ever be able to capture her heart like he had.

She had to tell him her heart was his; it always had been and it always would be. Her thoughts brought a smile to her face and she circled her foot in the water, kicking it up and splashing lightly on her body. She began to laugh as the droplets of water trickled down her face and she felt his love in her heart. She massaged her knee gently as it throbbed harder and her effort to bend it only agitated the pain more, but she had to get up and move.

She looked down at her Timex. "Jack should be here shortly," she said dreamily.

Her anticipation of leaving him in the fall for college only added to her anxiety, but they would make it work. As much as she loved him, though, she was thrilled at the prospect of becoming a teacher. Her extreme love for children and the innocent smiles on their faces warmed her heart and made her want to be the best educator possible. However, leaving Jack would be like leaving a part of herself behind.

She hoped that in time, her emptiness would pass quickly, and they'd stay in touch with each other at holidays, during the summers, and he could always come to Tuscaloosa to visit her.

She waited and waited... hoping and dreaming. The sun had begun to set slowly behind her. The evening had come and she knew she would eventually have to give up and go home, as much as it killed her to do so.

She dabbed away the sweat from her forehead and wondered, "Where could Jack be? He's late?"

~~~

"Jack, come on. We have to go, it's getting dark," Denise pointed out as the sun fell behind the tree-lined banks. "I don't know how to start the motor!"
~~~

Jack felt Denise shake him desperately, trying to awaken him from his inebriated state. He could hear her and knew what she was doing, but he didn't care.

"Oh, Denise," he laughed sheepishly as he stumbled around the boat. He fell clumsily on his knees and cried out from the pain.

"Jack! Don't be stupid!" she shouted out.

He grabbed the rope and gave it a quick jerk, firing up the motor. As intoxicated as he was, he cautiously steered the boat up the river to the dock. The boat gradually floated up to the wooden pier as Jack killed the motor and in a stupor tumbled over his seat.

"Hank!" Denise yelled across the water when she saw him sitting on the tailgate of his truck. "Help me... please," she pleaded.

"Denise?" Hank asked. "What the hell is going on here?"

"Oh, shut the hell up, Hank, and help me get Jack out of the boat," Denise snapped.

Jack watched as Hank grabbed the rope and threw it over the pylon. He lunged down into the boat, and both he and Denise pulled Jack to a standing position as they maneuvered his arms around their neck. The boat wobbled making it almost impossible to get him up and onto the pier. Jack fell to his knees as they got him on the deck and lifted him up again and across the dock. Everything around him was a blur. Hazy and unclear. He heard Hank scolding Denise.

"What the hell are you doing? Leave him alone. Shelby would be pissed if she knew you were with Jack and you know it."

"Hank, it's none of your damn business," Denise fired back as they both struggled to support his weight.

All Jack could do was to anchor his grip and tee-heed at the two of them sparring over him. It was all so ridiculous. If he weren't so damned drunk, he'd be laughing his ass off.

Denise let out a harrumph. "Besides, you know as well as I do that Shelby's going to dump him for some rich guy when she gets to college. It's the way it always happens. He's not good enough for her."

Jack shook his head over her words, not wanting to listen as they drug him over to the old shack to lay him down to sleep off his drunken stupor. Jack moaned as he hit the floor, but at least, there were some old quilts piled up that softened the blow.

"Maybe, but you don't have a right to interfere!" Hank shouted at Denise.

"You tell 'er, man," Jack slurred out.

"Listen, I have to go, I'm late to pick up, Wendy," Jack heard Hank say. "Just leave him here; he'll be fine until he comes to."

Through blinking eyes, Jack watched as Hank took one last glance at him. Denise just stood there with her hands on her hips.

"Now, what am I going to do?" she asked.

Jack laughed sardonically. "You heard the man. Better leave me alone."

~~~

Shelby waited late into the evening for Jack. The sun had long set and only the shimmer of the moonlight glittered across the water. An occasional flicker of headlights from passing cars gave off just enough light for her to see in the darkness.

"What if he shows up?" she whispered. She couldn't miss him not now. There was so much she had to say.

She swatted at the feisty mosquitoes nipping at her legs. Each passing car made her heartthrob, in hopes it would be Jack. She raised her arm as she struggled to see the tiny hands on her watch.

"I have to find him, something is wrong," she said to no one.

~~~

Jack grunted and moaned as he tried to sit up from the rough wooden floor of the old shelter. He wiped away the sweat that dribbled down his sides from the late afternoon's heat wave.

Groggy, he slowly blinked his eyes to focus and managed to stir long enough to see the silhouette of a woman. The sun had set and the room had darkened as Jack squinted to see. He noticed she tossed her hair over her shoulder and leaned back against the far wall without saying a word.

He smiled and muttered, "That's my Tootie."

He could barely make out the sound of the woman's voice.

"Jack, are you okay?" the woman asked softly.

He managed a smile, "Yep, Tootie, I'm goooood," his voice slurred as his head swayed.

He sniffed lightly as the faint smell of a lit cigarette filled the room.

"Tootie, what are you doing smoking?" Jack laughed as he wobbled from side to side. What was Shelby doing smoking? She'd never smoked before. Maybe she was loosening up and trying out something new. His eyes slowly blinked open and shut as he tried to gather his thoughts.

He could briefly see a faint light that flickered from the flame of a small candle that sat on an old crate, right before he fell backward with a harsh thump onto the wooden floor.

"Ugh," he moaned and then snickered from the fall.

He could hear her coming closer and then he groaned softly. He felt the gentle tug of his hair from her fingertips running across his head as she pushed it back and away from his forehead.

"Oh, Jack," he could faintly hear the woman's voice.

He sensed her closeness and suddenly he felt her hand as it made a gentle connection to his body. He could feel her fingers as they traveled down his hot and sweaty chest and then crawled across his abdomen. He twitched slightly as he felt the energy begin to flow through his body and he moaned in delight.

"Shelby," eased from his lips in a whisper as he reached out to her. He was pleasantly surprised when she cradled his face in her hands, and then placed a smooth and gentle kiss on his lips. He shivered from her touch. The kiss deepened and turned. Much more than the sweet crossroads they'd shared before. This kiss was full of passion and promise.

Overwhelmed by her kiss, he reached forward, and in his boggled state of mind, pulled her close. He opened his mouth and ravenously returned her kiss and muttered, "My Tootie."

"Whatever you say, Jack," she said between nips and soft bites at his lips.

He could feel her succumb to his grasp as he pulled her body close and they touched intimately. She sighed in pure ecstasy and relaxed into his embrace.

"Tootie, I've waited so long for you. I love you, Shelby," Jack said quietly as he could hear her moan with pleasure while his hands worked over her perfect body.

Jack grappled for her frame when he felt her gently tug at the string on his swimming trunks.

He could no longer resist as she pulled at his shorts. He mustered up his strength, lifted his hips, and rolled to his side to help her. Unfortunately, he lost his balance and tumbled over from his drunken stupor.

"Jack, you silly boy," she cooed out at him.

He laughed in spite of himself, glad that Shelby wasn't fussing at him and just going with the flow. He liked her this way... relaxed and randy.

He rolled over her warm and naked body and started stroking her hair back away from her face. With his eyes closed, he began to let his lips explore, kissing her torso. Oh, how he had waited for this for so long and now she was *really* his. His fingers caressed her breasts and then skimmed down and over her belly. He felt her jerk.

He blinked in the darkness trying to make out her face, but it was all a lovely blur. "Shelby, it will be okay, I promise, I love you. I've saved myself just for you, Tootie," Jack said with a sigh. "You don't have to be afraid, I promise."

Jack could hear her whimpers of delight as she pressed her hands on his back, pulling him back to her. He took that as a green light to go, go, go.

And there, in the low-lit room of the old shack, Jack did his best to surrender all of his love and passion to the woman he'd spent a lifetime loving. They moved together in the unified harmony he'd always known would work with them. Although it didn't last as long as he'd hoped—thanks to his alcohol intake. He shook and shuddered as sweat poured off him. She sighed in his ear and held him close. Spent, he collapsed on top of her, but not before he snuggled her lovely body into his and saying, "You're now mine, forever, Shell."

~~~

Shelby's knee felt tight as she tried to get up. Flustered from the pain, she limped to her car, sat down, and glanced across the river as she felt her heartbreak. What made her believe he would come? After all, he was the one who had been so unreasonable she thought as she drove away from the Kissing Bridge.

Not much goes on in Valley on Friday nights with the exception of the movie theater during the summer. She assumed he must be at the Ram's House restaurant, where they always hung out with friends.

She slowly pulled into the parking lot, put the Beetle Bug into park, and turned off the ignition. She got out and looked through the window. She saw all of their friends eating at a table in the corner, but there was no sign of Jack.

Shelby wobbled into the noisy restaurant filled with people chatting and laughing. Hank caught a glimpse of her coming toward them. "Oh, Lord, it's Shelby," he stuttered.

"Hey guys, have y'all seen Jack?" she asked. "I've been waiting for him at the Kissing Bridge."

"Have you talked to him?" Hank asked in surprise.
~~~

"No, he tried to call me, but I didn't take his calls. I wanted to see him instead," she said sadly.

"Oh... huh... ugh..." Hank scrambled for words. "I know he went fishing with Walter earlier today and they had a lot of beer. The last time I saw him, he was passed out on the floor of the shed at the dock," he said as he squirmed in his seat.

Everyone else shrugged their shoulders and nodded that they had not seen him.

"Okay, well if you see him, tell him I've been looking for him please?" Shelby said as she cleared her throat.

Having to make a quick stop in the restaurant restroom, Shelby was in the stall when she heard Wendy and Sadie talking as they entered the room.

"Poor Shelby, she loves Jack so much. I wish Denise would just leave him alone," Wendy sighed.

Shelby felt her eyes widen and she listened in silence.

"I know, Denise is such a slut," Sadie replied.

"Sadie, you have to promise not to say anything, but Hank said he saw Denise and Jack at the river and she had gotten him to take her out on the boat. When they came back, he was drunk as a coot. Hank had to help her get Jack into the old shack and then he left," Wendy said.

Shelby grasped her hand over her mouth as she felt her heart sink to her stomach. She felt lightheaded and tried desperately not to make a sound. But she was so overcome by Wendy's words that she couldn't help herself. She reached out and shoved the door of the stall open. She stood in shock looking straight into the faces of both girls.

"Oh, Shelby, I'm so sorry," Wendy gasped in shame.

Shelby, stunned by the news, quietly and without a whimper, rushed out the restroom door.

Shelby returned to her car, rattled by the words, "Denise and Jack." She had to find him; she couldn't go home until she did. She pleaded with God that it wasn't true. Jack wouldn't do that.

Shelby started her car, put it in reverse, and quickly backed out of the parking lot and headed straight for the boat ramp. She had wrestled with why he hadn't shown up at the Kissing Bridge, but now she knew he had been at the boat dock all day.

Shelby pulled onto the gravel road and continued down the hill to the old shelter. She gasped when she saw Denise's car parked next to the dock, as well as Jack's. Her friends hadn't been lying.

"Oh God, please no, Jack," she whimpered as her heart began to sink to her stomach. She turned off the headlights and motor as she rolled down the hill, trying to keep them from seeing her.

Her heart pounded and her thoughts raced out of control at the idea of Jack and Denise being together. She parked the car and quietly exited and bumped the door closed gently with her hip. She was overwhelmed with jitters as she limped toward the shed. She saw the flicker of a faint light emanating through the window. She crept up the stairs and across the porch to the door. She heard rumbling inside and reached for the door handle just as it flew open.

It frightened her, she jolted backward and saw Denise standing right before her eyes, topless and pulling up her bikini panties over her hips with one hand and holding a lit cigarette in her other hand. Shelby gasped at the sight of her.

"We've been expecting you, Shelby," Denise remarked sarcastically as she pushed the door open wider. "Well, Shelby don't you look all fancy-pancy," Denise said maliciously.

"What? We?" Shelby asked, confused.

Shelby pushed past Denise horrified. She covered her mouth in disbelief as she saw Jack's naked body lying face down on a quilt on the floor.

"Jack!" she cried in distress. She reached down and grabbed his limp arm and shook him, and called out his name. "Jack." Once again, she called his name. There was no response from him. "Denise, what the hell is going on here?" She cried as she shook him uncontrollably.

"Oh, for heaven's sake, Shelby, have you not ever seen someone passed out drunk and happy?" Denise sneered. "You know, it doesn't surprise me. You're nothing more than a little Miss Goody Two Shoes. Yes, that would explain it," Denise said as she laughed out loud. "You are so perfect and always telling Jack what to do. You should be ashamed of yourself and then you have the audacity to tell him how cute Richard Porter is."

"That's none of your business," Shelby said, trembling from head to toe.

Denise continued to belittle Shelby. "You think you're so high and mighty, going off to college and leaving Jack here. The only thing you ever think about is yourself."

Shelby was in tears and did her best to ignore Denise as she continued to try to jostle Jack awake, without success. "Oh, Jack, how could you let this happen?" Shelby said in anger to his passed out form. Then, she turned her wrath on the girl she'd never liked. "Denise, I asked you a question, what the hell have you done?"

"Oh, get a grip, Tootie," Denise struck back.

"Stop calling me that. Jack is the only one who says that."

"Yeah, that's what I understand," Denise said, as she continued to puff on her cigarette. "Well, on the side of the fence I grew up on, us ladies were always told to take care of our man or else he would go looking for it somewhere else. Besides, you're such a whiny bitch, always getting your way, but not this time," Denise replied angrily.

Shelby ignored Denise as she continued to get his attention. "Wake up!" she whispered in his face as she shook him. Crying uncontrollably, she knew in her heart, her worst nightmare had become a reality.

In anger, she shoved his shoulders against the wooden floor, and he moaned. She stood up, "Damn you, Jack, damn you for doing this to us!" she cried out with a high-pitched voice.

"Oh, and Jack wanted me to tell you, he was saving himself for you, but he just couldn't wait any longer." Denise laughed as she stood with one foot propped up against the wall.

Shelby grasped the wall as she rose in grueling pain from her knee. She stepped away, turned, and glared at his naked body as he lay on the old quilt. With a quick move of her foot, she gave him a swift kick in his bare ass.

She reached up to the heart necklace and held it tightly in her hand. Heartbroken, she quickly yanked it off her neck. She paused briefly as she looked down at the chain dangling from the palm of her hand as the tears flowed down her cheeks. She reached back and threw it toward him, landing just shy of his face in a small crack on the floor. "I hate you, Jack Emerson."

She grabbed for the door handle as she heard Denise. "You know, it's not often, but sometimes the good girls lose. It's too bad you just lost the best thing that will ever happen to you. You've lost Jack."

Shelby felt her emotions boiling over, shifting from hurt to anger. She was caught off guard by the cruel and heartless words, but it shouldn't surprise her coming from trash like Denise. Without hesitation, Shelby quickly turned, drew her hand back, and slapped Denise across the face. Then, for good measure, she lunged at her with both hands and gave her a shove as hard as she could. Denise tumbled backward, lost her balance, hit the back wall of the shack, and fell to the floor.

"You disgusting bitch! I hope you rot in hell," Shelby turned and hollered at her in anger.

Denise eyeballed Shelby with an evil look and shot back, "You whiny bitch."

Shelby rushed out the door and slammed it behind her. She ran with a limp across the gravel to her car. She stopped for a brief second as she looked back at the shack and with a heart-wrenching cry, "Damn you both!"

Shelby's hands trembled as she made the short drive home. She sat for a few minutes in her car before she picked her purse up off the seat and headed into her house. Her eyes swollen and her face streaked with mascara, she walked slowly up the back steps and opened the screen door leading to the kitchen.

Her mother gasped when she saw her face. "Oh Shelby, what's wrong, dear?" She rushed to her and wrapped her arms around her.

Shelby broke down and dropped her purse to the floor. She plopped into the chair at the table, putting her head in her hands. She was devastated.

"Oh, Mom, it's horrible, I don't think I can even talk about it right now," she cried.

"When you do want to talk about it, dear, I want you to know I'm here for you. I love you, Shelby," she said as she leaned closer and kissed her on the head.

"Everything just changed. Everything I'd planned and hoped for. I just don't know what I'm going to do," she wept, wobbling her head in disbelief. "But I'll figure it out."

Chapter Nine

The room was dark and Jack rolled over on the quilt as he began to stir. He opened his eyes and blinked several times unaware of his surroundings. He reached up, grabbed his temples with his hands, and moaned from the horrendous pounding in his forehead.

He joggled his head as he squinted and looked around in the darkness. He felt like he had been hit in the noggin with a baseball bat. He kept blinking several more times before he could get a glimpse of the dimly lit room. His neck was stiff and he twisted it from side to side, then he rolled it to stretch out the kinks from the hours he laid sprawled out on the hardwood floor.

The room was lit with only the flicker from a small candle that sat on the edge of a crate.

He belched out loud as he sat up on the dirty floor and gagged from the disgusting fumes coming from deep in the pit of his stomach from the over-consumption of beer. He grasped his abdomen, as he felt nauseated. “Ugh,” he said in misery.

His thoughts turned immediately from his aching body to feeling somewhat dazed by the darkened room, which he couldn’t readily identify.

“Oh, my God,” his breath caught in his throat when he noticed he was stark ass naked.

He snatched the quilt and covered himself up quickly while he searched to see if anyone else was around. The place was empty with the exception of the small, lit candle. He squinted as he noticed his swimming trunks lying on the floor across the room.

He grasped his watch as he eyed the small hand on the face, “Damn, it’s four in the morning!” he exclaimed with a squeal.

The room looked vaguely familiar and then it dawned on him that he was in the old shack at the boat dock. Jack was confused and couldn't understand what he was doing here at this time of the night... or morning, rather?

He scratched his head trying to jog his memory loose as he squeezed his eyes to the ache at the back of his skull. He remembered he had gone fishing with Walter and they had been drinking. A lot. They had returned from their afternoon of fishing to drop Walter off to go to work.

But, he didn't go to work. Obviously not.

He started to moan again from the turmoil of his gut as it continued to churn from the beer. He rubbed at it, hoping that would ease his discomfort.

He recounted; they had caught a mess of fish and he was tidying up the boat and was taking a quick break before unloading the cooler full of fish and then...

"Oh, no," he gasped as he sucked in a deep breath. "Denise."

It was beginning to come back to him now... he had been sitting in the boat and Denise had come prancing down the pier. She leaped and landed on the floor of the boat, rattling his attention. She had rubbed his knee and he felt she was getting frisky with her hand.

He could barely remember... when she asked him to take her out on the boat. Right. It was coming back to him. They had been drinking all afternoon... but that was the last thing he could remember.

"Oh, man," he said as he continued to rub his belly.

He stumbled as he stood up and shuffled over to pick up his swimming trunks. Confused... how'd they get there? What the hell was he doing butt ass naked?

"Oh Lord, please," he asked as he strained his brain to remember. He stepped one foot into his shorts and lost his balance, hitting the wall. He steadied himself and reached up with his other foot slipping it into his shorts. He pulled them up and over his hips and tied the string tightly around his waist.

Suddenly, he smiled when it started to come back to him. He could remember bits and pieces of the evening. They had finally done it he thought. Shelby had finally given in to him and opened up for their very first time and they made love. He felt as if his chest were bursting with all the love he felt gushing out and over her, and he hoped now she knew how much he loved her. He grinned again at the thought. He just wished he hadn't been drunk when it happened for the first time. Then in a flash, he had a frightening thought. Was it just a dream?

He searched the room for clues when he noticed several cigarette butts thrown about the floor. He reached down, picked one up, and held it close to the candle's flame as he read the name brand. They were nothing like the kind he smoked.

"Damn, I don't smoke Virginia Slims. Those are girl cigarettes."

He cringed at the frightening thought as he recognized them being the same type of cigarettes Denise smoked. Okay, no big deal. She'd been here smoking. Nothing wrong with that, right? He didn't want to hear the answer his brain returned to him, though.

Perplexed at his situation, his hand pinched his lips between his thumb and index finger. "Damn, what have I done?" he wondered as he shook his head quickly to jar his thoughts.

Jack imagined the worst-case scenario; did Denise have something to do with this or was it, Shelby?

Maybe the cigarette butts were from some other time, he tried to reason. If so, then who would have been here and left the candle burning like that with him passed out?

He argued in the silent turmoil and he knew he had to sweep away the thoughts of being with Denise from the floor of his mind. He knew better than to get tangled up with the likes of her. He loved Shelby and that was that.

Still in a daze, he rubbed his face trying to wake up. He headed for the door, but remembered the candle was still burning. He walked back, leaned over, and blew the flame out.

Seconds later, Jack leaped into the driver's seat of his car and hit the ignition. He moved the gearshift and put it in reverse, quickly backing his car away from the shelter and up the hill.

It was in the wee hours of the night when he turned onto Highway 29 as he cautiously headed home.

The night air blew gently on his face as he leaned his head toward the open window.

He had hoped the fresh air would help relieve his nausea and awaken him from the numbness of his body.

A collision of thoughts unraveled a slew of emotions. He had to get to the bottom of this. Maybe it was Shelby; if it was she would have stayed with him as late as she could have, but she wouldn't have left the candle burning. She was too safety conscious and she would have surely blown it out before she left.

Then again, maybe it was Hank or Walter. They were just dumb enough to leave him there with it still burning. Wait a minute, they wouldn't have undressed him. Or would they have as a joke or something?

"Yes, they would have done that," he said as he tried to reason their actions. Then again they were always playing pranks and so he chalked them up as nothing more than jokers. Now, he was convinced. This was exactly their prankster character. Even though his rationale was shaky given the situation.

He pulled into the long drive of his home and parked his car. He leaned back against the headrest. "Yep, Hank and Walter were up to something. Just wait until I get my grubby hands on you two," he snarled out.

~~~

It was early Saturday morning with the dawn breaking way for another warm summer day. Shelby watched the white eyelet curtains over the bay window swaying with the gentle breeze coming through the opening.

Shelby laid somberly on her side with her hands tucked under her cheek as she riveted her eyes ahead in a daze. The flood of emotions increasingly tortured her throughout the night and there had not been much sleep. It had been a long and tough one.

She had tossed and turned for hours in the blackness, lying awake. The time had slowly passed, much like a snail slithering through the darkness, one millimeter at a time.

However, morning had awakened and the sun began to creep boldly into her window, as it shone brightly on her face. She blinked softly from the light. Her body was numb and still in shock over the previous night's scene of Denise and Jack together at the old shelter.

Her heart ached and the thought of Denise sickened her when she recalled the vision of seeing her and Jack naked and in the same room. Her stomach roiled again for good measure now as she replayed the image.

The early morning sunshine always brought delight to Shelby's heart, but not this time. She had no desire for the night to end and especially for the day to begin.

"Oh, Jack, how could you have done this to us?" Shelby asked silently.

She'd had so many hopes and dreams for them and yearned for this whole incident to be just a hallucination, one she could toss out of her mind. It was anything but, though. She knew it. The totality of the nightmare transformed into reality crushed her feelings of hope.
~~~

The sun rays came shining through the glass as she climbed out of bed and picked up her pillow. She snuggled it under her arm as she sat down at the window. She twisted the knob on her radio, adjusted the volume down low, and placed it on the windowsill. She picked up her feet and rested them on the bench, wrapping her arms around her knees, leaning down to rest her chin on them.

Feelings of hopelessness filled her heart. It was unbearable. She needed to understand what happened. She wanted to be comforted. She needed Jack.

The sight of the street below filled her thoughts and she recounted her many memories of Jack while she listened to the soothing music.

She agonized over the pain in her heart and she had no idea what she was going to do next, but she knew she had to be strong.

Her heart had been fatally wounded by the overwhelming grief caused by Jack and Denise's profound and deceitful behavior. She couldn't bring herself to call it, what it was... *sex.*

She wanted to be consoled and know everything was going to be okay. The last thing she wanted was sympathy or pity. She just couldn't bear the pain of telling anyone. Not right now, she had to figure it out on her own.

~~~

Jack was startled from a deep sleep when Hank busted through his bedroom door.

"Hey," he said as the door flew open. "Your mom let me in."

"What the hell, Hank?" Jack said annoyed as he sat straight up in his bed and grabbed his head.

"I'm sorry, but I had to see you. Did you see Shelby last night? She was looking for you, man," he inquired nervously.

He was barely awake. "Huh, I don't know," he said confused as he fell back on the bed and threw a pillow over his face.

"What do you mean, you don't know? She came by the Ram's House looking for you about eight thirty," Hank asked in surprise.

"Look, I told you I don't remember seeing Shelby last night." But he couldn't say if he had or if it was a dream. Jack, wide-awake now, sat up quickly when he realized what Hank was asking. He garnered his thoughts, and then asked, "What do you know about last night?"

Hank sat at the foot of the bed once he realized Jack was not quite with the program.
~~~

Jack pressed his friend. "What do you know about last night?"

"Shelby had gone to meet you at the Kissing Bridge and when you didn't show up, she came looking for you. We were all at the Ram's House eating and she wanted to know if we had seen you," Hank explained. "I didn't know what to tell her."

"Go on," Jack said.

"I told her the last time I saw you, you were passed out on the floor in the old shelter because you had been drinking all day," he said as he paused.

Jack cocked his head to the side. "And?"

"No, I didn't tell her you were with Denise," Hank admitted. "If that's what you mean."

"Denise? What are you talking about?" Jack grumbled.

Jack reached up and grabbed Hank by the collar. "Tell me that it was you and Walter who played the joke on me!" he said as he nodded his head yes.

"What joke?" Hank asked with a frown on his face.

"You know the joke, right?" Jack said glaring into his friend's eyes. The look Hank returned was a dead giveaway as Jack gently let go of his shirt.

"No, I don't know what joke you're talking about," Hank replied.

Jack frantically asked, "Where was Walter last night?"

"He was at work until eleven. "Why?"

"Oh, my God," Jack wailed as he sprang from the bed throwing the blanket across the room and scrambled to the window. "It *is* true. It wasn't my imagination. Holy shit."

"Wait, Jack, that's not all," Hank said as his eyes and voice followed Jack across the room. "Wendy and Sadie went to the bathroom and didn't know Shelby was there and they said something about you being with Denise, and when she heard them, she came out of the stall and ran out upset. They thought she had already left the restaurant."

Jack let out a long sigh all the way from his gut. "So, Shelby found out from the girls that I was with Denise?"

"Yep, apparently," Hanks said, scratching his head.

Jack nipped his lips as he paced the floor.

"What are you going to do?" Hank asked.

Jack slowly sat down on the bed and dropped his head. "I woke up about four this morning at the shack. No one was there, but me. There was a lit candle sitting on an old crate near where I was laid out." Jack shook his head in disbelief. "I was butt ass naked with a quilt laid over me when I came to."

"Seriously?" Hank asked, almost with a laugh in his voice.

"Yeah, that's what I said. And this isn't funny! My shorts were across the room on the floor and there were a bunch of cigarette butts all over the floor. I checked them out and they were the same brand Denise smokes."

"Jack, you don't think..." Hanks words trailed off.

"Damn I fear the worst man. I can't believe I got so drunk and I'm scared to death to think I did it with Denise," he snapped back.

"You really don't remember?" Hank asked in surprise.

"I thought it was Shelby," he said softly. "Yeah, it had to have been her. I remember calling her by her name."

"Are you sure?" Hank asked with a shocked look on his face.

"It's a blur. I can remember bits and pieces, but that's it." In his heart, he hoped and prayed that it was his sweet Shelby that he'd experienced such life-changing closeness.

They both sat on the bed in silence for a short time.

Hank turned to face him and looked him squarely in the eyes. "Did you sleep with Denise?"

"I don't know... God, please don't let it be so," he said sadly, as he lowered his head in shame. "I have to call Shelby," he said as he reached for the phone.

Hank grabbed it out of his hand. "Wait, you need to find out from Denise what went on before you talk to Shelby."

Jack stopped and thought for a minute and then slowly placed the phone down on the cradle.

"I have to go now," Hank said as he stood up from the bed and slapped Jack on the shoulder. "Try to remember the details, okay, and call me when you figure it all out."

"Okay, I will. Thanks, man," he replied as he shook Hank's hand.

Jack sat silently on the edge of his unmade bed. His hands covered his face as his mind raced tumultuously trying desperately to recall every detail of the night before.

"I hope I haven't royally screwed up."

~~~

It was late on Sunday afternoon and Shelby couldn't stop thinking about Jack. Why did he do this? Was he still mad about the Fourth of July? She was confused as to what she could have
~~~

done so badly that it would push him into the arms of someone else... especially Denise.

Shelby heard a gentle knock on her bedroom door. "Shelby, are you okay? May I come in?" her mom asked.

She got up from the window seat and limped across the floor. She unlocked the door and opened it to see her mom standing there with a tray full of food.

"Aww, Mom," she said relieved to see a smile greeting her. It was what she needed to lift her spirits.

"I'm sorry to bother you, sweetie, but I thought 'I'd check on you and see if you want some lunch," she said, reaching over and kissing Shelby on the forehead. "Here are a few things you might want to eat when you get to feeling better."

She glanced down at the tray full of goodies that had obviously been made with love, care, and concern in mind. "Thanks, Mom, but I'm not very hungry right now."

"I know, but you need to eat."

Shelby reached up and gave her a big hug, almost knocking the tray out of her hands. Frances laid the food on the window seat and turned back to take Shelby in her arms.

"I'll try to eat something later," she said to her mom.

"Do you feel like talking about it?" Frances inquired as she dipped her head to look Shelby in the eyes.

"No, I'm not ready yet," Shelby replied.

"Well, okay then, I'll just leave you alone and you can let me know when you're ready. I love you, Shelby."

"I love you, too, Mom," Shelby responded as she closed the door behind her.

Far from hungry, Shelby lifted the small lid covering her dinner. Fried chicken and a hefty serving of mashed potatoes were piled on the plate. She smiled as she thought about Jack, and how he would have cheered at the sight of such a feast.

Her hands gripped the lid tightly. Suddenly, she felt hazy and began to tremble. She released the lid from her grip and it toppled over the food. It was at that point that she lost control over her body and collapsed in a weakened state and fell to the floor on her knees. She had finally succumbed to her shattered and broken heart. A vast flood of tears flowed heavily from her eyes in a weeping state of agony for the loss of the man she was to love forever as everything went black.

~~~
~~~

Later that afternoon, Jack was heartbroken as he struggled to piece together the puzzle of the previous night's events. He wrung his hands together as he paced the floor of his bedroom. He still had not completely put it all together and it only had him more confused. He stood before the window in a daze, as he conceptualized the blunder of events.

His mind wandered as he remembered Hank and Denise dragging him across the pier and he could hear Hank fussing at her, about something. Then, he recalled the hard floor of the old shack where they dropped him and he passed out.

When he'd awakened, it had been hot as hell, and he had sweat pouring from his body, and then something about a cigarette, a woman's voice, and he was amazingly happy Shelby had come for him. Who was smoking? He knew it couldn't have been Shelby. Or could it? Had she loosened up and tried a cigarette? No, not his Tootie.

Frazzled, he shook the thought from his mind as he focused harder on the woman. She had touched him and he shuddered in pleasure, just as he had always dreamed it would be with Shelby. He called out to her, "Tootie," he remembered that and then she kissed him and then he, he kissed...

"Ohhh, my God!" he declared in horror as he carved out the silhouette of Denise's face in his mind. It hadn't been Shelby at all. It was Denise. He gasped, terrified of his recollection of what had transpired. "Please God, no!" he cried out, pleading. "What in the hell have I done?"

Finally unable to keep the remnants of yesterday's activities down, he ran to the bathroom and wretched up his guts. Torrents of guilt cascaded from him as the sour beer and guilty conscience emptied from his stomach. When he finished, he leaned back and against the porcelain tub, hoping the coolness of it would soothe him. But nothing would make him feel better. Not now. Not ever.

Had he really slept with Denise thinking it was Shelby?

Dumbfounded, he dropped his head in shame. He got up, splashed some cold water on his face, and then returned to bed.

"No, no, no!" he exclaimed in a heart-wrenching tone as he slammed his fist on the bed. "Damn you, Denise!"

He was devastated, and he could barely utter his words. He could only hope this was just a bad dream. He wondered what he was going to do. Hank was right, he had to get in touch with Denise quickly and find out what she knew.

He had to be savvy to avoid any suspicion that he couldn't remember what happened. He needed to hear her side of the story to confirm if anything transpired or not. He hoped and prayed it was just a nightmare.

The thought of having sex with Denise drew harsh chills over his body. He quickly scrambled to the shower and he frantically scrubbed every inch of his skin. He had to get her cooties off him.

Shelby could never find out about this, he thought as the idea of that preyed upon him. Hank had said Shelby already *did* know, or, at least, had the idea planted in her head. At that realization, Jack broke down and stood quietly as the hot water rushed over his naked body.

He could barely look at himself in the mirror from the shame and his hands trembled as he tried to shave. "Damn you, Jack!" he said furiously at his image in the mirror. His hands shook in anger as he threw the razor in the sink.

"I've got to call Denise," he said, as he tried to think of someone who would have her phone number. He didn't know her grandmother's name so he couldn't look it up in the phone book.

"Jackie," he whispered as he recalled that the two girls hung out in school. "Carlson," he whispered as he looked up Jackie's last name in the phone book. He called Jackie and she gave him Denise's phone number.

It was late Sunday afternoon, so there was a slim chance she wouldn't be home. He pleaded in silence that she would be there. He grabbed the phone and dialed the number. The phone rang on the other end. An elderly woman's voice answered.

"Hello?"

"Yes ma'am, this is Jack. Is Denise there?" he asked as his voice began to tremble.

"No, I'm sorry she's not," the woman replied.

"Do you know when she will be home?"

"She's gone to Dothan to spend a few days with her mother. I can have her call you when she gets back."

Jack's heart sank to his stomach, as he managed to say, "Yes, please, tell her I need to talk to her as soon as she gets back."

"This is Jack?" she asked.

"Yes ma'am," he said softly.

"Okay, I'll let her know, dear."

He was heavy-hearted over whether he should call Shelby now. She was obviously aware of him being with Denise. He reached up and rubbed his forehead as it ached from all the mind-boggling noise bouncing around in his skull.

He sat quietly all afternoon in his bedroom as he thought about Shelby. She hadn't returned his calls, but she had gone to the bridge. That was before she heard Wendy and Sadie talking about him and Denise. For Shelby to have gone to the bridge meant she had forgiven him for his silly behavior on Thursday at the picnic.

He loved her with all his heart and he knew that he'd hurt her. Now, how was he going to make this stupid mistake up to her? He was so ashamed; he just didn't know what to do.

He checked his watch; it was seven-thirty and it was getting late. Since Shelby went to church, he knew she'd be home by now. As much as he feared the unknown, his heart prompted him to call her. It was the least he could do. He had to know.

He inhaled a big gulp of air and coughed slightly as he reached down to pick up the phone. He could feel his hands shaking as he dialed her phone number.

"Hello," Joel answered.

"Mr. Harrelson, this is Jack. Is Shelby there?"

"Yes, she is, but she's not taking any calls right now. I'll tell her you called." Joel said and hung up the phone.

"Wait! Please Mr. Harrelson," Jack cried out, but it was too late; the connection went dead.

Jack was shocked; he had never experienced anyone hanging up on him. This could only mean one thing. Shelby was pissed off at him and for good reason. How much did she know? As far as he knew, she only heard the girls talking about him and Denise.

How was he going to get out of this?

Monday morning came too quickly as Jack arrived for work at the mill. He couldn't wait for his lunch break. He needed to see Shelby and he knew he would have to run by Johnson's Grocery to see if she was there.

Chapter Ten

Shelby made her way down the stairs to the kitchen where the aroma of coffee filled the room. She was up and dressed by nine a.m. She took her place at the table while her mom poured her a fresh cup of coffee. She picked up the creamer, poured it into the steaming liquid.

"Thank you, Mom," she said as she smiled.

"You're welcome, sweetie. Are you okay?" she asked with a concerned tone in her voice.

Shelby nodded yes, not wanting to elaborate.

Thoughts of Jack encompassed her mind as she began to daydream. They had been together for over six years. They had made promises and said crazy things to each other like "nothing could ever come between us," and "our love will last a lifetime;" the kind of silly words you say when you're young high school sweethearts. She'd meant every promise she had ever made to Jack. But now, she had doubts about the ones he had made to her.

No one had ever warned her how hard it was going to be growing up and facing adult challenges. A shadow of grief fell on her face as she stirred her coffee vigorously. Around and around with the teaspoon, much like the tumultuous emotions from the last few days. A mixture of feelings—heartbreak to anger—churned inside of her and she knew she had to deal with them. She was just not in a hurry to do so.

She was sad and afraid she would run into Jack. She wasn't ready to see him yet, but she knew he would be at work all day. So would she, and he would know that her shift ended at four o'clock. She contemplated calling in sick, but they usually only had two cashiers on Mondays and she didn't want to leave them stranded.

Besides, her mother had taught her to be a person of her word. One of many lessons. She recalled her mother saying.

"Shelby, if you tell someone you are going to do something, you must do it, and you've got to be true to your word."

"I have to go now, Mom, I love you," she said feeling hurt in her heart.

~~~

Jack anguished over the time as he paced up and down the floor of the mill's spinning room, waiting impatiently for his break. The whistle blew and he flew like a bat out of hell from the doors. He scrambled to his car, where he jerked the gearshift into drive, spinning across the parking lot headed for the grocery store.

He had hoped he could talk to Denise before he spoke to Shelby, but it was killing him and he just couldn't take another minute without seeing Shelby. Even though it only took ten minutes to Johnson's Grocery, it felt like an hour, as he weaved in and out of traffic on his mad dash.

"Oh, God, please let her be here," he said with a sigh. His heart began to beat out of his chest as he came to a stop. He grasped for another deep breath and forcing it from his lungs when he shifted the gear into park and leaped out of the car, slamming the door behind him. He rushed across the parking lot and through the automatic doors as they swooshed opened. He could see Shelby with her back to him as she helped the customers through the checkout line.

He walked up behind her and paused. He listened as he heard her speaking softly to the lady in the checkout line.

"That'll be $22.95," she said sweetly to the customer.

He hoped she'd address him in such a friendly manner. He could feel her gentle way with people and to hear the softness of her voice was music to his ears. His heart melted when he saw her face and her undeniably beautiful smile. He yearned to hold her in his arms just one more time, hoping to make everything right.

"Please talk to me, Shelby," he whispered under his lips as he slowly approached the register.

"Thanks and come again," he heard Shelby say to the woman holding a brown paper bag. The lady stopped and witnessed him standing there, which drew Shelby's attention as she turned around to see what was holding up her line.

"Jack," he heard her say, almost as a curse.

All eyes were now on Shelby as she felt her heart skip a beat and then her body began to quiver. Her breath went awry, and uneven. She could feel her toes, legs, fingertips, and lips go numb.
~~~

Her stomach gave way to the jitters. The sight of him completely obliterated her world. She could faintly hear his voice again.

"Shelby," Jack called out her name softly as he reached for her. He could see distress in her eyes as she struggled to speak while she slowly stepped back from his reach.

"No, Jack, please go away," she demanded and threw her hands out toward him to stop him from coming any closer.

Shelby was aware that everyone around them had paused to watch and listen to their exchange. It wasn't every day there was this much drama in the small town.

"Shell, please come talk to me," he pleaded. "I promise just for a min–"

She quickly interrupted his words before he could finish. "We have nothing to talk about, Jack," she said angrily. "You have to leave. I'm working." She twisted back toward her register.

"We have to talk, Shell," he shouted out louder.

Shelby felt her face flush and fear welled up inside her as she caught the look in Mr. Johnson's eyes as he rounded the corner of the aisle to find out what all the commotion was about.

"Shelby, what is going on here?" he asked.

"Nothing, Mr. Johnson. Jack was just leaving," she replied with a fake smile. She quickly faced Jack again and said, "You really have to leave. Now."

"Shelby," Jack nearly said in a whimper.

She turned her back on him. She was determined not to cry. Not here. Not at work. Not in front of people. Not for Jack to see.

"Jack, son, you're going to have to leave," Mr. Johnson said authoritatively. "We're quite busy today."

"Wait, sir. I need to talk to Shelby. It won't take but a minute," he said in distress.

Mr. Johnson stood tall and firm. "Son, I said you're going to have to take your business elsewhere. Now, go on and don't make me have to call your dad," he warned as he stepped toward Jack.

Jack threw his hands up in defeat and urgently replied, "I'm sorry, Mr. Johnson. I'll leave now. Please don't be mad at Shelby." Jack leaned around Mr. Johnson as he took a step backward. With one last plea, he yelled, "Shelby, please call me. I love you!"

Shelby stood frozen like an icicle hanging from the eaves of a roof on a cold, freezing morning. She hung her head low and closed her eyes as she heard Jack's voice trailing off as he left the store. Her heart felt like it was being ripped from her chest.

Shaken from the embarrassing incident, she swiftly spun

around and unexpectedly caught a glimpse of none other than Richard Porter staring her square in the eyes. She could sense a bit of sympathy from him and she wondered for a split second if it was for her.

Frightened by his presence, Shelby felt lost and alone and turned to silently solicit a quick break, when she saw Stella nodding yes and moving in to take over the register. Shelby grabbed the back of her apron, untied it, and tossed it on the counter. She felt the pain from embarrassment as she rushed past Richard and down the hall to the break room.

A few minutes later, she found herself sitting quietly all alone in the large open room. It had been heart-wrenching to see Mr. Johnson escort Jack out of the store. She had never expected anything like this to happen, at least not here at work, nor the feeling her heart now endured.

Bitterness, intermixed with emotions of anger, began to surface and she stood abruptly and began to pace the floor of the break room. She thought about all the things that Jack had done over the last few days.

She was not about to take the blame for his actions. For the first time, she wasn't going to give in and smooth over his bad behavior like she had always done in the past. He wasn't some kid anymore; he was a man and had to take responsibility for the things that he had done.

Suddenly it was obvious; the atrocities of his behavior were unforgivable in her mind. "They are his and his alone. How could he have been so stupid?" she angrily grumbled.

She was determined to somehow manage and try to survive the chilling and devastating force of emotions that threatened to overcome her. Her shattered heart was all she had left and she knew it was a matter of picking up the pieces and moving on.

~~~

Jack clutched his hands together as he lingered in his car. He closed his eyes and let the lyrics from the radio roll off his heart to carry him back to a time when he first realized his love for Shelby. He honestly loved her, as the voice of Olivia Newton-John's hit, "*I Honestly Love You,*" fell intimately on his heart. He slumped down in the seat as he replayed the scene over in his mind. *Damn, Jack, you screwed it up again!*

He ached over how the love of his life had nothing to say to him and her words penetrated his soul. This wasn't the Shelby he
~~~

knew. It was the Shelby he had created with his actions.

She had a way of smoothing things over when they were on the outs. Just like going to the Kissing Bridge on Friday was her way of making up, even after he had been so mean to her at the celebration the day before. He knew in his heart that she would be there, so why hadn't he been? How could he have stood her up?

He anguished over the situation with Denise. It was evident Shelby was angry with him and he had to find out somehow and some way about what all she knew.

This is complicated, he thought. But, there was no way he was giving up this easily on her. He was madly in love with her and she was the one person he wanted to spend the rest of his life with.

The thing was he had to do *something* to convince Shelby how much he loved her. He'd send her flowers, buy her whatever she wanted, or take her wherever she wanted to go. He had to make it up to her.

The escapade with Denise was a misunderstanding and they would clear it all up just as soon as she returned home, he tried to reason with himself.

He felt his eyes water as he turned on the ignition. Heartbroken, he lifted his head toward the store, smiled, and quietly whispered, "I love you, Tootie."

He was about to pull away when the sight of Richard Porter strutting out of Johnson's Grocery store suddenly startled him. He didn't see him earlier in the store.

"What the hell?" Jack murmured suspiciously when he realized Richard had nothing in his hands. He was struck with an avalanche of emotions.

~~~

During the next three days following the heartsick scene, Jack tried to call Shelby and even drove past her home on a few occasions. He hoped she would see him from her window seat and come out to greet him. But, it hadn't happened.

Nursing a broken heart, he longed to just hear her voice... to put his arms around her... to tell her how much he loved her... that it had all been just a terrible mistake.

Despite his confusion, he was sure it would all be cleared up as soon as he heard from Denise. Surely, she'd help him make things right.

It was late Friday afternoon and Jack punched the time clock as he dashed out of the mill. He wanted to rush home, shower and
~~~

shave, and head straight for the Kissing Bridge. With hope all but lost, his heart still yearned for Shelby to be there.

Within an hour, Jack was clean and refreshed from the long day at the mill. He pulled his car into the gravel-lined drive of the Kissing Bridge and parked.

"It won't be long now," he said with a knowing smile.

Jack had been uptight as he waited for Denise to call him, but he hadn't heard from her despite his repeated calls to her grandmother. He thought about how it really didn't matter what had happened between him and Denise. His heart and soul still belonged to Shelby, and there was nothing Denise could say to change that.

Jack climbed out of his car and walked worriedly over to the sandbags on the side of the river. He kicked off his flip-flops and tossed them behind him. He plopped down on the hard surface of the bags and slowly slid both feet into the cold rushing water of the river when a shiver of chills ran up his legs.

He sat quietly on the bank; a thought cascaded down on him of how he and Shelby had spent nearly half of their lives together. He couldn't imagine them not spending the rest of their lives together. It had never been an option.

He was jarred out of his deep thoughts when he heard the toot of a car horn behind him. His heart skipped a beat as he speedily stood up and turned around to face the noise. He knew Shelby would be getting out of her car and would rush to him.

But instead, he was shaken at the sight of Denise. He saw her climbing out of her car. She slammed the door and she walked toward him.

"Oh, my God," he whispered silently to himself.

He could see her smiling, and she seemed different today, as she got closer to him.

"Hey, Jack," she said dreamily. He noticed her eyes met his and he quickly turned from her gaze.

"Oh, hey, Denise," he said hesitating. This was the last thing he needed, especially if Shelby were on her way here, as well.

"You don't seem to be happy to see me," she commented. "My grandmother told me you called several times. I'm sorry, but I had gone down to visit my mom. I guess I should have said I was leaving for the week before I left," she explained as she took a step toward him.

He wondered what that meant. Why was she being so casual with him? She was never this calm.

"What's wrong?" she asked with a puzzled look on her face.

He struggled for the words; he wasn't prepared to talk to her right now. "Look, Denise, I'm waiting on Shelby now, so you have to go. You can't be here when she gets here," he said urgently, motioning his hands in the air for her to leave.

"Wait," she said. "What are you talking about? I thought you wanted to see *me,*" she said sounding surprised.

"I do, but not right this minute. We need to talk, but I just can't talk to you right now," he said as he felt his head bobbling.

"So, what's the deal with you and Shelby? Are y'all back together? What about us?" she asked sarcastically.

Confused, he replied. "What do you mean, what about us? There is no us. Shelby and I've always been together, why would you ask me that?"

Denise stabbed her fists to her hips and cocked her head defiantly. "For heaven's sake, you two had a fight and you weren't speaking and then you and I..." her words trailed off.

"Wait, what about you and me?" he shouted, interrupting her words.

He noticed Denise's smile soured. "You don't remember?" she asked with an eyebrow lifted and a startled look on her face. "At the boat dock... we had gone out fishing... and then... in the old shack..." she nodded her head at him.

"Go on," he said, nodding along with her. "What happened, Denise?" he demanded.

Denise's face reflected her struggle, to be honest. He could tell she was beginning to get nervous and flustered. He too became jittery and began to agonize over what she had to say.

"Please, Jack. Can we sit down and talk about it?" she asked as she cleared her throat.

"No, tell me what happened," he demanded. "Now!"

"Okay, but you have to tell me what you remember."

"Spit it out, Denise!" he growled at her, livid from the frustrating situation.

"Okay, okay," she said backpedaling. "That night when we were together, I thought you were sincere. I know I was and I thought it meant something to you..."

Her words fell heavy on his heart, as the anticipation of what was coming next slowly began to sink in. He braced himself as he closed his eyes and listened.

"I have to tell you how much you mean to me, Jack, I fell in love with you the first day I met you. Please, you have to understand you mean the world to me. I wouldn't be here today if it weren't for you. I love you," she said loudly.

"No!" he growled out as she continued.

Denise reached out for him, stepping closer and closer. "The last time we were together, you made love to me in the old shelter."

He cringed at her words. To hear her say them out loud made them more real.

"Oh, Jack, it was wonderful. You held me in your arms and I could feel your love. Your body was warm against mine..." Denise said, trying to get nearer to him.

"Stop! "Tell me it didn't happen. You have to tell me it was just a nightmare," he shouted in disbelief as he rolled his eyes at her.

He put both his hands over his ears, to keep from comprehending what he feared the most, it wasn't a dream, but a reality. They *had* sex. The words pounded in his head.

"I love you, Jack," Denise snapped back at him once again.

Jack stood tall and shook his finger in her face, anger fueling his every word. "You manipulated me and took advantage of me. For God's sake, Denise, you knew I was drunk. But no, all you cared about was *you*. You know I love Shelby and she is the one I had saved myself for and you stole that from her... from us." He could see the tears welling up in her eyes, but he didn't care. He wanted her to hurt as much as she had hurt him.

Denise barely blinked, though. No tears escaped her eyes, as she was somehow strangely confident in the words she was saying to him.

He couldn't take it. "How could you be so cruel? I've never done anything but be your friend. Now, look what you've done. You should be ashamed of yourself. I can't stand to look at you. Just go, Denise. I don't ever want to see you again!" he cried out.

He turned his back to her in a state of denial even though he could hear her plea's for him to talk to her. There was just no way he could look at her now.

"Jack, don't be that way..."

"Please go away, Denise," he appealed her. With his fists clenched, he crossed his arms and laid them against his chest as he felt his heart explode like a balloon being popped by a sharp needle, right into thin air.

Jack's body began to shudder. The guilt of his actions tormented him deep in his soul. As he trembled from the shame it became evident and clear he was having an emotional heart attack. It took his breath away as he sank to the ground on his knees and lowered his head in shame. He felt weak and sick to his stomach and feared he'd never breathe again from the pain in his chest. He was so ashamed of committing the greatest atrocity in a loving relationship. A woman he despised had seduced him. And the woman he'd spent his life loving, had turned her back on him—rightly so.

Memories and hurtful emotions collided within his mind, leaving his storybook Romeo and Juliet romance in shambles. But then again, those two didn't have a happy ending either.

~~~

Shelby couldn't shake the realization that Jack had gone all the way with Denise. But the evidence of them naked and alone in the old shelter spoke for itself and made her sick to her stomach. She blamed him for their screwed up relationship.

"How could this happen? It can't happen again. No, it won't happen again!" She jerked her head to interrupt her insane thinking as she sat alone in her room a week after all the chaos.

The weeks that followed were hard for Shelby. She was constantly wrapped up in a patchwork of emotions characterized by the turmoil her heart has endured.

Every year, in late August, her family went on their favorite vacation to Panama City Beach, Florida. Shelby couldn't wait for a week away from it all, Jack, work, and Denise. The thought of time away at the beach renewed her heart. She had to be strong now and stand tall and walk in faith that all had happened was for the best as she recalled her mom's words.

"Shelby, God is close to the brokenhearted and saves those crushed in spirit. So try not to worry so much. What is meant to happen will happen. It's your willingness to let it be and forgiving Jack that will ultimately give you peace."

The words floated around in her mind like a lost survivor in the open waters trying to find his way. She had no idea where all this was going. But faith would be her driving force and leaving for college was the right thing for the next step of her life.

The weekend of September fourteenth was only two weeks away and she would be leaving for Tuscaloosa. The jittered feelings of her broken heart, compounded with all the commotion over her move was all she could deal with. She still anguished over Jack. But the excitement of college was turning her focus now. She couldn't let all the discord of the summer interfere with her
~~~

schoolwork and transition into a new world.

She continued to work at Johnson's, even though things were different now. While her heart wasn't into it anymore, it did fill the days until she left for college. Mr. Johnson had banned Jack from the store during all of her shifts and that saddened her.

And then, there was that silly guy, Richard...

She smiled as she pulled into the parking lot on her first day back to work after vacation. She parked the VW, got out of the car, and hurried into the store with a renewed perspective.

Within the hour, Richard walked through the automatic doors; cool as the air conditioning that rushed out to greet him.

"Hey Shelby, how was the beach?" he asked with excitement.

She smiled at him as he approached her. "It was wonderful. I had a great time."

"Cool, so are you over Jack now?" he inquired.

She peered at him under her eyelashes. "Richard, we are not going to talk about that," she said shyly as she tilted her head. She had to be the mature one.

"Okay, just asking," he said as his hands shot up in the air.

Damn, why is he so cute? she wondered as their eyes met.

"No, seriously Shelby. You doing okay?" he asked with a concerned look on his face.

"Yes, Richard, I'm fine."

"Have you talked to him?" he asked.

"No," she replied with sadness in her voice.

"Aww... Shelby, I'm sorry. I know it hurts and I wish there was something I could do to make it all better for you," Richard said as he looked deeply into her eyes.

Hearing him say that reminded her she had to be strong and try to pick up the pieces of her shattered heart.

"It's okay, it'll all work out the way it's supposed to," she spoke softly holding on to her hope for reconciliation.

"Well, smile then," he chimed out with a big grin on his face. She returned one of her own as he turned and walked away.

~~~

Shelby spent hours of reminiscing over the Labor Day weekend while she packed for her move to college. She would set out Tuesday morning on her new adventure.

She packed some and then took a break to sit in her window seat. There, her mind was jammed with thoughts of days gone by...
~~~

of the hot summer evenings playing hide-and-seek with neighborhood friends, tubing down the Chattahoochee River, swinging on the tire swing out back, and, yes, heartbroken and lonely thoughts of Jack.

She'd always dreamed Jack would be helping her pack up and then he would set out in his Mustang to escort her on the long drive to Tuscaloosa. She'd show him around Tutwiler, the dorm where she would be staying, and he'd come visit her on weekends.

Tomorrow, she would load up her car and drive away on her own. It had been a long and emotional weekend and Shelby was exhausted from all the details of her move. She zipped up her last duffle bag, letting it drop to the floor as she propped her feet up and wrapped her arms around her legs, resting her chin on her knees. She closed her eyes and said a prayer.

She shook away the sadness and replaced her thoughts with excitement for the new experience that would begin in just a few hours. Her plan was to spend some time with her mom and dad in the morning and then make a quick stop by the Kissing Bridge before heading out of town. She felt it was appropriate since she'd spent her most memorable times there with Jack.

~~~

Jack lay in his bed and in spite of his inner pain and having to deal with all the confusion and sadness, he often wondered for the millionth time: *will we ever have a second chance for love?*

He ached for Shelby... to put his arms around her... tell her how much he loved her... and, most of all, that it all had just been a terrible nightmare and a regretful mistake.

~~~

It was almost noon and Shelby picked up the last duffle bag from the floor of her bedroom and threw it over her shoulder. She turned around to take a quick overview of her things.

She smiled, as she gazed around the room. Today was the day and for the first time, she would be living on her own. She had waited all her life for this day, and it was here now, with bittersweet emotions of happiness and sadness all wrapped up in one. Happy anticipation for her new adventure, but sadness for leaving the man she wanted to spend the rest of her life with. But he'd turned his back on her, so she owed it to herself to see what the future held for her.

She walked through the door and closed it behind her. She took each step slowly down the staircase, occasionally lingering on flashbacks of a little girl running up and down the steps. This was home and her safe haven and she was going to miss it.

She was startled out of her musing to hear her mother call her from the kitchen.

"Shelby."

"Yes, Mom," she called back.

She rounded the corner and walked into the kitchen to find both her parents standing there eagerly waiting.

"Come here, sweetie," her dad said softly as he motioned for her. She dropped the bag from her shoulder and ran straight into their open arms as she fell into their embrace. Tears of joy and sadness flooded their faces. Standing together, she held her parents with every bit of strength she had in her.

"Oh, Mom and Dad, I love you so much and I'm going to miss you both," she said

"We love you too, dear," her mother said tenderly.

"Shelby we love you, sweetie," Joel said as he choked on his words.

For the next few minutes, they stood quietly in the midst of their home as they embraced each other. Shelby was overwhelmed by their love and she wondered how the heck she was going to survive each day without their "I love yous."

They all squeezed tightly one last time and then broke away and cheered, "Roll Tide." They laughed as she scooped up her last bag and they walked out the back door to her car.

Shelby tossed her knapsack into the passenger seat, turned, and blew them a kiss. She slipped into her car, pulled out of the driveway, and headed down 23rd Drive as she watched the waves from her parents in her rearview mirror. She headed south on Highway 29 and drove toward the Kissing Bridge. She needed to go by just one more time before she left.

She made her way down the gravel drive and parked the Bug. She stepped out and walked calmly over to the sandbags. She began to tremble from the overwhelming emotions bottled up inside her heart. God, she was going to miss this place. She was going to miss Jack holding her hand and his gentle kisses.

In a deluge of emotions, she quickly raced back toward her car. She was shocked when she saw Jack's car speeding down the drive.

"Oh, God, no!" she moaned silently under her breath. She'd

been so good at evading his attempts to talk to her. She couldn't do this, not now. So, she scrambled for the door handle.

Jack rolled down his window and hollered out at her, "Shelby, please wait!"

She didn't do as he said. Instead, she hurried into her car, started the ignition, and put the gear in drive. Jack leaped from his car and rushed toward her. Her heart melted from just seeing him.

As he approached, he hollered, "Shelby, I love you! Please don't leave me!"

She glanced back and caught a glimpse of his face as she slowly pulled away. Their eyes met.

Jack lunged at the car and reached his hand out toward the closed window as he ran alongside her as she was driving off.

He begged her not to leave...

Shelby reached up with her hand and together their touch met the window simultaneously. She was unable to utter a word and through her own tear-filled eyes, she moved her lips, "I love you, Jack."

"Then you have to forgive me!" he pleaded.

But she couldn't. She just... no... she couldn't. It was over. Time to move on. Time to start her new life. Time for Jack to grow up and be the man she knew he could be.

She turned her head away from his eyes to avoid the onslaught of new emotions and accelerated away from him and up the hill.

Without looking back, she turned north on Highway 29 and headed out of town.

Chapter Eleven

Just four hours later, Shelby drove up Highway 82 and passed the sign that read, "Welcome to Tuscaloosa." She smiled. "Heck yeah, I made it!" She was super excited and couldn't believe she was finally here. Her arrival in Tuscaloosa was just the beginning of her first steps in college life. She was on her own now and would be making all her own decisions, which felt kind of liberating. It would be a new exploration of different cultural concepts for her and the thought of it was gratifying.

Having lost Jack, the love of her life, over the summer to another girl reminded her of a time she had experienced long ago, after she had lost her best friend, Gina. It felt like déjà vu all over again as she turned her car off McFarland Boulevard and onto University Drive, past the official University of Alabama brick sign. She was alone once again.

She had experienced a good bit of guilt and grief over the last month for leaving Jack, but she had to hold tight to her faith that it was the right thing to do. It was time for her to put Shelby first, to stretch her wings and fly.

With the sound of the radio blasting from the speakers in her car, she weaved her way through campus, taking in the sight of it and hardly believing she was actually here. She turned off Bryant Drive and pulled into the Julia Tutwiler dormitory parking lot. This was the main housing unit for incoming freshmen girls their first year in school. Station wagons filled the parking lot with parents helping their daughters carry in suitcases, boxes, and stuffed animals into their new home.

Shelby searched the crowded area for a spot to tuck her Beetle Bug safely into. Three rows deep, she found a space and crept into the tiny nook. She reached up and turned the ignition off. Still humming to the music of "*Rock On*," by David Essex, she stepped out into the warm mid-September air and did a happy dance in her baby blue knee knockers.

She lifted her sunglasses off her nose and pushed them into her hair. She snickered as she lost her balance from the new platform shoes she had bought earlier in the week. But, she just couldn't stop dancing as the music still lingered in her mind.

"Whoa," she laughed out loud and looked around to see if anyone had caught a glimpse of her silliness. Good, no one noticed.

She turned quickly and covered her eyes with her hand to block out the glare from the bright sun setting in the western sky. She had been told the tall building that stood before her was one of the latest and greatest modern luxury dormitories now found on many campuses across the country.

She was ecstatic that she would call Tutwiler home for the next year, and she smiled at all the thoughts rambling around in her mind.

She reached into the front seat of her car and grabbed her purse, heading for the front door of the dormitory, bouncing along in excitement. There were girls everywhere as she made her way to the check-in table.

"Hi, I'm Shelby Harrelson," she announced to the young lady who stood directly behind the round desk. Shelby noticed several girls worked in unison with each other as they flipped through the cardboard bins to locate the move-in packets. It appeared they had plenty of experience doing this kind of thing.

"Hey Shelby, let me get your packet," she said with a smile as she turned to the boxes on the table behind her.

Shelby gazed around the crowded lobby with people coming and going. Noisy chatter and laughter of their voices filled her ears. *Wow, this is going to be a blast*, she thought as she waited.

"Okay, Shelby, here you go. Your room is on the seventh floor and your roommate is JoJo Williams, but she hasn't checked in yet. Everything you need is in your folder, but if you have any questions, just let us know. The elevators are right there and we have luggage carts to help move your stuff, as well," she said as she handed Shelby her packet and pointed.

Excitement rushed through Shelby as she walked away. She reached into the folder and removed her key. She glanced at it as it dangled in her hand and her mind zeroed in on the shape and feel of it... the key to her new life. She stood in the line for the elevators, weaving her way through all the chaos, bumping into several girls on the way. She finally crammed into one and reached over a girl with a blue bandana scarf on her head to press the button for her floor.

The elevator zipped along, stopping on every floor; it seemed, as Shelby's anticipation amped up even more. Within minutes, the door opened and she stepped out into the main lobby of the seventh floor along with several other girls with their arms filled with suitcases and pillows. She smiled and shook her head at all the craziness.

She followed the sign for where her room should be located. When she reached her room, trembling from the buzz, she placed the key in the lock and opened the door. The sunshine blared through the room as she pushed in.

"Oh, my Lord," she gasped full of energy as she ran toward the window. The view was fabulous as she stood and gazed out the glass at the panorama of the nearby cemetery and the famed Denny Stadium across the street. She whizzed around and plopped down on the bed, kicked off her platforms, and fell back on the bed with both her arms stretched out by her side.

"This bed's mine," she said as she bounced her body up and down on the twin mattress.

She was overjoyed with a feeling that she had landed in the middle of a candy store. There were so many things to choose from and this was definitely the sweet life she'd planned for.

She was startled by a noise in the hall and sat up quickly, as a brown-haired girl with a big smile stepped in through the wide open door.

"Hey, I'm JoJo, you must be Shelby," the girl said as she stretched her hand out to her.

"Yes, it's me. Hey, JoJo. I'm glad to meet you," she said as she shook her new roommate's hand.

JoJo tossed her pillows on the other bed, threw down her duffle bag, and said, "It looks like you've claimed that bed so I'll claim this one. How about that?" she asked.

"Great, I'll take it," Shelby responded with a nod.

"I'm so excited to be here, how about you?" Shelby asked with a grin.

"You have no idea how glad I am to be here. I'm finally on my own. My older sister has just about driven me crazy," she said sarcastically and rolled her eyes.

Shelby laughed out loud and thought it was an odd statement to make, but shrugged it off.

"So, Shelby, where are you from?" JoJo asked as she sat down on the bed and crossed her legs Indian style.

"Valley, Alabama," Shelby replied. "Where are you from?"

"Valley's not too far from where I grew up in Montgomery, but I don't live there anymore," JoJo admitted. Shelby could see her expression change and she noticed a hint of sadness in her voice.

"Oh wow! My parents used to take me with them when my dad went to his meetings there. He's a deacon at our church back home. So, do your parents live there now?" Shelby asked enthusiastically.

"Well, no. We used to, but I live with my sister, Sandra, in LaGrange, Georgia. My mom passed away when I was fourteen," she said softly.

"Oh, I'm so sorry," Shelby, said as her voice trailed off.

"It's okay, it's been a while now, and I'm kind of getting through it," JoJo said as she brushed her face. "It's days like this that I really miss her."

"I can't imagine what it would be like if my mom died," Shelby replied sympathetically.

"Sometimes it's still hard to believe she's gone," JoJo said sadly, as she scanned the scenery out the window.

"Wow, so what about your dad?" Shelby asked with a bit of curiosity.

"Don't know where he's at," she replied with a long sigh. JoJo's hesitant tone of voice made Shelby's heart soften and she changed the subject. She didn't press her for more information and hoped JoJo would talk about it when she was ready to.

Shelby remembered her mom's words only a few short weeks earlier: "If you want to talk, know that I'm here."

She turned to JoJo and smiled. "Well, if you ever need to talk about it JoJo, know that I'm here for you."

"Thanks," she replied and returned a smile.

"Do you have any siblings?" JoJo asked.

"Oh, no. I'm an only child," she replied happily. "My dad used to tell me they weren't sure they could have any more kids because they gave me all their love."

"How about you?" Shelby inquired.

"Just Sandra, she's older than me and drives me crazy sometimes," she replied clenching her jaw.

The girls chatted for the next hour as they unloaded all their belongings from their cars and carried them up to their new home.

Boxes and duffle bags filled the small dorm room as if they had packed their entire life in just a few cartons. They would stop occasionally for a quick break and conversation about themselves.

Shelby removed a framed picture of her parents from one of her boxes and placed it on her nightstand. She looked down and smiled, feeling so blessed to have them both only a few hours away. She wondered what had happened to JoJo's mom since she didn't really divulge that information. The thoughts raced through Shelby's mind over and over while they continued to unpack.

Hours later and all pooped out from the hustle and bustle of the move, they both fell down exhausted on their beds to take an inventory of the things that still needed to be organized and put away.

"Oh, my goodness, what are we going to do with all our stuff?" Shelby asked in a state of amazement.

"I don't know," JoJo said. "Let's not worry about that right now."

Shelby glanced over at the pile of clothes that still needed to be hung up in the small wardrobe and folded away into the few drawers she'd claimed as her own, but there was no one to tell her she *had* to do it right away.

"Hey, let's go get something to eat," JoJo said after standing up from her bed and walking over to the window. Shelby joined her new friend as they stood together peering out on the campus where they would spend the next four years.

"Maybe have an ice cream cone," JoJo said as she turned to Shelby.

"Ice cream? Heck yeah, that's a nifty idea. I'd loveeee some," Shelby said as her eyes widened and met JoJo's. The cold taste of a cone filled with the creamy flavored milk was just what she wanted.

"Me too," JoJo said back at her.

All the restaurants and shops on University Boulevard were just a short walk from the dormitory. Shelby soaked up the sights of the large sorority houses and the even grander football stadium as they wandered down the sidewalk and made their way into a small diner on the corner. They both ordered two large scoops of chocolate in a cone.

The room was loud with all the chatter of the students and the music played in the background. The two girls sat for a bit laughing and slurping up the ice cream dripping down the sides of the cones in sheer delight.

JoJo leaned forward. "So, are you going through Rush?"

"Yes, I am, but I really don't know that much about it," she admitted with a frown on her face. "I really want to, JoJo. My Aunt Beverly was in a sorority back in 1965. My mom never went to college, though. She met my dad, they got married, and six years later they had me," she said and lifted both her shoulders in a shrug. "My aunt used to tell me lots of stories of all the wild things they did back in the day. I always said when I went to college I wanted to be in a sorority. So, that's all I know. Aunt Beverly would be so proud of me if I were able to get in one. It really doesn't matter to my mom. She just said to go for it if I wanted to."

"I can tell you just about anything you want to know about it," JoJo said as she took a bite of her cone. She appeared confident as she continued. "Sandra was in one when she was here and it was during the time when Mom died, so she felt like they were her family and she's still committed to all of it today. She said if it hadn't been for her sorority sisters, she doesn't think she would have made it through everything." JoJo offered the information and then shifted her attention out the window of the diner.

"Aww, that's sweet," Shelby returned with a tinge of curiosity.

"Yep. Sororities are real big on being your home away from home. They are like your family while you are here. Especially when things get tough," JoJo pronounced.

"Wow, that's kind of cool," Shelby, said excitedly. "Being the only child, I've never had a roommate or a sister, so this is going to be fun. Tell me exactly what Rush is."

They talked on as they finished up their ice cream.

"Okay, so it starts out on the first day," JoJo began. "I think there are like sixteen sororities right now, so on Monday and Tuesday, they have what they call Ice Water Teas, where you literally get rushed through each of the sorority houses. Wednesday morning, you'll get invitations back to some of the residences and you have to pick only eight parties you think you would like to go to. The same thing happens on Thursday when you'll have four parties to pick from and then Friday night is Serious Night."

"What's that?" Shelby asked. It already seemed like the whole process was pretty serious.

JoJo licked ice cream off her finger. "Well, we dress up in our formals and go to real serious parties at only two sororities.

It's a crazy rush all week to get through every sorority. You never have a minute of time to yourself and you meet hundreds of girls. So many that all of their names and faces start to run together. By the end of the week, you're exhausted," JoJo said, winded from all the explaining.

Shelby wiped her lips one more time and tossed her ice cream drenched napkin in the trash container as they left the diner. "Wow, that's pretty intense," she replied.

"Yes it is, but from what Sandra said, it's a lot of fun and you will never forget it," JoJo told her.

Tired and quiet, they moseyed along the low-lit sidewalk making their way back to the dormitory. Shelby's thoughts drifted to the ice cream place back home and how she and Jack would go there after church on Wednesday nights.

Shelby smiled at the thought of how Jack would smash his ice cream in her face when she would take a taste of his favorite flavor—strawberry—and then, he would reach up, wipe her face with his napkin, and kiss her on the nose. Those were the days and she missed them, but she was in a different world now. At least, she had the memories and nothing could take them away.

~~~

The first few days on campus, Shelby felt like a lost puppy, but JoJo charged forward, like a big sister, and guided her around. Shelby was delighted.

At six a.m. on the Monday morning of Rush, the tiny room echoed with the rattling sound of Shelby's bedside alarm. The noise startled her out of her deep sleep as she quickly slammed down the button on the back of the clock. She rolled over and noticed JoJo had now stirred.

"Who's ready to Rush?" JoJo asked from underneath her pillow.

Shelby stretched. "I'm in no rush to do anything," she kidded. From all JoJo had warned her about the week ahead, they were about to enter the total chaos that was known as Sorority Rush. There would be no time for resting as they spent five days learning about the sixteen sororities on campus, meeting the members, and making sure they pledged the "right" club, the one they'd feel the most at home in.

Everything had to be perfect. Her smile. Her clothes. Her hair. Her makeup. Her introduction. She would be socially judged; where she was from, people she knew, her grades, her clothes,
~~~

everything. Shelby was all but ready to chicken out, but JoJo assured her, if she played her cards just right, it was a piece of cake and she would help her through it. Maybe they would even pledge the same organization.

They had made all the plans over the weekend and were ready to push forward, as JoJo put it. Shelby worried about whether her formal dress was going to be fashionable enough, and what if they didn't like where she was from. Valley was not your typical socially acceptable place to live. Fortunately, Shelby had a perky personality going for her and hoped this would land her the sorority she wanted.

The next few days were definitely a rush... running from one sorority to the next, being herded around and trying to decide which sisterhood to go back to. The anticipation of waiting to see who wanted her back and then dwindling down the whole process into just two houses to decide between. Her mind was flustered from all the craziness.

It was Friday afternoon, and the waitress appeared with their beverages at the Dreamland Bar-B-Que. JoJo grabbed her cold glass of sweet tea and raised her mason jar in a toasting gesture. Shelby lifted her glass, as well.

"This is the best sweet tea ever," JoJo exclaimed as their jars clanked.

"It is," Shelby said in agreement, as they gulped down the drink. "I really needed this. It's been awfully hot today and I need a break," Shelby said hastily as she wiped the sweat from her forehead.

"Oh, no you don't. We still have to get back to the dorm, shower, and get ready for Serious Night," JoJo said to her.

"Why do they call it that?" Shelby wondered.

JoJo picked up the ribs from her plate and explained. "They call it Serious Night because it's when each of your final two choices really open up the can of emotions to persuade you to join them instead of someone else. My sister told me they make you miss your mama and home and let you know you've got a group of new sisters waiting to welcome you in."

Shelby's heart pounded in her chest in anticipation of the night ahead. It had been hard enough for her to break her ties with Valley, her family... and Jack. Knowing she might be about to get a brand new extended family, a home away from home, brightened her outlook and relieved the pressure in her lungs.

"Hurry up and gulp down your sandwich, we have to go," JoJo said hurriedly. She was the one who kept Shelby on track.

JoJo was right; they did not have a minute to spare as they arrived on Sorority Row. The place was filled with girls all dressed in the frills and fancies of their long formals and high heel shoes that sparkled from the sun's rays setting over the horizon. The street was blocked off from car traffic and was packed with hundreds of girls stumbling along in their high heels on the sidewalks as the anticipation of the evening events grew among them. Their facial expressions were a dead giveaway as they restlessly waited for each sorority to open their doors and for the sisters to pour out of the houses, dressed alike, with candles in their hands, singing songs of welcome, friendship, and sisterhood.

The night had been long, and Shelby's feet ached from the three-inch heels she had bought for tonight's activities. She really needed Kappa Delta Omega, who was her first choice, to see she could be a great contribution to the affiliation and a valued sorority sister. Although, she liked her second selection, Phi Mu Sigma, too.

"What the hell was I thinking, buying these shoes?" she complained to JoJo after it was all over and they took the long walk from Sorority Row over to The Ferguson Student Center. There, in the ballroom, the remaining rushees filed into the quiet room and sat to themselves with a blank Rush card. They contemplated one of the biggest decisions they would make to date in their life.

"Okay," Shelby whispered to herself as she began to mull over both organizations. It was time to choose which one of the two would best fit her. She pondered over each one.

God came first in her life and her faith was an important factor in her decision-making. He had many times shown her a better way of living, so she had to make sure she was doing the right thing. Love and compassion for people were two of Shelby's greatest assets. Being an only child, she craved love and support from people. She was relentless in ministering to the needy the way God wanted her to do. These were extremely important values and she would not compromise or waiver from them. Kappa Delta Omega and Phi Mu Sigma both portrayed many of the same qualities she looked for in her own life. It was commitments like these that she knew in her heart would secure her future.

Being a loyal leader and creating life-long bonds were exciting factors and having guidance from her sisters throughout her life played a significant influence on her decision as well. She resolved that either sorority would be a perfect fit as she held her card tightly.

Both made her feel special in their own way. "This is so confusing," she said as she focused on the blank card she held in her hand. This had to be the hardest decision she had ever made. Her heartstrings began to gently tug at her. She was going to have to make a decision now. She took the pen and wrote:

1st Choice – Kappa Delta Omega
2nd Choice – Phi Mu Sigma

Shelby turned her card in about the same time JoJo did, and then they headed back to Tutwiler together.

Shelby let out a long breath as they crossed the quad. "Well, I hope I made the right decision."

JoJo poised and firm, promised her, "You did great, and I think you're going to do just fine tomorrow. I'm confident you and I both are going to get the sorority we want."

"I sure hope so. I had no idea it was going to be like this. All the hoop-la, skits, singing, clapping, and cheering. I don't know if I'm cut out to be a member of a whole house full of girls. I'm an only child, so having a hundred sisters might be really weird," Shelby said with a sigh. "I'm not sure one of the two sororities I went to tonight will even choose me."

JoJo busted out laughing. "Quit being such a wimp, Shelby. This will be all over tomorrow and you'll find a wonderful new home. You're a big girl now and you have to start acting like it."

Shelby was surprised by JoJo's comments. Even though she knew how outspoken JoJo could be, it still left her feeling a bit jittery. She knew she'd grown up quickly over the last few months, given all the things she'd gone through with Jack.

Back at Tutwiler, they stepped into the elevator and pressed the seven button. It was all Shelby could do to make it back to the room. Her feet throbbed from the pain of the new shoes—that were completely broken in by now—and a few minutes later, they were both passed out on the twin beds in the dark room.

~~~

At ten o'clock on Saturday morning, the two girls waited nervously by the phone in the lounge, along with several other girls, hoping it didn't ring to tell them they'd been cut from Rush.
~~~

That meant that neither of the clubs they went to the night before had offered them a bid to be a member. Shelby held her pillow in her grip, twisting the lace on the end as she prayed for the phone *not* to ring. JoJo held her stuffed teddy bear, torturing his ear as she tugged on it.

JoJo looked at the time. "It's ten minutes of noon," she reported. "I might die waiting."

Shelby knew from the rules that if they hadn't gotten a phone call by noon, then they were in! Her excitement grew and she was actually looking forward now to what her social future on campus would be.

"One more minute," JoJo reported, eyeballing the clock.

Shelby gawked at the phone... but nothing.

When the noon hour had passed, both girls, expressing their enthusiasm, hugged each other in the middle of the room. "Guess we got somewhere to go," JoJo said.

They hurriedly got dressed in shorts, T-shirts, and their tennis shoes and headed back to the ballroom at The Ferguson Center for the big reveal.

"JoJo which sorority are you hoping for?" Shelby asked as they crossed Bryant Drive on their way over.

"Kappa Delta Omega," JoJo said. "How about you?"

Shelby's eyes grew wide. "Oh, my gosh! Me too, I had no idea that's the one you wanted, too," Shelby replied.

"I suicided, Shelby," JoJo told her. "I hope like hell I get it."

"What does that mean?" Shelby asked, fearing her roommate might take her own life if she didn't get in the one she wanted.

"It means I put Kappa Delta Omega as my only choice."

That was something the rush counselors had advised against. Shelby just hoped it worked out in JoJo's favor. "What if you don't get it?"

"I will, watch and see," JoJo erupted with the confidence of a satisfying win.

Shelby didn't have the nerve like JoJo to suicide one; she just hoped she could get in a least one of the two she'd been to. Both had great reputations on campus, were known for their strong academics, service to the community, and they were rumored to have the best parties on campus with the best-looking frat guys.

Shelby and JoJo held hands as they climbed the stairs to the third level of Ferguson and made their way to their designated spots in the ballroom. Each rushee had an assigned number throughout the process, so Shelby and JoJo parted ways.

Shelby found her seat and saw a small, white envelope on the cushion. As the hundreds of other girls filed excitedly into the room, Shelby squirmed around, wondering what sorority had offered her a bid to join them.

A rush counselor took the stage before them and spoke through the microphone. "Welcome to Bid Day, rushees! This is what you've been waiting for all week, so I won't delay any further. On the count of three, you're to stand up, open your envelope, read the name of your new home, and then take off running to Sorority Row where your new sisters will be waiting for you."

Shelby's skin itched with anticipation and exhilaration all at once. She glanced across the many heads of ponytails and braids in brunette, red, and blond to try to see JoJo, but she couldn't make her out.

"Ready?" the counselor asked through the microphone. "One... two... threeeeee!"

Pandemonium erupted throughout the ballroom as the sound of hundreds of envelopes being torn sounded out. Chairs toppled as girls jumped for joy, hugged, and then took off running out of the room.

Shelby breathed a sigh and pulled her finger along the edge of the envelope. She reached in and took the card out, flipping it over. Her heart stopped for a brief second as she gratefully read the name on the invitation:

Kappa Delta Omega.

"Oh, my God!" she shouted out, not believing how jazzed she was at this point.

She wanted to find JoJo and run to Sorority Row with her, but there was no way to find her in the utter chaos of arms and legs, and flying ponytails.

Shelby ran alongside the pack of girls nearby as they sped out of the Ferguson parking lot, around the Gorgas Library, through the quad, and across University Boulevard. The campus police had the street blocked off with barriers and blue lights so the herd of girls wouldn't be kept from their new homes.

The Kappa Delta Omega building was on the bend in the road on Sorority Row—a gorgeous white Georgian mansion with an expansive porch and four white columns. She rounded the corner and saw pink and green balloons decorating the front lawn of ΚΔΩ.

"Welcome home!" the ΚΔΩ sisters shouted at her as she was engulfed in hugs and kisses.

One sister handed Shelby a T-shirt that said "Pledge Day" on it in ΚΔΩ pink and green letters. She slipped it over her head and joined in the celebration.

"Shelby! Oh, my God!" she heard someone in the distance.

She turned around to see her roommate, beaming a smile at her from cheek to cheek, wearing her own ΚΔΩ T-shirt.

"JoJo! You got in, too." Shelby clapped furiously and hugged her roommate.

"Told ya, doll," JoJo said with a wink.

The girls sang out in delight as they grabbed each other by the shoulders in a joyful bounce. There was music, food, and drinks and so many new people to meet. Friends and sisters forever. Shelby was ecstatic by all that she had been through during the week. She was so glad now that she'd done this, but so grateful that it was all over.

She and JoJo were sorority sisters. They were roommates, but best of all, they were friends.

Shelby was having the time of her life and there was no time for looking back.

~~~

Shelby was completely engrossed in her studies now as well as life in the sorority—meals, pledge meetings, frat parties—and she'd finally settled down from all the newness of college life. However, now, she was distracted by a knock at the door of her room.

"Shelby, you got a call on the hall phone," the girl's voice sounded out from the other side of the door.

Shelby leaped from her bed and tossed her notebook on the desk. *Who could be calling me?* She wondered. She'd just talked to her mom the night before. She ran down the hall to the lounge near the elevators.

"Hello," Shelby said breathlessly as she grabbed the dangling handset.

"Shelby, hey it's Mary," she heard her best friend sing out.

"Mary, oh, my gosh, girl, I'm so glad you called. How are you?"

"I'm great," Mary said. "I love it here in Athens. What about you?"

"I'm having a blast and I love college," Shelby said, excited to hear her voice.
~~~

"Me too, it's so much fun. You are *not* going to believe who I have in two of my classes here at UGA," Mary said with a quirky laugh.

"I don't know, who?"

"Richard Porter," she all but laughed out loud through the phone. Shelby threw her head to the side and held the phone away from her ear as Mary continued to speak loudly.

"No, for real?" Shelby asked inquisitively once Mary calmed down.

"Oh, my Lord, Shelby. All he talks about is you. He must be madly in love with you, girl. I can't get any work done in class. He's always asking about you and wants to know if I've talked to you or if you're coming to Athens to visit. He goes on and on."

"Really?" Shelby asked with a smile on her face. She didn't know how to respond. She felt a twinge of eagerness to learn more. She had no idea how Richard felt about her.

"Yep."

"I didn't know he liked me?" Shelby admitted, although, come to think of it, he had visited the grocery store a lot without buying anything.

"Well, he's head over heels crazy about you and he wants to see you," Mary pointed out.

Shelby's hand shook a bit. "He wants to see me?"

"Yes, that's what I said and he wanted me to see if it would be okay if he and I drove over to Tuscaloosa for the Florida State game on the Saturday after next. I think he said it was October 12th. He was hoping Georgia would play Alabama, but they aren't on the schedule this year. I would love to come see you, Shelby."

"Oh gosh..." Shelby said hesitantly. What should she do? This was all so sudden.

"Come on, Shell," Mary said. "He likes you and wants to see you. You and Jack are over and done with and you need to just move on."

Her smile quickly faded as she thought about Jack. "No, don't do this, Shelby," she whispered to herself.

"Hmm... okay, you're right Mary," Shelby said, knowing her friend pretty well. "Yes, y'all come on over. I can't wait to see you. I've got so much to tell you," she said.

"Yes! Yes!" Mary exclaimed. "We'll call you in a week or so and let you know when we will be there. I miss you, Shelby."

"I miss you, too, Mary. You take care and we'll talk soon," Shelby said feeling a bit perky.

JoJo leaned forward as Shelby came through the door. "Okay, so who was it?" she asked.

"Well, aren't we just the nosey one?" Shelby said. "It was my best friend, Mary, from home. She's at UGA in Athens and she called to check on me."

"Dang, I was hoping it was a guy," JoJo said disappointedly.

"Yeah, right," Shelby said flatly, trying to push her roommate off.

"So, tell me, Shelby, do you have a boyfriend?"

"No," she said, quick to answer. "Do you?" Shelby asked back.

"Nope, neither do I," JoJo replied. "Not yet."

Chapter Twelve

The cool breeze of mid-October danced across the open waters of the Chattahoochee as Jack sat soberly watching the barge move down the swift current of the river. He was sure it was headed for Columbus. He half-smiled right before he took a sip of his soda. His thoughts rambled as he mused over the many times he and Shelby sat alone here at the Kissing Bridge and talked about their future. He set the can down as he followed his thoughts back in time.

He could hear her voice as if she was sitting right next to him. "Someday we are going to get married and have four kids. What do you think, Jack?" he recalled as a vision of her beautiful smile replayed in his mind.

He remembered his reply clearly. "I think four might be a bit too many, Shelby. At least one, though," he had said with a snicker.

"Well, one day you're going to be the sheriff, just like your dad, and our kids are going to love having you as a father. We're going to build us a house and I'm going to teach at Shawmut Elementary," Shelby had declared.

He didn't think much about her words of their future back then; it was just too grown up for him to be thinking about things like that. He would just nod in agreement. Whatever his beautiful Shelby wanted was perfectly fine with him. Sometimes it made him feel uncomfortable though when she spoke so confidently of their future. He'd feared that he wouldn't be able to give her all that she wanted.

How right he'd been.

The horn from the barge blew loudly and it shook him out of his thoughts when it drifted out of sight down the river.

He wondered how she was doing... how school was... did she enjoy it... did she ever think about him anymore? He would give anything now to turn back the clock to have just one more chance to hold her in his arms. He remembered how his heart would melt when he would kiss her gently on the lips.

He would do whatever it took to make it all up to her. He promised. She'd been gone for a month now and he missed her dearly. It was like she had vanished without a trace. Like a part of him had been amputated. He even drove by her folks' house on the weekends several times to see if she had come home for a visit.

He never saw her car, though. He managed for a brief instant to whisper her name "Tootie."

He could no longer bear the heartbreak of sitting alone at the Kissing Bridge and decided it was time for him to leave. Maybe the next time he came, it would be with Shelby. He smiled at the thought and stood up from the sandbags, got in his car, and drove home. When he pulled up in front of his parent's home late in the afternoon, he noticed a familiar-looking car sitting in the front of the sidewalk. Was it Denise's?

"Oh great..." he muttered under his breath.

He parked the Mustang, got out, ran up the steps of the porch, and opened the wooden front door. As he stepped into the foyer, he turned to see Denise, her grandmother, Mrs. Hollis, and his mom and dad. His dad stood in front of the fireplace with Denise and Mrs. Hollis sitting comfortably on the sofa. His mother sat in the tall winged-back chair facing her guests with an uneasy look on her face.

"Jack, we've been waiting for you," his dad called out to him in a deep and serious voice.

He could see the expressions on their faces as he entered the room and wondered just what was going on here. He glanced down at Denise, but she turned her head away.

Once again his dad said, "Come in and have a seat, son. We need to talk."

He quickly searched his mother's eyes.

"Mom, are you okay?" Jack asked as he stepped toward her.

"Jack, have a seat. This is a serious matter that we all need to discuss. Mrs. Hollis kindly asked to stop by and talk about this."

This? "Talk about what, Dad?"

His father stretched tall and authoritative. "Well, Mrs. Hollis says her granddaughter, Denise, is with child, and that you had something to do with it." His father's voice was stern and resonated through the room.

"With child? Does that mean what I think it means?" he quickly asked, looking for a response from his dad.

"Jack, I'm pregnant," Denise said flatly interrupting his words.

He turned to Denise with a panicked look in his eyes. "What?"

"You heard me," she said.

"No way, Denise. Say it ain't true," he said.

He could feel the pain in her eyes as she lowered her head again to the floor, ashamed to meet his eyes. She began to cry.

Anger seethed through Jack's veins. "Denise, I don't believe it. You're a..." His words stopped and he quickly turned to Mrs. Hollis.

"I'm a what, Jack?" Slamming her hands on the sofa, Denise shouted out, "A whore? Is that what you were going to say as if I just sleep around with everyone? I know what people say about me, but it's not true. You're the only guy I've ever been with!" she belted out in anger.

Jack was petrified and turned to his dad and then quickly to his mother as he could hear her sob softly.

"I don't believe you," Jack snapped. "This can't be true."

"Son, that's enough now. You can't go blaming Denise. Calling her names isn't going to get us anywhere. If you've been with her, then you know. We have to figure it all out. The question now is... have you been with Denise?" His dad asked firmly and looked him squarely in the eyes.

Jack gawked at her angrily as she continued to hang her head low. "I'm not sure, Dad. The only time I could ever have been with her was the day I got drunk when Walter and I went out fishing after the Fourth of July celebration. We had been drinking beer all day. Walter had to leave and go to work, so we came back into the pier and Denise asked me to take her out for a boat ride. I remember taking her out and then, the next thing I remember, I was waking up butt-naked in the old shack at the boat dock. I was by myself. It's all I can say for sure," Jack admitted.

"Jack, I was the one who lit the candle and left it on the crate. I was the one you were with, not Shelby, even though you kept calling me by her name," Denise said, almost as if she were enjoying his pain.

Jack sat on the couch and dropped his head in his hands as he rested them on his knees. He shook his head trying to dislodge the truth. "This can't be true," he repeated.

"You know if it is, then you have to do the right thing by this girl," his dad said sympathetically.

Jack looked up at his dad terrified by his words. He knew exactly what that statement meant. He *was* a southern gentleman, after all. He frantically tried to gather his thoughts from this horrible news. No way could he marry Denise. He was going to marry Shelby. He couldn't. *No, I won't marry her,* he said to himself, trying desperately to make sense of all of this.

"She tricked me," Jack snapped back at his dad. "I didn't have any idea what happened until a week later when she told me. I thought I was with Shelby that night," he confessed angrily. "Why did you do this, Denise? You know I love Shelby," he cried out and faced her.

"I love you, Jack," she responded softly. "I told you how I felt about you and how much you meant to me from the first time I met you."

He watched as Mrs. Hollis gazed at his dad. "Sheriff Emerson, I know y'all will do the right thing by Denise. We're going to go now and let y'all have some time together. I'll keep in touch."

Denise stood up. "I'm sorry, Jack," she said as she took a step in front of her grandmother. "I didn't mean for this to happen."

They both walked out the front door.

The room was silent after the door closed behind them with the exception of Mrs. Emerson's heartbroken sobs. Jack couldn't believe he'd done this to his parents, to himself, and to Shelby. "Oh God, what have I done?" he asked softly.

"Dad, you got to believe me, Denise is always pulling crap. I don't think I slept with her; it's probably some other guy's baby. Now, she's knocked up and wants me to be responsible for it? She probably hates the guy who did it and I'm the one who gets blamed for it. Just because she loves me, well that's a crock of shit, Dad," he said in anger.

"Mind your mouth, son."

Jack trembled as he recalled. "Shelby warned me about Denise and told me she was no good, but no... I wouldn't listen. The only thing I'm guilty of is being her friend. I felt sorry for her. Now, look where I'm at," he said as he furled his fists at his side.

"Oh, dear," his mother said with a long sigh.

"I've got to get out of here for a while," he said as he paced the floor. He peered at his mother and walked over to her. He knelt before her and wrapped his arms around her. He felt her body tremble as he held her in his arms. His heart grieved at the thought of hurting his mother. The most perfect person in the world to him.

"Oh, Jack," she struggled to speak. He reached up with his hand and took her chin in his index finger as he lifted her head and looked into her eyes.

"Mom, I promise it's all going to be okay. Please don't worry. It's all a big mistake and we'll work it out," he said sadly, as he kissed her on her forehead.

He stood up and stepped toward his dad who was leaning against the mantle with his head down. "Dad, you have to believe me. It will all be okay."

Jack stuck his hands in his front pockets and lowered his eyes in shame. He walked into the foyer and paused, shaking his thoughts out of his mind. His hand trembled as he reached for the door handle, opened it wide, and stepped out onto the front porch. He gently closed the door behind him. A burst of tears flooded his eyes as they rushed down his face. He had never felt so alone and ashamed as he did right then.

He had ruined his life, his parents' life, and surely Shelby's life, as well. The guilt poured over him like a pot of boiling water... as his body shivered.

He leaped off the porch, ran toward his car, flew open the door, and hopped in. He quickly started the ignition and slammed the gearshift into drive. He spun the Mustang out into the street as the sound of his tires squealing resonated in his ears.

He sped down Highway 29 toward the Kissing Bridge. All he could think about was Shelby and the love they had shared. Now, he had ruined all hope for their reconciliation.

He needed to sit on the sandbags and hold their memories close in his thoughts. He had to figure it all out.

"How will I ever be able to tell Shelby about this?" he whispered as he drew in a deep breath and exhaled it rapidly.

He drove down the gravel drive to the Kissing Bridge and parked his car. He got out, walked over to the river's edge, and slowly sat down on the bank. He felt pain in his chest as the guilt welled up inside him as he lowered his head. He was nauseated. He felt like his body was going to rupture as tears continued to flood his eyes like water rushing over the edge of a waterfall as they landed on his jeans.

"You gave me your heart, Shelby," he said as he wept. "You loved me... you protected me... you believed in me... you were everything to me... we had it all... this just can't be the end. I promise to make this up to you... somehow... someday."

The sun began to lower on the horizon. Jack shivered from the cool October evening. He wrapped his jacket closer to his chest and folded his arms. He sat in silence, as he pondered what he was going to do.

"What if I *am* the father?" he asked out loud.

It was time for him to be a man. It was what Shelby had tried to get him to do. He just didn't know this was how it would happen. Shelby was always right, she tried so hard to protect him, and he loved everything about her.

However, she was gone now. She had left him with a shattered heart and all alone. Maybe it was true what they always said, "God has a plan."

It was late when Jack arrived home and all the lights were out with the exception of the low-lit porch light his mother always left on for him when he came home late. He stepped quietly across the porch, opened the front door, and stepped into the foyer.

He started up the staircase when he was startled by his mother's voice, calling out from the living room.

"Jack, please come here," she said sniffling. Jack stopped and slowly turned to see her silhouette in the chair. He walked over and turned on the lamp sitting on the end table as he sat down on the sofa.

"Mom," he said as he cleared his throat.

"It's okay, Jack," she said softly as she reached for his hand. She took it and folded it in hers. "You don't have to say anything. I just want you to know how much I love you."

"No, I've ruined our lives, I really don't know if I'm the baby's dad. I was so drunk," he said sadly. He could feel her gently patting his hand to comfort him.

"I feel so alone and ashamed. I don't know what I'm going to do," he admitted as he looked into his mother's deep blue eyes.

"Sweetheart, it's going to be okay. This is normal for you to feel this way. You just need a few days to think it out. Always remember to do what is right Jack. Remind yourself often what the Lord says about those in pain. 'He hears the cries of the broken-hearted,'" she said cautiously. She lifted his hands to her cheek and then kissed the back of his knuckles. "We will get through this together. Your dad and I have talked and we will help in any way we can," she spoke softly to him.

The next few days were the hardest times for Jack.

He was faced with so many people telling him what was best. "Do the right thing," echoed in his mind over and over.

However, the right thing meant he had to completely let go of the hope of any sort of future with Shelby by marrying Denise.

Wait. What about Shelby? She was the one he loved... how could he possibly walk away from the love of his life and marry someone he didn't even know that well, much less have any feelings for? Just like that.

Because now there was a baby, that was why.

A tiny, innocent little baby girl or boy, his baby, his baby, bombarded his mind.

A gift from God.

Jack's heart anguished over everything he had done and the mistakes he had made in the past. He needed to learn to deal with the situation and leave them in the past where they belonged. Admitting his mistakes would put him on the path to making better choices.

His first priority was to figure out how to let Shelby know. He had to tell her before she found out some other way.

It was going to be the hardest thing he had ever done.

However, it was the right thing.

Chapter Thirteen

Shelby rolled over in her comfy bed, stretched out her arms, and rubbed her eyes. The sun peered through the window this late Sunday morning. She and JoJo had partied into the wee hours of the morning with the Alpha Delta frat brothers. She chuckled when she recalled the wild and crazy party the night before. She turned to face JoJo, who had just plopped back down on her bunk.

"Oh, my headaches," JoJo, said with a sigh. "It's been a while since I chugged beer like that."

"You were so funny," Shelby said as she snickered out loud.

"Go ahead and laugh, my friend. Just wait until you do it. I'm going to get you back," JoJo said with a villainous tone in her voice. She lay motionless on her bed as Shelby refreshed her memory of the night before.

Shelby cackled. "You and that guy, Phillip, were completely out of control." "I dated a guy in high school who used to get drunk all the time, then get sick and puke everywhere. I would get so mad at him; he would think it was funny. Then, later he would complain about how bad he felt," Shelby said, slapping her hand on the bed.

"I could only get down a few beers, and that was enough for me. They said I would get silly and stupid acting and then want to go to sleep," Shelby admitted shyly, thinking about how Jack would help her on those occasions.

"So, did you ever get really drunk, Shelby?" JoJo asked with a suspicious tone in her voice.

"Oh, a few times," Shelby admitted. She grinned recalling the times she and Mary would join in with the guys. "For heaven's sake, my parents never knew it, though. Thank goodness and I only drank when I would spend the night with Mary," Shelby said.

"Oh, Shelby," JoJo laughed as she shook her head. "You're such a sheltered child, girl. I bet you never did anything wrong, did you?" she asked as she cut her eyes toward Shelby.

"I wasn't an angel if that's what you mean," she fired back with a hint of sarcasm. She reached down and pulled the blanket up over her neck. "But I was careful not to get caught when I stepped out on the edge." She rolled her eyes at JoJo.

"Oh, give me a break, Shell," JoJo remarked. "You think last night was wild? Just wait until you get to know the people here. You're going to see some really off the wall things."

Shelby thought about JoJo's remark and wondered what could be wilder than last night? *Oh well, I guess I'll find out soon enough,* she thought. She rolled over and closed her eyes to catch a few more zzzz's, but her thoughts went straight to Jack.

She fell back in time as she reminisced. Jack had held her hair back when she got sick and barfed all over herself from the three beers she drank the first time she got drunk.

Oh gosh, she recalled the awful experience in her mind. It was sweltering that night and the heat only made it worse. She had stripped down to her tank top and bathing suit bottoms trying to cool off, but not before she upchucked all over herself at the pier that night.

"That's my girl," Jack acted like a hyena howling in the night. He had wiped the puke from her face when she was finished and helped Mary get her back to her house where she spent the night in front of the toilet.

Shelby had woken up late in the afternoon the next day unable to relive the events of the previous night. She couldn't understand where the small bruises on her chest just below her chin had come from. Mary reminded her, "It's from where you hugged the toilet all night."

It had been Shelby's first time being drunk and her last if she had anything to do with it... she recalled. If that was what going out on Saturday night partying was all about, she didn't want anything to do with it. It wasn't as if she got any brownie points or anything like that... she remembered.

~~~

Late that Sunday afternoon, chatter in the lounge among the girls was mostly about the wild parties Saturday night. Shelby smiled as she reached for the phone and dialed Mary's number.
~~~

"May I speak to Mary Jeffers," Shelby asked excitedly.

"Hold on and let me get her," the girl's voice said on the other end. As she waited patiently for Mary to answer, her thoughts turned to Richard. She recalled the last time she had seen him was the day after her family's summer vacation. He was so sweet to stop by the store and check in on her. Now, he wanted to see her. Was Mary playing with her or could it be true?

"Hello," Mary answered.

"Mary, hey, it's Shelby." Excited to hear her best friend's voice.

"Shelby, I was just thinking about you. I saw Richard last night at Chi Pi frat party and he said he couldn't wait until Saturday when we drive over to Tuscaloosa. We're still on right?"

"You bet," Shelby replied quickly. "I'm so homesick, Mary, I can't wait to see you. So, is there anything new with Richard? I really want to know what you think of him," Shelby said hesitantly.

"He seems like a great guy from what I can tell. Everyone here likes him a lot and all the girls are after him. I think you and he would make a great couple," Mary admitted.

"Hold on, not so fast. We're not a couple. You know I've never had a boyfriend other than Jack and that scares me a bit," she said as she waited for a response from Mary.

"I think you're going to have a great time with Richard. Our plans are to leave at nine a.m. Saturday morning. Let me know what gate at the stadium to meet you at."

"Let's meet at Denny Chimes, then we'll hang out on the quad until the game starts," Shelby said excitedly. "I'm so happy you're coming."

"Me too, Shell," Mary replied.

"Okay then, call me right before y'all leave," Shelby said as they said their goodbyes.

She hung up the phone and walked over to the window. She had a strange feeling something new was about to happen as she gazed out the glass.

Thoughts of Richard weaved in and out of her mind. She remembered the first time she'd met him and how his dreamy, bright green eyes caught her attention. He was tall and thin, with the physique of an athlete. His last word to her resonated in her mind. "Smile," he said when he looked into her eyes, and she recalled just how it made her feel. Special. She just didn't know how special until now. Feeling like a beautiful rose, a yellow one to be exact, towering tall above all the others on the lushness of a bush blowing gently in the breeze, swaying to the music of Mother

Nature. It made her feel beautiful and free.

Yes, she was free, and she smiled at the thought.

~~~

Shelby stood in front of the main entrance to Denny Stadium at one o'clock sharp as she and Mary had planned. She nervously bit her lip in anticipation of seeing her and Richard. It had been a long week and Shelby's excitement was overwhelming. She paced the sidewalk, peered down at her wristwatch, and nodded. She was right on time.

Spectators lined up in front of the main entrance waiting for the gates to open to rush into their seats. Shouts of "Roll Tide" blared out among the crowds of people. Everyone was dressed in the UA colors of crimson and white and it was hard to see anything but those hues around her.

"Shelby," Mary yelled from afar, as she made her way through the crowds of people.

"Oh, my gosh, Mary, over here!" Shelby said wishing her voice were louder, as the two rushed into each other's arms. They maneuvered around like two kindergartners returning to school after summer vacation. After their joyous welcoming reunion, Shelby turned to Richard, smiled gently, and stepped forward as Richard reached out with his arms and took her into his embrace for a friendly hug.

"It's good to see you, Shelby," Richard said with a smile on his face. Shelby could feel his gentleness as he wrapped his arms around her and hugged her. His tender squeeze made her feel good. Even though Jack had been the only one... she had felt good about... until now.

"It's great to see you, Richard. How have you been?" she asked giddily. She stepped backward as Richard let go of his embrace, and grasped her hands in his. Shelby felt his hesitation to let her go and she wasn't in any hurry to push away either. He stepped forward and kissed her unexpectedly on the cheek. Shelby blushed as he winked at her and moved away. Her heart fluttered briefly at his closeness.

It was a reunion she hadn't expected, at least from Richard. They had barely known each other. But she had to admit she enjoyed his attention.

"Have y'all eaten?" Shelby asked once the homecoming had settled.
~~~

"No, we're starving," Mary, admitted. "Where's a good place to eat?"

"There's a diner not far from here," Shelby said as she pointed in the direction of University Boulevard.

"Great let's get a bite to eat before the game," Richard called out in agreement.

Shelby could feel Richard's eyes following her as they turned and headed down the street. She felt his hand touch the curve of her back as they weaved through the crowd. Shelby felt his nearness and she blinked her eyes briefly at the sensation of his touch. She felt safe with his gentleness.

The line was long at the diner as they waited hungrily. They chatted about home... about school... about Greek life and it was no time before they found themselves seated with menus in their hand.

"Okay, this is my treat. Order anything you like," Richard said, as he looked Shelby in the eyes.

"Hmm... I want the cheeseburger, French fries, and a Coke," Mary said handing the menu to the waitress. Shelby scanned the list of items while the young girl stood tapping her pencil on her pad. "I'll have the Bar-B-Que sandwich, chips, and a Sprite," Shelby said as she turned to see Richard peeking over the menu.

"I'll have the same as the lady here," he said to the waitress.

Before long, the table was filled with their drinks. Shelby watched as Richard reached down, picked up his soda, and hoisted the glass for a toast. Mary quickly lifted hers and Shelby followed next.

"Roll Tide," Richard shouted.

They all laughed, knowing it was odd for those words to come out of the mouth of a Georgia Bulldog. He then turned to Mary and leaned in toward her and they both cupped their hand over their mouth and whispered something to each other.

"Wait, what are y'all saying? No secrets," Shelby said and frowned at her two friends.

Mary and Richard both whispered together, "Go Dawgs."

The three burst into laughter again. Shelby's eyes went straight to them, this was exactly what she needed and she was thrilled to have both seated across the table from her. In the blink of an eye, her spirits had been lifted and it brought joy to her heart. She was sure of happier times to come.

Shelby wasn't even finished eating when Mary caught a glimpse of a guy across the room. She moved quickly to her feet, flapping her hand in the air, and hollered. "It's Justin, hey Justin," her voice emitted loudly across the room to catch the attention of a young man seated at the end of the bar. "Sorry guys, but I've got to talk to this one," she smiled down at the two of them.

"Who's that guy?" Richard asked with a puzzled smirk that made Shelby laugh. She knew they had probably lost Mary's company for the rest of the afternoon. "He's a guy from back home she has been in love with him since junior high," Shelby said and then sipped her soda. "Justin Reese. I could tell you some tales about those two." She nodded as she smiled at Richard.

"Some really juicy ones huh?" Richard asked.

Shelby returned his smile and said, "You got that right."

Ten minutes later, when they walked over to the end of the bar to rescue Mary, the chatter and laughter were sure giveaways they were going to be unsuccessful with this extrication.

"Mary, we're leaving, the game starts in thirty minutes. Are you coming?" Shelby inquired as she interrupted their soirée.

"Look who I found," Mary said, pointing to Justin.

"Hey, Justin," Shelby replied in a hospitable tone. She hadn't ever cared much for Justin, but because Mary was crazy about him, she tolerated his presence.

"Hey, Shelby, who's your friend?" Justin asked. Shelby felt sure he was just being nosey.

She cleared her throat. "This is Richard."

"Nice to meet you, Justin," Richard said extending his hand in a friendly shake.

She could see the curiosity in Justin's eyes. He would probably run back to Valley and shoot his mouth off to Jack. Which, of course, would be perfectly fine with her if he did.

"Mary, we're heading back to the stadium, are you ready?" Shelby asked.

"Hmm, how about I meet the two of you later? Justin and I have some catching up to do. I tell you what, see you back at the main entrance right after the game is over?" she asked. Shelby could sense she and Richard weren't invited to join them.

Shelby thought for a minute and then immediately said. "Okay, that works for us," as she turned for an approval from Richard.

"Yeah, yeah, that would be great," Richard, said.

"Then, we'll see you later," Shelby said thinking she needed a beer right about now. She was going to be spending the afternoon with Richard. Alone.

Shelby and Richard stood there a bit longer, and they couldn't help but be entertained by Mary, riding ever so tightly to Justin's arm, like a saddle on a horse being harnessed down.

As they turned to walk away, Mary gave Shelby a thumb up and a silly wink.

She set me up Shelby thought and grinned. She shook her head in disbelief and shot back a wink of her own.

The whole world suddenly brightened.

Shelby was like an emerging butterfly. Somehow, she could see herself in a new light, and it made her feel different about who she was. She felt Richard's hand once again touch the curve of her back while they made their way through the crowd to their seats just minutes before kickoff.

Out of nowhere, Shelby felt guilt rising in the pit of her stomach. She had never gone out with another guy. But the truth was, right now she just didn't care. She was here with Richard and she was going to have a wonderful time. Nothing was going to get in her way. No memories... no guilt. She didn't need anyone's permission and she was satisfied with her decision.

The game ended and the announcer roared, "Alabama 8 and Florida State 7."

Shelby and Richard sprang from their seats and grabbed each other in a playful hug, ecstatic over the win, as they cheered along with the crowd.

It had been a seat chiller. The cheers, "Roll Tide" echoed across the stadium. Richard had really gotten into the game, which she loved. She reached for her belongings and noticed they were leaving with much more than they had arrived with.

Richard had made their time special. He had been so sweet to buy her a football program and pompoms in red and white, along with snacks they had munched on during the game. She swept everything into her arms as he helped her zigzag through the mob of people, chanting, and celebrating Alabama's win.

Through the main entrance, they waited where they had promised to meet Mary. Honestly, Shelby was a bit saddened that their day had come to a close. In a few short minutes, Mary would meet them and she and Richard would head back to Athens. She wasn't sure she wanted the evening to end yet.

"Here, let's sit over there on the bench while we wait on Mary," Richard suggested as he pointed toward an empty seat.

The crowd began to thin some while they sat and waited for Mary. Silence filled the air around them. At first, it felt a bit awkward.

"Shelby," Richard said, softly breaking the silence. "I've had a wonderful time today."

She leaned back into the bench and smiled at his comment. "I have too, Richard," she said dreamily. She watched him closely when he looked down and took her hand gently into his while their fingers entwined together. Shelby felt a rush of goosebumps. What was it about him that made her feel so giddy?

Shelby felt the gentle squeeze of his fingers. "I was hoping you would see me. I know the last time we saw each..." his voice stopped. *Here it comes,* she thought as she cringed at what was coming next. "Well, you remember," he said sympathetically.

She waited as he paused.

"I wanted to ask about you and Jack," Richard said in a hesitant tone of voice. She could feel his reluctance to hear her response.

She turned and looked him squarely in the eyes and spoke softly. "Richard, we broke up four months ago, and if it's okay, I would rather not spoil our evening by talking about Jack and the past. I'm good. I have to look forward and not backward," she said confidently.

She could barely see his eyes in the reflection of the lights still glistening from the stadium. But it was the glittering of his handsome green eyes that told her he was thrilled. She hoped her response satisfied his curiosity and relieved his apprehension when he suddenly responded. "That's what I was hoping to hear."

Still holding her hands, he lightly squeezed them as he lifted them up to his lips and kissed the back of her hand. She turned to study his face against the backdrop of the dimly lit streetlight. She saw his eyes close gently and she elongated her next breath and let out a sigh of contentment.

There was no doubt in her mind he was thinking about them kissing. They were alone now. The droves of people had vanished into the darkness. A few couples sat on blankets thrown on the grass around them. There were gentle whispers, quiet, and intimate moments flanking the area.

It was only seconds later when Richard leaned forward and gazed into her eyes. She felt his touch as he lifted her chin in his hand and closer to his mouth and kissed her ever so gently on the lips. There was a split second of hesitation, but it passed rapidly. She gave in to his kiss and it was pleasantly breathtaking and she knew it was so right.

Shelby shivered from his kiss and he instantly responded tenderly.

"Are you cold?" he asked.

She tried to hide it—no, she wasn't—but she didn't want him to know it was the kiss and not the chill in the air.

"Yes, just a bit," she whispered. She watched him as he stood up, removed his jacket, and covered her shoulders.

"There," he said apologetically. "Maybe this will help." He brushed aside a strand of hair blowing in her face.

She couldn't resist his gentleness and with his every move, she soaked up all his attention. He wrapped his arms closely around her shoulders and rubbed them in an attempt to create a little friction to keep her warm. *All will be well*, she thought while she embraced his touch and then laid her head on his shoulder.

Mary was late. Shelby appreciated her tardiness, something she hadn't been so tolerant of in years past, but tonight she was grateful. It had given her and Richard time together.

It was after midnight when Shelby stood alone on the front sidewalk of Tutwiler dorm. She smiled and waved as Mary and Richard drove out of sight in his black Corvette Stingray. Shelby envied Mary for an instant and within seconds, the taillights disappeared into the darkness.

It had become clear to Shelby... Richard had a heart for romance. She sensed his yearning for her by the gentle touch of his hands. She knew he cared when he asked about Jack. She could tell from his sweet kiss that he was a man with a tender heart. A side of him she had never known.

Had she really begun to move on from Jack? Would Richard now be the one who had awakened her heartbroken spirit?

She shivered from the cold night air and crossed her arms around her. She rubbed the back of them with her hands up and down to warm herself as she brushed off the coldness. She gazed up into the clear October sky as the stars twinkled and the full moon shone down brightly. The scent of fall filled the air.

With a slow, deep breath, she inhaled and let out a cheerful sigh, smiled, and walked to the front door of the dormitory.

Chapter Fourteen

Jack sat quietly at the Kissing Bridge late in the evening. He shivered at the cool October chill, reached up, and pulled his jacket collar tightly around his neck. The breeze had moved in late that afternoon and now had begun to make small ripples of white caps on the river as the brightness of the moon glistened off the water. His heart was actually missing beats as he sat on the sandbags staring at nothing. Never, in all the years he and Shelby had been together, did he ever believe—

It sunk in suddenly; he had to let her go. He sucked in a deep breath and let out a loud sigh.

He was startled, by the touch of a hand on his shoulder. He quickly turned to find his father's silhouette standing tall against the full moon's light.

"You, okay son?" Sheriff Emerson asked.

"Not really, Dad," Jack said as he sipped in another deep breath. He saw his dad step forward and sit down next to him on the bank.

"You can't wait any longer, Jack," the sheriff said in an authoritative, but gentle tone.

"I know, Dad."

He felt himself falling apart, and the thought of having to let go of Shelby scared him to death. For days now, he had tried to bury his emotions and was desperate to figure out how he would tell her what he had done. God, he knew what would happen when she found out. He wasn't ready to let her go, but the time had come and he had to make the hardest decision he had ever made in his life. It hurt him more than he could stand, letting her go, but he didn't know any other way out.

"Dad, if you were me, what would you do?" he asked as he looked into his dad's eyes.

Sheriff Emerson was a wise man and Jack respected what he had to say. Even though they had had their differences, Jack knew his dad wanted only the best for him. He watched as his dad drew in a deep breath, looked across the water, and replied.

"Son, think of it this way. If I had gotten your mother pregnant, would you have wanted me to do the right thing and marry her?"

Jack answered without hesitation. "Absolutely, Dad," he said quickly before he realized what he had just spoken. He could see his father's expression with his response. It was in that flash of time, he understood what his dad had just asked him. There was no way he ever wanted to be faced with that question from his son or daughter.

"I hear you, Dad," Jack said knowing what he had to do as he nodded his head.

"Good, son, I knew you would. I'm going to leave you alone now. Don't be too late coming in. You know how your mother worries about you."

"I won't. I'll be home shortly," Jack said sadly. "Dad, thank you and know I love you."

"I love you, too, son."

Jack sat for a few more minutes. "No more waiting," he said. "I have to get this behind me." He stood up firmly and headed home.

When he finished showering and dressing for bed, he hesitantly walked over to the small desk in the corner of his room. He turned on the tiny desk light, opened his notebook, and pulled out a piece of paper. He began to write as tears rolled down his face.

~~~

Over the next month, Shelby visited Richard a few times in Athens and he had in return driven over to Tuscaloosa to see her, as well. Their relationship grew like a bean sprouting in a freshly tilled garden.

Shelby enjoyed spending time with Richard when she wasn't studying or wrapped up in her sorority duties. He treated her like a princess and she loved all the attention. There was no doubt in her mind that Richard's mother was someone to respect. After all, she had taught him how to treat a lady; she had thought that on several occasions and mentioned it to Mary.
~~~

Mary, of course, had conveniently made herself unavailable to them during Shelby's visits to Athens, other than to check in and say hello when Shelby spent the weekends at her place.

It was the weekend before the Thanksgiving break. Shelby stressed over the craziness of her life, even though she loved every minute; the time she spent with Richard, college and classes, and all her obligations to the sorority. She was overwhelmed and overjoyed. Shelby was up and getting dressed to head to her only class on Friday. She was excited to see Richard this weekend before they both headed home for the holidays.

There was a knock on the door. Shelby reached for the handle and opened it. There in the doorway was JoJo with her arms full of bright, long-stemmed yellow roses all fanned out in a bouquet that took Shelby's breath away.

JoJo's voice escaped from behind the bouquet. "These are for you, Shelby," she said as she tried to peek around the elaborate cluster of roses.

"Oh, my," Shelby squealed, as she reached to take them. They were absolutely stunning.

"I kind of peeked at the card. They're from Richard. I just couldn't help myself," JoJo said handing them to Shelby.

Shelby gasped at the overwhelming bunch of roses. She had never seen this many flowers in a bouquet in her life.

She managed to close the door behind her, made her way to the desk, and set them down, with JoJo right on her heels. The bouquet was so big it literally covered the table. She stepped back after setting them down and reached for the card pinned on the front sash. She opened it and shouted in excitement.

"You are one lucky girl, Shelby," JoJo said happily.

"Oh, they are beautiful," she babbled. The card read:

Shelby, I hope you enjoy the flowers. They are a token of my apology for not being able to come for the weekend as we had planned. My professor has me working on one of my accelerated classes and I have to finish a project this weekend and turn it into him before he leaves on Monday. I miss you and I'll call you when you get home. Be safe and we'll talk soon.

Love
Richard

"Oh, dang it," Shelby whispered as she let out a sigh of disappointment. She smiled though when she felt the softness of the beautiful yellow petals that beamed at her in a majestic show of beauty. "What a wonderful gesture, apology accepted," she murmured as she finished getting ready for class. She knew how important and diligent he was toward his studies. After all, he was working on his core classes in hopes of getting into John Marshall Law School a year earlier than he anticipated.

It was just hours later when Shelby rushed out of the classroom, down the hall, and threw open the door into the bright sunlight blaring down on this late November afternoon.

It had been a crazy week, but now she was going home for the first time since she had left back in September. She missed her parents and home. It wasn't until just then that she realized how much she had missed them. She had been living in a different world here. There had been no time to feel homesick. At least not until now...

She packed her Beetle Bug with a week's worth of clothing. She secured her big bright bouquet of roses on the floorboard of the front seat to keep them from falling over. She backed her Bug out of her parking spot and headed south on 82. She was going home. She had bittersweet feelings buzzing in her stomach. She was excited to see her parents, but there were also thoughts of Jack as she drove home to Valley.

~~~

The sun was setting in her eyes as she turned onto 23rd Drive and she was almost home. She had been gone for a long time and she couldn't be happier. She smiled as she pulled into the drive of her parents' house. She parked her car next to her dad's, wiggled out of her seat, and ran toward the back door.

She pulled on the screen door and as it flew open, she called out, "I'm home, Mom and Dad!" She ran into the kitchen and saw her mother turn her way. "Shelby, you made it home." She could see the excitement in her mom's face as they grabbed one another and held on tightly. Shelby needed that hug more than anything. She loved the many times her mom would hold her.

Just as they released their embrace, Shelby saw her dad come through the door and with both of his arms reaching for her. Shelby ran straight into his big bear hug. "Oh, Daddy, I've missed you so much," she said overjoyed "It feels so good to be home, you have no idea how much, " she said turning to face her mother.

"It sure hasn't been the same here," Joel said. She watched as he reached up and wiped his eyes.
~~~

Shelby and her dad sat down at the table as Frances poured glasses of sweet tea, walked over, and handed each one a drink.

"We have so much to get caught up on," Frances said as she joined them at the table.

"I know," Shelby replied, relieved she was finally home.

"So much has happened since I've been gone. My classes are going great. I love college. JoJo and I made it into the same sorority and they have kept me so busy, but I'm enjoying every minute of it. They are like my family away from home. I spend every evening doing something with them," she said as she sipped her tea. "I've made a lot of new friends, just in the few months, I've been away. Especially my sisters."

"Sisters?" Joel asked with a puzzled look on his face. Shelby smiled as she realized he wasn't familiar with sororities.

"Yes, Dad, we are a house full of girls," Shelby explained. "It's like a club and we act as if we are a family while we're at college and we pledge to be close throughout our lives," she said laughing.

"I see," he said. Shelby could tell it wasn't anything he had any interest in knowing more.

"Dad, it's great and they take good care of me," Shelby explained.

He shook his head at her and smiled.

Sitting and talking to her parents for the next few hours warmed her heart. Frances buzzed around the kitchen fixing supper. Shelby had missed these times. But she was home now for a week and she was going to enjoy every minute of their presence.

She had told them just about everything she had done over the last few months, in just a few short hours, with the exception of dating Richard. She wasn't sure she was quite ready to tell them about him.

Joel stood up, walked over to the desk, and picked up a small pile of mail. He handed it to Shelby. "Here's your mail, dear," he said in a reserved tone of voice.

"Wow, I actually have mail," she said laughingly. As she sorted through each envelope, one caught her eye as she read the return name and address: Jack Emerson, Valley, Alabama.

She stopped as she felt her heart tumble to her stomach. She was sure her dad had noticed her reaction, when he asked, "Are you okay, Shelby?"

She stumbled on her words. "Ahhh... yes, Daddy," she said quietly as she stared at the envelope. She hurriedly finished going through the small stack emotionless, trying to hold her composure. She held tightly to the mail, as they began to tidy up the kitchen before bedtime.

Shelby hugged and kissed her parents goodnight as Joel turned and carried her duffle bag up to her room.

She opened the door, flipped on the light, and stepped in quietly. She glanced around the room. It looked the same as the day she'd left. Her dad handed her the duffle bag and she laid it on the floor next to the window seat.

"Thank you, Daddy," she said and reached up and kissed him on the cheek.

"I saw the letter from Jack. I hope all is okay," he said.

"Oh, yes I'm sure it is," Shelby managed to reply.

"Have you talked to him since you left?"

"No, I haven't. It's been months," she said sadly.

"Well, just know that God has his plans for you and try to be sensitive to Jack's feelings," he said as he walked out and closed the door gently behind him. Shelby felt it was an odd statement from her dad. Why did he seem so concerned about Jack?

Shelby removed the envelope from the stack, walked over to the window seat, sat, and propped her feet against the wall as she held the envelope in her hand. What did Jack have to say? Why did her dad act so funny about the envelope?

She tore the back of the envelope open, took out the letter, and began to read it.

To my darling Shelby... the love of my life...

It's late at night and I've just come back from the Kissing Bridge. I've taken my shower and I'm sitting here at my desk writing to you.

I've wanted to talk to you and hold you in my arms so many times over the last four months. To tell you how much I love you. But it appears there has never been an opportunity for us, for whatever reasons. I guess it's God's way and plan for our lives.

Shelby, I realize you've given up on me. I know you and I may never get back together. It's terribly hard for me to accept, knowing you may never come home to me. Something that was never a question or a concern for me just a few short months ago. I knew you were mine.

I need you to understand what's going on in my life now. I've had to come to some real grown-up decisions. Many times, you often talked about how I needed to grow up and be the man I was meant to be. I just want to share with you what I've been thinking.

There are no words that could possibly describe my love for you. I feel like we have had the greatest love story. A Romeo and Juliet kind of a love and I have to admit we never really had a bad time. However, now over the last few months, our love story has been shattered by the craziness of my life.

We had the misunderstanding on the Fourth of July. I was the fool for treating you so badly over my jealousy. Hank told me how you overheard the girls in the bathroom at the Ram's House that I had been with Denise the day after. It was a rough ride and even though I had gone through it all, I still felt safe and confident in our relationship. We had everything going for us, Shelby.

Since then, it has been like a roller coaster ride of emotions running completely out of control on a track to nowhere. The pain is so bad, but what's even worse for me is I miss you desperately. Every day, I waited to hear from you... a call, a letter, just something and I never heard from you. I know it's over. But my heart would explode with joy, even now, if I could look up and see your smile or just hear your voice one more time.

At night, I lay here thinking of you and often wondering how we would have lived our lives together had things been different. I go out every day hiding my loneliness and broken heart. Hoping one day.

But that one day—

I'm afraid that one day has been misplaced like a needle in a haystack.

Shelby, there are no words that can express my love for you while at the same time justifying my actions. Even though I've spent many hours suppressing the truth, the truth must come out.

The night I spent with Denise, I had more to drink than I should have. To describe it better, I was wasted and couldn't remember anything when I woke up the next morning. I had no idea that Denise had been there with me. At first, I thought Walter and Hank had played a terrible joke on me when I came to in the old shelter early the next morning. I believed I had lived through a nightmare and that I hadn't spent the night with Denise.

Shelby, the truth is I did spend the night with her. And I'm so ashamed to admit; I thought and believed I was with you. I really did. I had no idea it was Denise.

Shelby's heart broke from his words and she laid the letter down on her lap. There it was in writing. It was the truth; he had been with Denise as she thought. She had hoped and prayed it was just a game Denise had played to make her mad.

She was startled out of her thoughts as the phone rang out loudly. It sounded out a second time and Shelby focused her eyes on the phone, hesitant to answer it in the midst of the critical juncture. She was hoping to absorb what Jack was trying to tell her. The phone rang again. She set the letter down on the window seat, bent over, and picked up the phone.

"Helloooo," she said getting impatient with the sound.

"Shelby?" The male voice inquired with a tone of hesitation.

"Yeah," she said out of character.

"It's me, Richard," he said.

"Oh, hi, Richard," Shelby said trying to gain her composure and add some excitement in her voice. "I'm sorry; I was in the middle of something when the phone rang. It kind of startled me. I'm so glad you called," she said as her thoughts raced back to Jack's letter sitting next to her.

"Well, I'm glad. I was afraid something was wrong when you answered. I wasn't sure it was you, right at first. Is everything okay?" he asked.

"Oh, yes. It is now," she said with a smile on her face. She swooshed away the thoughts of Jack and relaxed in the joy that Richard had called her.

"Great, I wanted to check on you and make sure you got home okay. I was worried about you driving by yourself. And I wanted to tell you how disappointed I was when I couldn't come this weekend," he said apologetically.

"Richard, it's okay I understand," she said.

"Shelby, there is something I wanted to tell you before we left for the Thanksgiving break. I'm sorry, I didn't have the opportunity to see you before you left," he said in a soft tone.

Her thoughts raced like wild. *Oh, my gosh. Here it comes... he's going to dump me like Jack just did in his letter.* Her heart skipped several beats like a pebble skimming on the top of a pool of water. She breathed in and let out a big sigh as she awaited his response.

"I wanted to tell you how much you mean to me. I really, really care about you, Shelby. I always have, even from the first day I met you at Johnson's. I knew you were in love with Jack, so I never pursued you. But then, you told me you and Jack had broken it off," Richard stopped for a split second.

Shelby looked around her room as she listened to Richard. There were mementos everywhere of bits and pieces of her life with Jack—photographs of them, ones she left behind before going off to college, secretly hoping they would work things out when she came home for the holidays.

Then, he continued. "I have to tell you I was the happiest guy in the world when I heard those words and I want you to know I'm absolutely crazy about you," he said.

Shelby gasped as she listened and placed her hand over her mouth in awe. Somehow, she could feel his emotions and the sincerity in his words as they zipped through the phone line and into her ear. He had a very sensitive style about him, she thought.

"I can't stop thinking about you. And it sometimes gets in the way of my studying and I have to force myself to get back to my work when my mind wanders off to you. I know this may sound weird, but I miss you and want to be with you all the time. I know I'm probably babbling now, but I just had to tell you how I felt," Richard said with passion in his voice.

Her heart filled with warm feelings, as she concentrated on the way he spoke. Her smile brightened and stretched across her face. "Richard, that is so sweet, and you have no idea how much I really needed to hear this right now. I feel the same way about you. I was disappointed when you couldn't come. I was actually afraid you were going to say you didn't want to see me anymore. It scared me a little. But now, it's okay. I miss you, too," she said shyly into the phone.

"Really, Shelby? You feel the same way?" he asked.

"I do, and I mean it," Shelby said, confident in her decision to let him know.

"That means a lot to me. I was afraid you wouldn't feel the same way," he admitted.

"I do and I'm so glad you called," she said pleasantly.

"Great, will you be my girlfriend then?" he asked.

Shelby happily replied. "Yes, I will, Richard."

She could hear his voice as he declared, "You're my girlfriend and I'm so happy, you just don't know," he replied.

"Me too," she said as she grinned.

"I won't keep you. I just wanted to tell you how I felt and make sure you made it home okay. Now, go to bed and get some rest," he said sweetly.

"Aww... thank you and I'm tickled pink you called. I'm going to bed shortly," she said with a big smile on her face.

"Bye now," he said his voice trailing off.

"Bye, Richard." She placed the phone down on the receiver and leaned back against the wall of her window seat, crossing her arms, and stretching out her feet.

She couldn't believe it. She and Richard were now boyfriend and girlfriend. She had never had a boyfriend other than Jack. A vision of his face popped into her thoughts as she remembered his letter. She picked it up and continued to read.

But, there is a new development that has forced me into writing this letter. This news has my heart in shambles.

Know that my decision to let you go has torn me apart. Yet, I must let you go for the sake of someone else. And, because of them, I must do what is right. I love you, Shelby, with all my heart, and I will never stop loving you.

There is someone else I must think about before my own feelings. It's my child. I must put my baby first above me. Yes, Denise is pregnant...

Shelby gasped and covered her mouth with her fingers as she read the letter. "*Denise is pregnant.*"

"Oh, my Lord, Jack," she said as she agonized over the news, and she continued to read:

Shelby, it doesn't change how I feel about you. I had always dreamt of you and I having our own child someday. I know deep in my heart someday will never come. I guess it just wasn't in God's plan. I know in my heart you will never forgive me, and I'm okay with that. I just hope someday we can look back and know how much we meant to each other.

I love you, Shelby, with all my heart.

Love,
Jack

Shelby leaned her head against the wall of the window seat as she wiped away the deluge of tears now flowing from her eyes.

"How could this have happened to us?" she asked in a whisper as she lowered her head totally heartbroken. She wasn't quite sure what it was, but there had been a gut feeling something wasn't right and now she knew in her heart they were through and their lives would take new curves in the road.

Chapter Fifteen

While home for the Christmas holiday, Shelby got word that Jack and Denise had set the date for the wedding ceremony.

"Have you heard?" Mary asked cautiously.

"About Jack and Denise, you mean?" Shelby asked as she cleared her throat.

"Yeah," Mary said quietly.

Shelby and Mary were eating lunch at the Ram's House when her friend decided to share the news. Shelby picked up her fork and tossed the French fries around on her plate before she glanced up at Mary.

"Yes, I heard it's sometime in January right?" she asked looking in Mary's direction. She saw Mary's expression of sadness.

"Saturday, January twenty-fifth," Mary confirmed. "Are you sure you're okay?" she asked with concern in her voice.

"Mary, of course, I'm sure. I'm good. Really," Shelby said confidently. "I'm glad he decided to do the right thing and marry her. Jack is a good man and I know he'll take good care of them. I would be lying if I didn't admit that I wished he was marrying me. But, you know what? I'm really okay with it now. I'm having a blast with Richard. Honestly, I have a secret to tell you," she said sheepishly.

She could see the curiosity in Mary's face. "What?" Mary asked. "Tell me right now."

Shelby smiled and without even a second of hesitation responded. "I think I'm crazy in love with Richard."

"No way," Mary said, wide-eyed.

"Shhh... don't tell anyone," Shelby said shyly as she covered her mouth with her fingers. "We've shared a lot about ourselves with each other. He's told me all about his life growing up, and how hard it was to be the son of a Brigadier General and live under his authority. It's a military thing Richard had told her. They traveled the world until they finally settled down at Fort Benning. He and his dad don't get along very well, but he's crazy about his mother and he tells me all the time how much I remind him of her. He said it was one of the reasons he liked me from the first time he ever saw me. As a matter of fact, I'm going to meet his parents on New Year's Day."

"Oh, Shelby, I'm so glad for you both. You deserve to be happy, girl." Mary's excitement was written all over her face and Shelby watched her when she pushed her chair away and rushed around the table to give her a hug.

To see the emotions in Mary's face confirmed she had made the right decision to let Jack go and move on with her life. And it made Shelby feel good that Mary approved of Richard and she should, after all, since she was the one who hooked them up.

"Jack is getting married and I'm crazy in love with Richard. Who would have imagined that?" Shelby burst out with excitement. They kept chatting as they finished their lunch and hung out together.

Shelby knew in her heart that God had a plan for them. And, it apparently wasn't going to be for her and Jack to be together. She never questioned the Lord's will; rather she always tried to have faith that it would turn out exactly as it should.

Jack would always be her first love. The only love she had ever known, until now. Every emotion and memory were now ready to be stored away in a chamber of her heart.

She was ready to move on.

"You know, I love Richard in a different way than Jack," she said sheepishly.

"And just how is that?" Mary asked.

'I'm not really sure. It just is. He has stolen my heart. It's kind of like he courts me, instead of just going with me. He sends me flowers, writes me notes, he wines and dines me with romantic dinners, and he's so tenderhearted. He is such a charmer. I just never know what he is going to come up with next and I absolutely love feeling that way," Shelby said dreamily.

"Dang, Shelby, you *are* crazy about him," Mary said a little surprised. "I was afraid you wouldn't be able to let Jack go, but it sounds like you have."

"Honestly, I think I have," Shelby said with confidence.

"Then, I think you're doing the right thing," she replied.

Shelby smiled feeling convinced she had made the best decision. Mary hugged her again and said, "I'm so proud of you."

Shelby had many hopes and dreams for her future and they were just beginning.

~~~

Jack stood staring out the window of his bedroom.

"In a few hours, I'll be married to Denise," he said to no one.

He pulled his hair back away from his forehead as he ran his fingers through the shaggy dark brown curls.

His thoughts were of how he was going to say, "I do" when he really didn't want to. They had haunted him for some time now.

Denise had chosen January twenty-fifth, for some silly reason, something about it being her Grandparents' wedding day fifty years ago on her dad's side of the family. It saddened him to think about how his wedding day was supposed to be an extraordinary time, but he wasn't feeling so special right now. He was startled when he heard a knock at the door, pulling him out of his thoughts.

"Jack, it's me, son. May I come in?" his dad asked. Jack walked over to the door and opened it without a word. "Are you about ready to head over to the church?"

"I guess so," Jack replied with sadness in his voice. He was marrying a woman he didn't love. But, his baby was what was important. He had to keep reminding himself it was the only reason he was marrying her. Even though he knew in his heart how much Denise was madly in love with him. She had made him help her with the wedding plans, and doctor visits and all the other things young married couples with a baby on the way did together. She had made him attend those weird breathing classes, and it amazed him how breathing was such a big part of delivering a baby. She had him committed to all the domestic chores of a husband. He had to admit she was doing everything the right way.

"Son, I know this is hard for you, but you have to keep that innocent baby in mind today. I can promise you; as soon as he or she gets here, you are going to be ecstatic when you hold him or her in your arms. That I can attest to," Sheriff Emerson said with a smile on his face.

Jack felt the closeness of his dad as he reached up and they hugged tightly. Jack smiled and said, "Thank you, Dad; it really helps me keep things in perspective."
~~~

His dad grabbed him by the shoulder and gave him a gentle nudge. "I'm so proud of you."

Jack smiled as he picked up his suit jacket and threw it over his shoulder.

The church was just a ten-minute ride and they sat silently in the front seat of his dad's pickup truck while they drove down Highway 29.

As they passed the Kissing Bridge, Jack felt a sharp pain in his chest as if a knife had pierced his heart. And, it ached for Shelby. He focused intensely on the bridge until it was no longer in sight. He turned his face away from his dad to hide the water now clouding his eyes.

He felt a gentle touch as his dad reached over and laid his hand on his shoulder. "Son, try to love Denise and give her a chance, would you?" his dad asked. "At least for the baby's sake."

The words echoed in Jack's mind and he made no attempt to respond.

It was no time before Jack was standing in the foyer of the church. He picked up the wedding program sitting on the small table outside the sanctuary and read:

Evelyn Denise Davenport
&
Jackson Daniel Emerson
United in Marriage
January 25, 1975

Jack stood staring down at the white note he held in his hand and recalled his dad's last request. He laid the note card down on the table and silently walked to the front of the church to take his place.

With his dad as his best man, they stood beside each other as the wedding march began to play. The congregation stood and Denise appeared in the doorway. Her elegance took Jack aback.

There was something about her today, she looked different—besides being five months pregnant—but she also had a glow about her. He always thought she was pretty; it was just her ways he didn't like. But now, as she walked slowly down the aisle toward him, he could feel his heart reaching out to her. Something he just couldn't explain. He smiled, as his breath exhaled, and let out a small sigh. Finally, Jack had to admit she was a beautiful woman.

~~~
~~~

Spring break couldn't arrive fast enough for Shelby. It was just a few weeks away and Richard had promised to take her, Mary, and JoJo to Panama City Beach where they could stay in his parents' beach house. She thought about the warm welcome she had received from his folks back on New Year's Day. His mother was exactly how he had described her. His dad... well, the jury was still out on him.

A shout from behind the door startled Shelby as she heard a girl's voice. "Telephone, Shelby." She scrambled from her bed, rushed down the hall, and grabbed the phone.

"Hello," she said loudly.

"Shelby, hey, it's Richard. I wanted to make sure we're still set for spring break."

"Heck yeah and I can't wait," she declared with excitement in her voice.

"Awesome, I picked up the keys from Mom last weekend. So, we can head straight down from Tuscaloosa on Friday evening if you want. Or we can wait and leave on Saturday. Just let me know which day," he said.

"Saturday would be better for me," she remarked remembering her project was due that Friday.

"Okay, great. I probably won't get to see you until then, I have a bunch of work to do before I leave," he said.

"Well, okay then," she said disappointedly. She always looked forward to seeing him, but she knew she would be spending the whole week with him.

"I miss you, Shelby, and I can't wait to see you," he said. She felt her heartthrob at his words.

"I miss you, too. Bye, Richard," she said as she hung up the phone.

~~~

It was a cool April morning and the first day of their Spring Break. They piled all the luggage into their cars. Shelby rode with Richard and Mary rode with JoJo.

It was cloudy that morning when they arrived in Panama City. Richard pulled up to a gated entrance. He got out of the car and punched in a code and the iron gate began to slowly open in front of them.

"Wow!" Shelby exclaimed, as she watched Richard walk back to the car and they drove through the gate. They couldn't see the
~~~

house until they veered around the tall tropical bushes and trees lining the circular drive. There stood a tall, majestic two-story white mansion with tall, round columns at the front entrance. Shelby was speechless as she sat observing the display of beauty right before her eyes. She had never seen anything so gorgeous.

"Oh my goodness, Richard, I've never seen anything so beautiful," she admitted almost choking on her words. She reached for the door handle and opened it slowly to step out of the car. She never took her eyes from the estate.

She heard car doors slam shut behind her and the girls' loud squeals of joy.

"I'm glad you like it," he said excitedly. Within seconds, he walked over and put his arms around her waist. Shelby turned and put her arms around him and gently kissed him on the lips.

"It's beautiful, it looks like something out of a magazine," she said giddily. She couldn't help but wonder what it was like to own such a lovely piece of architecture. It was theirs just the four of them for the next week and it was more than she could have ever imagined.

It was every bit as beautiful on the inside as it was on the outside. The six-bedroom, six-bath home had everything you could ever need. The veranda in the back opened to an in-ground pool with a view of the ocean just beyond. She laughed after she had pinched herself several times to make sure she wasn't dreaming.

"Oh, my God," JoJo said in disbelief, as they explored the kitchen. "Shelby, did you know about this?" JoJo asked when Richard had left the room.

"No, I had no idea it was like this when he said his parents owned a house at the beach," Shelby said.

"Can you believe this place?" Mary asked in awe, as she inspected the big open den.

"I know, I'm just as blown away about it as y'all are," Shelby replied.

It wasn't long before Richard reappeared and gave them all a tour of the house and grounds. It was like the home appeared right out of the pages of a magazine. Nothing she had ever seen before could compare. Fabulous was merely a token description of its opulence.

"Richard, why didn't you tell me the house was so elegant?" Shelby asked when they were finally alone.

"Would it have mattered if I had told you? Would you have not come?" he asked as they sat together on one of the chaises at the edge of the pool.

"No, not really," she said shyly as she turned to look him in the eyes. Richard was more than she had ever dreamed of. He was handsome, witty, intelligent, and now, apparently, wealthy needed to be added to his list of qualities. She smiled at him as he reached around her waist and pulled her close to him.

"Good, I'm glad," he said holding her against his chest. Shelby leaned over and picked up her glass of wine, Richard took his beer in his, and they toasted their evening. "Here's to a wonderful time," he said as their glasses clinked together. He had definitely wooed her off her feet.

This was the first time she and Richard had gone away together. Even though she had her own room, she could tell Richard wanted her to stay with him.

The evening progressed as they talked about the things they wanted to do in life. Several glasses of wine and beer later and tightly tucked into each other's arms, Richard whispered, "Shelby, would you stay with me tonight?"

Shelby's heart melted from the softness of his voice as she paused and considered his request. She strained to see out and over the dunes toward the ocean watching the moon now slightly above the horizon of the water, as she thought about it. She knew it was just a matter of time before this moment would come. It was kind of scary for her given the fact she was still a virgin, but in her heart, she felt like she was ready.

She could tell he was a bit nervous to hear her response. He reached up and gently touched her chin and turned her head back to face his and their eyes met.

"I love you, Shelby, with all my heart. I promise you, I will be gentle and I won't hurt you," Richard said as he smiled. Shelby could no longer resist. She wanted him as much as he wanted her.

"Yes, Richard. I will," she said, as she leaned forward and closed her eyes as their lips met. She could feel his energy through their kiss. This was the first time he had spoken the words *"I love you"* and she exploded inside with delight and knew exactly what was in her heart.

"I love you, too, Richard," she whispered in his ear.

They sat for a bit longer, and then Richard stood up and looked down into her eyes. He motioned for her hand, she gently laid hers into his, and he helped her stand up. He wrapped his arm around her as they slowly walked into the house and up the grand staircase that laced the two-story foyer and down the hall to his bedroom.

~~~

The next evening, the four friends sat around the pool soaking up the last remnants of the sun as it began to set on the horizon. The phone rang in the house and Richard hesitated to answer, but felt he might better, in case something was up. Shelby followed him into the kitchen.

"Hello," Richard said. "Yes, sir," he spoke and nodded. Shelby listened in. "Really?" he asked surprised. Shelby was curious now as to whom he could be talking to. "I think I can make that if you believe it will work out," Richard said with excitement in his voice. Shelby shrugged her shoulders dying to find out who it was. "Yes, sir. I'll be there."

Shelby saw the look on Richard's face as he hung up the phone.

"What, what!" Shelby asked surprised.

"I apparently have impressed the law school I wanted to attend and they have scheduled an interview with me to offer me an accelerated program to shave a year and a half of my college credits. Professor Stokes thinks I have a really good chance and there have only been three others that have ever been offered this program."

"Richard, that's amazing!" Shelby shouted out.

He held up his hand to stop her. "The thing is, I have to go back to school on Tuesday to prepare for the interview on Friday. They are going to help me through a mock interview process," Richard explained. She could tell this was something he really felt good about.

"That's awesome, Richard," Shelby said. "I'm so proud of you."

"Yes, it is, but that means I can't stay here for spring break with you," he said sadly.

"It's okay. I understand," she replied feeling disappointed.

"Listen, I'll go back on Tuesday and you and the girls stay here and have fun," he told her.

"Really? You would let us do that? Will it be okay with your parents?" Shelby asked.

"I know it will be fine with them. They really like you," he admitted to her.

~~~

Richard had only been gone for a few hours on Tuesday when the gate buzzer rang out loud. Shelby reached over to the intercom and pressed the button, just as Richard had instructed her. "Yes," she said.

"Ma'am, I have some flowers for a Miss Shelby Harrelson," the voice came through the speaker.

"Oh, okay," she said as she pressed the button for the gate to open.

The doorbell rang a few minutes later as Shelby reached the foyer. She opened the door and the young man handed her a big bouquet of spring flowers full of roses, lilies, and carnations. She grinned as she took them in her hands, walked into the kitchen, and set them on the counter. By this time, JoJo and Mary had heard all the commotion and followed her into the room.

She grabbed the card and read it:

To my darling Shelby,

I'm sorry I had to leave you this week. I hope you enjoy the flowers and your time at the beach. I left an envelope in the spoon drawer in the kitchen. It's a little something for you and the girls to enjoy.

I'll miss you, but know I will be thinking about you all the time I'm away.

I love you,
Richard

Shelby covered her mouth as she read his last words *"I love you"* again.

The girls delighted in her gift. "Damn, Shelby, this guy's got the hots for you, girl!" JoJo exclaimed.

"What did he leave in the envelope?" Mary asked eagerly.

Shelby laughed when she realized she wasn't sure which of the ninety-five drawers was the spoon drawer. All three girls began pulling them open two at a time, like kids hunting Easter eggs.

"Here it is," JoJo said with a grin on her face from across the room. Shelby scrambled around the long island that stretched across the center of the huge kitchen. She tore open the envelope and looked inside. There were three crisp one hundred dollar bills with a note.

I know this isn't much, but take it and you and the girls enjoy spring break.

Love, Richard

Shelby was overwhelmed with emotions. The house... the flowers... the first time he said, "*I love you*"... the first time they'd ever made love... and now the money. He was amazing, and she couldn't for the life of her understand what she had done to have someone like Richard fall in love with her. She smiled and handed the envelope to Mary.

She stood and watched the girls' expression as they opened it and read the note. She knew in her heart that none of them would have ever had this kind of opportunity if it hadn't been for Richard. She was so blessed.

The next morning while Shelby enjoyed soaking up the sun's rays, she reached over and sipped her orange juice. She had never known anyone wealthy. This was a new way of life for her. Besides, she was just a girl from Valley, Alabama, and there were definitely no wealthy people living there.

Richard was from a different world than her. To hear him tell her about it fascinated her. She couldn't have ever imagined living the life he'd had growing up. He had traveled the world, his parents owned a huge home in Columbus, people respected his dad, the Brigadier General, and now sitting here in the beach house they owned was like living in a fantasy world. Her only reservation, "*Would she be able to fit into his life of high society*?" She only hoped so.

~~~

The week had come to an end and the girls were all packed up and ready for their journey back to Tuscaloosa. Shelby was kneeling down cleaning out the trash in JoJo's car when she noticed a small newspaper lying upside down on the floor. She reached down and picked it up. *The Valley News*. Shelby sat back on her feet as she flipped through the pages when she noticed a big circle drawn around an announcement and began to read:

Trevor Jackson Emerson born April 5, 1975, to the proud parents, Jack and Denise Emerson of Langdale.
~~~

Shelby breathed out in a long sigh. "Congratulations, Jack," she whispered. She closed the newspaper and tossed it into the trash bag as she could feel the tears welling up in her eyes. "No, don't do this, Shelby," she said firmly. She stood up, carried the trash bag into the house, and dumped it in the kitchen bin. She looked around the estate and declared, "This is my life now!"

On the long drive back to Tuscaloosa, Shelby sat quietly by herself in the backseat of JoJo's car. Mary and JoJo chatted and sang songs along with the radio. All she could think about was the birth announcement of Trevor.

"Life sure hasn't turned out the way I'd planned it," she whispered to her heavenly friend Gina, under her breath. "It seems life keeps throwing curve balls at me, and I just keep dodging them. I sure didn't expect to be dating a wealthy guy," she admitted.

Chapter Sixteen

It was only a few weeks until summer vacation. Shelby had decided not to take any classes, but to go home to Valley for the summer. Richard would be staying in Athens working on his degree. His interview went well and he had been accepted into the accelerated program offered to him by the law school, which basically meant he would be an attorney two years sooner.

Shelby felt she needed a break from all the craziness of her freshman year. She missed Valley and her parents and she was homesick, she had to admit.

The days quickly passed and she found herself sad as she finished packing up her things from her dorm. JoJo had left early in the day to head home for the summer break. Shelby now sat alone on her bed and looked around at the small room. She smiled and with a big shout out, "What a hell of a year!" She stood up and grabbed her duffle bag, threw it over her shoulder, and walked out the room closing the door behind her.

~~~

It was a warm June evening and Jack sat quietly on the porch of his parents' home as he held Trevor in his arms in the porch swing. He was two months old and growing like a weed. Jack recalled his dad's words clearly:

"Nothing in the world matters more than when you hold that baby in your arms."

He beamed down at Trevor while he lay asleep. Underneath his long lashes, he had deep, brown eyes and a head full of brown shaggy hair. Jack smiled when he remembered his mother say, "He looks just like you did when you were born."
~~~

No words could express the love and emotions he had for this little boy. The last few months had been nothing but pure pleasure. Jack could hardly wait to get home every afternoon from work so he could hold and play with him.

He and Denise were living with his parents temporarily until they could save enough money for a place of their own. The arrangement had worked very well for them. Denise and his mother got along great and he was thankful for that. And, it was good to have the support of his parents. Sheriff Emerson was absolutely beside himself and was ecstatic to be a grandpa, and of course, Martha was the perfect grandma.

Jack had begun to give Denise a chance and he had seen such a huge difference in her since they had gotten married and had Trevor. He couldn't deny it and he honestly felt they had grown a lot closer now. He felt like he loved her in a special way, although he knew in his heart that it would take time.

"Trevor Jackson Emerson, you are my world, son, and I will always love and take care of you," Jack whispered down at him.

He glanced up and saw Denise standing in the doorway. She stepped out, walked over, and sat next to him on the swing. She reached up and kissed Jack on the forehead. He could tell it made her heart melt to hear him say those words. He took her hand, kissed the back of it, and held it close to his face.

"Thank you, Denise, for giving me such a wonderful gift," he said as he peered over at her. "I'm so sorry for doubting you and for treating you the way I did early on. I'm really grateful to you for all you have done for us," he said. "I'm so ashamed of the way I've acted. Please forgive me? I do love you, Denise," he said as their eyes met. "I promise to always take care of you and Trevor. I mean that."

"Oh, Jack," she said. "You have no idea how much that means to me."

"I know it's not been easy, and we are going to have a few struggles financially, but know I will do whatever it takes to make it work for us," he said confidently.

She leaned in toward him and Trevor and wrapped her arms around his shoulders and he held her tightly in his arm.

The emotions from her embrace were like finding something you had lost, only to have it finally make its way back to you. They were now a real family; he could feel it in his heart and he was more than grateful.

~~~
~~~

Shelby's only reservation over returning home for summer break was the fear of running into Jack and Denise. She was nervous about how she would react. She didn't want to unleash a can of old emotions. The thoughts kept popping in her head on the four-hour drive home to Valley.

However, the desire to be home with her parents was much greater than her fear of seeing the newlyweds. After all, she had Richard now and they were madly in love. She was confident their relationship was strong and would help her get past any encounter with Jack.

Roberta Flack's 1974 hit "*Killing Me Softly with His Song*" played from the car stereo as she drove the back roads home.

Shelby was going to spend the summer with her parents; she wasn't going to work like she had last year. Then, in the fall, she would head back to school and be involved with all the college stuff. There would be sorority Rush from the other side—inside the sorority—football games to attend, new classes to enjoy, and then the holidays. It would be spring break again and another great time planned at the Porter's beach house. Before she knew it, she'd be finished with her sophomore year at Alabama.

"Whoa, wait this is all going too fast," she said as she laughed out loud and focused on her driving. There were so many busy things happening in the near future and she was glad she would have this time to relax.

~~~

Sure enough, everything fell right into place just as she and Richard had planned. It was no time at all before she had finished her sophomore year in the spring of 1976. Her life now was a big schedule of events that Richard had planned for them. She knew exactly what, when, where, and why about the future. Everything was neatly slated on a calendar. She loved how Richard was so meticulously organized and it kept her on track.

Once again, though, Shelby had decided to take off the summer and spend it in Valley. She had loved being home last summer with her mom and dad. Her favorite thing to do was help her mom in her flower garden. And, she was looking forward to another great lazy summer.

Richard had always been open for her to spend her summer any way she wanted, even though he tried to talk her into taking summer classes to help her get through college sooner.
~~~

"I know, but I'm not in any hurry to finish. Besides, I have obligations to the Kappa Delta Omegas and you know how important that is to me. Anyway, I always do what you want during the year. I think I should get to spend my summers the way I want to," Shelby reminded him when they had talked the evening before she left Tuscaloosa.

"I guess you're right then," Richard admitted.

~~~

It was the Bicentennial and the big Fourth of July Celebration in Valley. However, this year, the festivities had grown and they had to move the event from the circle in Shawmut to a new venue in front of the Langdale Textile Mill. This way, there would be ample room for everyone attending.

"Richard, you are going to be able to come for the celebration this week, right?" Shelby asked, sitting in the window seat of her room.

"Yes! Mom and the General are coming up from Columbus that day, too," he said with excitement in his voice.

"You're kidding me," she said suspiciously. "What made the General want to come?"

"Well, you know him. No one ever knows why the General does the things he does," Richard said with a laugh.

"We're going to have a blast no matter what," Shelby said.

The next couple of days were quite busy for Shelby; she had volunteered to help set up the kid's booths. She had to admit how much she loved children and thought Richard might be right and maybe next year she would take some summer classes so she could finish up early and go into teaching sooner. Children had always had a special place in her heart.

She was working on the kid's "Go Fish" booth when thoughts of Jack popped into her mind. She wondered how he and Denise were doing. Trevor would be about sixteen- months old now. He would probably love fishing. Her heart melted as she thought about him. *I bet he's just like Jack*, she thought as she smiled. She wondered if Jack and Denise would bring him to the celebration. Surely, they would. After all, it was all about family fun.

~~~

Jack had been working late in the evenings at Sweet's Bar-B-Que Restaurant after finishing his shift at the mill. They were still living with his parents. Jack had to admit, everything was good at first with their arrangements. They all got along. Everyone helped take care of Trevor and there was never a time he didn't have someone drooling over him. Yet, Jack could see all the pressure from being a new mom, not having a place of her own, and their financial situation had started to take a toll on Denise. She had been working long hours at the bowling alley in the evenings. His mom and dad kept Trevor at night while they both worked and then Denise would have him during the day.

But a few months ago, Denise injured her back at work and that only added to their struggles. He could tell she wasn't happy by the way she was quick to snap at him these days. They had been saving every dime and he knew it was time to find a place of their own. He had decided they would go looking right after the Fourth. He knew he would be too busy until after the holiday. Mr. Sweet had him scheduled to work during the celebration.

"Jack, you need to be here about four a.m. to get the meat on the grill. You got any problems with that?" Mr. Sweet asked in a gruff old voice as he cut his eyes at Jack.

"No sir, no problem, I'll be here bright-eyed and bushy-tailed," he said trying to smile through it.

"That's my guy," Mr. Sweet said as he turned and walked away.

Jack was exhausted, but he wasn't about to let Mr. Sweet know. He was just thankful to have the extra income. He desperately needed it now more than ever. He made a promise to take care of Denise and Trevor and he wasn't about to let them down. Not now.

~~~

Crowds of people filled the streets in front of Langdale Mill the morning of the Fourth of July. The Bicentennial Celebration was well underway. The streets were closed off around the mill. The music blared over the loudspeakers as the band played on center stage. Kids were everywhere running and playing. The scent of the smoke of the barbecue grill behind Sweet's restaurant permeated the air. The laughter from the crowd enjoying the afternoon activities filled the streets surrounding the mill.

Jack had already been at work for eight hours with only a few hours of sleep. Before that, he had gotten up with Trevor at
~~~

one a.m. He put him back to bed and lay back down about an hour later, but it wasn't restful.

Working long hours with little sleep was wearing him down quickly. He was overwhelmed and never thought it would be so hard to take care of a family. Come to think about it, he had no idea what the hell he was doing either.

Jack wiped the sweat from his forehead as he unloaded the Boston butts from the grill and took them to the back door of the restaurant. It was his turn to take a break and he made himself a glass of iced tea, walked out back, and sat in the lawn chair behind the grill.

As he sipped his tea, his thoughts somehow went to Shelby. He wondered what she was up to and where she was. He couldn't believe that just two years ago they were together at the celebration. That horrible, horrible night...

"God, how could I have been so stupid," he said to no one as he squinted from the sweat rolling down his face and into his eyes. "Shelby and I had it all going for us and I screwed it up," he remembered too clearly. "Damn, now I've gotten myself into a heap of shit and I don't know what to do," he whispered.

Shelby would know what to do. Of course, if he had only listened to her, he wouldn't be in the situation he was in now. But, the reality of it all was he had made his bed and he now had to lie in it. He shook his head in disbelief.

Jack had not finished his break yet when Denise showed up with Trevor in tow.

"Denise, you okay?" He could tell she didn't seem herself.

"Here, hold him for a minute. I've had him all morning and I need a break. My back is killing me," she said in an annoyed tone of voice. Jack scooped Trevor up in his arms and checked to make sure he was okay. Jack saw his son smile back at him and it warmed his heart. He watched as Denise flopped over into his chair with the coordination of a wet noodle.

"Denise!" Jack cried out, hoping no one heard him. "Have you been taking pain pills again?" he asked sternly.

"Oh, Jack, I had to, I told you my back is hurting," she said. Denise looked like shit as he reached for her chin to turn her face to his. Her hair was a mess; it was obvious she hadn't washed it in a week. Her make-up was smudged all around her eyes and they were bloodshot, too. She could barely stand up straight.

It was an all too familiar sight these days and he just didn't know what to do.

"You're a mess, Denise. Go home," Jack scolded as he spun around and walked through the door leading to the restaurant kitchen with Trevor in his arms. Jack heard a commotion behind him and turned to find Denise had fallen out of the chair and was now sprawled out on the ground. He was disgusted with her and just wanted to get away. He shook his head and kept going.

~~~

"Hey, Richard, let's go over to Sweet's for lunch," Shelby said as they walked past all the booths. Both sets of parents followed closely behind. It was refreshing seeing them all together and getting along. Shelby wasn't sure if her dad was taking a liking to the General, or not. At least, he was tolerating him well.

"That's great. Let's do it," Richard said.

"Mom and Dad, Mr. and Mrs. Porter, let's go across the street for lunch, does that work for y'all?" she asked as she whipped around and started walking backward to face them. "They've got the best barbecue in town."

"Sounds good to me," Joel shouted back in her direction.

"Yes, dear, the General and I would love to try it out," Mrs. Porter replied.

"Good," Shelby said with a smile almost tripping over her feet when she turned back around. She took Richard by the arm and wrapped her hands around his as they crossed the street.

They had to wait in line for about ten minutes when Richard said, "I need to run to the car. I'll be right back."

"Why do you need to go to the car?" Shelby asked.

"I forget to get something I wanted to show you. I'll be real quick." And then, he raced away toward his car.

The hostess seated them in the back corner of the room. They chatted about different things and in no time at all the food was served. Richard had returned and settled in next to Shelby. She was curious about what he had forgotten.

"The food is wonderful, Shelby. You did good in recommending this place," the General said in a deep voice as he saluted her with a half-eaten pork rib.

Shelby turned and smiled when she saw Richard staring at her. The waitress stopped to inquire about dessert and everyone declined.

"For heaven's sake, not me," Mrs. Porter said as she held her stomach.
~~~

"Me either," Frances dittoed. Shelby noticed Joel just raised his hand and declined.

"I'm good, too," the General replied. "This is on me," the General said as he grabbed the tab and everyone thanked him for his generosity.

They all sat silently for a few minutes when the General turned to everyone and announced, "I think Richard may have a sweet dessert for us, though."

Shelby was surprised as she saw everyone's eyes move directly to Richard. He shoved the chair back and stood up. He seemed a bit nervous and it puzzled her.

"Are you okay?" she asked looking up at him. She followed his eyes as he knelt to the floor in front of her. Shelby was surprised to find that everyone in the restaurant had turned to watch them and she felt her face flush.

"Oh, my goodness," Shelby mumbled. Richard removed a small black box from his pocket and she knew what was coming next...

"Shelby, will you marry me?" he asked as he slowly opened the box to reveal the most beautiful diamond she had ever seen. It was huge. It was gorgeous. Her breath caught in her throat and surely her heart was going to stop beating. She felt like he was going to ask her at some point, but she hadn't expected it now. Today. Here in front of all these people. But that would explain why the General and Mrs. Porter wanted to come to the celebration.

Without hesitation, she said, "Oh my, Richard, yes!" Her voice echoed throughout the room and the place erupted into cheers. She grabbed him around the neck and they kissed. When he pulled back, he took the ring from the box. Shelby tried to hold her hand steady as Richard gently slipped the ring on her shaking finger.

"Shelby, I love you," Richard whispered to her.

She scurried to her feet and hugged him around the neck, and said, "I love you, too, Richard."

The crowd was shouting at the beautiful proposal they had just witnessed. Everyone congratulated them and a lot of people gave her hugs. One man even offered to pick up their tab. Frances and Mrs. Porter each reached for their own hugs and kisses. The General and Joel both shook Richard's hand in approval.

It was just a short few minutes later when they gathered their things and started out the door. Shelby noticed Richard stopped for a split second and turned to look back into the restaurant.

"What is it?" she asked him.

He spun back to her and wrapped his protective arm around her, hustling her out. "Nothing you need to worry about."

~~~

Through all the commotion that surrounded the proposal, Jack stood speechless and heartbroken. Just inside the kitchen door, he cringed at what he had just heard. He had witnessed the only woman he would ever love in his life take the hand of another man. And there wasn't a damn thing he could do about it.

He put his head down on Trevor's small head, hiding so no one could see the pain in his face. He returned to the kitchen and rushed out the back door of the restaurant.
~~~

Chapter Seventeen

Jack spent the next several weeks searching for a place for Denise and him. He had worked long, hard hours and saved enough for them to get their own home. Even though most of the time Denise was found to be in her own world and didn't care much for helping.

He hoped once they moved into their space, she would be relieved of some of the pressure. She could relax and maybe she could fight off the foothold the pain pills had on her life. At least, that was his reasoning.

He thought about all the things that he could do to help her. He knew how much she liked him rubbing her back down with lotion. He would do most of the housework and watch after Trevor and let her rest as much as she needed to in order to get better. After all, she insisted it was what she needed more than anything was for them to be alone, just the three of them.

He had quit work at Sweet's after the Fourth of July so he could be home in the evenings to help with Trevor. The little guy was going to pre-school at the church until noon every day and Denise would only have him for a few hours on her own until Jack got off work at the mill.

Jack found a perfect place for them outside of town not far from his parents. It was a small, three bedroom, one bath house with a fenced-in backyard. It needed some work, but he was pretty handy and knew if he used some elbow grease, he could fix it up nicely for them. He couldn't wait to get off work and share the news with Denise.

The rest of the afternoon sped by at the mill and Jack was excited and couldn't wait to get home to talk to Denise about the house. She hadn't been much for helping him with the search. Most of the time, she would say. "Whatever you find will be good with me." Her demeanor was always indifferent these days.

As Jack unfortunately predicted, when he arrived home, he found his mom in the kitchen making dinner and watching over Trevor and no sign of Denise. Trevor meant the world to Martha. Jack could see it in her eyes.

"Hey, Mom," he said as he walked into the kitchen and hugged her while she stirred the pot of potatoes on the stove. "How's my man?" he asked waving his hand at two and half-year-old Trevor, proudly sitting on the counter helping his Nanny. Jack raised his hand as Trevor gestured a high-five.

"Dadddddddy..." Trevor squealed out in delight back at him, his beautiful smile melting Jack's heart. There was nothing in the world that captivated him more than Trevor.

"Where's Denise?" he asked, looking over at his mother.

"She's asleep," Martha snapped quickly and rolled her eyes at him. He could sense her annoyance. He watched her move around the kitchen and knew she was disappointed in the entire situation by the way she was slamming things around. It wasn't like his mother to be this way.

"I'm sorry you have to do this, Mom," Jack said apologetically. "I promise this is all going to better soon. I got Denise, Trevor, and me a house out on the corner of Highway 29 and Ben Brown Road. It's nothing great, but I can fix it up so it will be perfect for us," he told her.

"Jack, what are you going to do about Denise?" She turned and untied her apron, threw it down on the counter, and squinted her eyes at him. "Son, you've got to get her some help."

Jack was startled by her words, yet he knew she was right. If he could just get them moved into their own place, he felt that would certainly make matters easier. Or so he hoped. Was he being foolish?

Hurt by his mother's words, he stood ashamed. He reached over and wrapped Trevor in his arms. Holding him tightly, he turned to his mother and said, "I don't know what to do, Mom."

Martha let out a sigh and then went to him. "You know your dad and I will do anything for you, but now, something has to be done about Denise and her behavior before it reflects poorly on all of us. Your dad's the sheriff and people are beginning to talk about Denise. This could hurt his job."

He stepped around the island in the kitchen with his precious Trevor in one arm, and leaned over and hugged her with his other arm. "I'm going to take care of everything," he vowed. His parents had been supportive of him and now he knew it was time for him to deal with the problems Denise was causing. "Right now," he added.

"What are you going to do?" she asked with a frown.

"Don't you worry. I'll take care of it," he said confidently. He apologized for all they had to go through with Denise and he assured his mother that things were going to work out.

Martha nodded in understanding.

~~~

The next morning came quickly. Denise had awakened earlier and was lying in bed next to Jack watching TV. He rolled over and put his arm around her. He noticed she made no attempt to return his loving gesture.

"Hey, I found us a place just outside of Langdale. It's got a big backyard where we can plant a garden and have a swing for Trevor to play on," Jack told her, hoping she would be receptive.

"You did?" she asked and turned to face him without a stitch of emotion over the news. "Good, we need to move out soon. I'm not sure I can stay here much longer. This place is a hellhole and your mother is a bitch." She got up out of the bed, walked over to the dresser, and lit up a cigarette. Then, she sat down in the armchair across the room.

Her words sliced through his heart like a pair of scissors cutting through a pile of papers. He closed his eyes to hold back his anger and disappointment. How could she be so insensitive?

He could feel her despair and desperation to get out of the house and he tried to defuse the situation. "I told you I'd take care of everything and I did. I'll get us moved in as fast as I can. All you have to do is relax." He lay back on the bed, placed his arms over his head, and crossed them under his neck as he fluffed the pillow.

It broke his heart to see Denise this way. She had always been a young and confident woman. He could remember how she would irritate the hell out of Shelby with her witty remarks. He smiled at the thought. What had happened to Denise? She was different now and he wanted the old feisty Denise back.

He was sure the move would do it.

~~~

Shelby had been busy and overwhelmed with endless days of classes, nights spent with sorority sisters, and visiting Richard in Athens on the weekends. She felt like she'd had enough emotional and physical stress piled on her to fill a dump truck.

The summer spent in Valley had been exactly what Shelby needed, though. Even with all the excitement of Richard's proposal and the pre-planning stages of the wedding, she was able to take it easy and enjoy her time at home. While school was a bit hectic she had to admit she loved her life even if it were crazy.

Shelby tugged at her sweatshirt and pulled the hood up and over her head to mask the cold air from her ears. She and JoJo were on their way to meet their other sorority sisters to finalize the details of the bake sale coming up on Saturday morning before the football game.

"Is Richard coming to the game Saturday?" JoJo asked.

"No, he's so wrapped up in his studies. I think he's going to turn into a bookworm one day," Shelby said laughing. "Mary's coming, though, and she'll be able to hang out with us. Did I ever tell you she's in ΚΔΩ too at UGA?"

"No, dang, I didn't know that. That's great," JoJo, replied. "You know, Shelby, we should get the girls together and introduce them to Mary. Maybe we could all stay at the house on the sleeping porch. That way everyone could meet her. After all, you've known her since the sixth grade even if she is a sister from a different chapter. What do you think?"

"That would be awesome," Shelby, said eagerly. "You know... you, Mary, and my sorority sisters are my closest friends. Y'all mean the world to me. If anything were to happen to my parents I wouldn't have anyone but all of you. I just want us to always be friends no matter what. You know what I mean? I don't want us to finish college, then go our separate ways, and never keep in touch. I guess I'm a softy when it comes to family and friends. I just don't have a big family. I have an aunt, uncle, and cousin in Valley and my dad has a few cousins in Mobile, but that's pretty much it," Shelby admitted.

"Wow, that's your whole family?" JoJo questioned her. "Let's talk to Amy, Jenna, and Rachel and see what they think."

"Great, then I could call Mary and let her know as soon as we see what they say," Shelby was filled with excitement as they approached the sorority house.

As usual JoJo, Shelby, Amy, Jenna, and Rachel sat cheerfully around the table as Jenna, the philanthropy chairman, finalized the plans for the bake sale. Afterward, they sat around chit chatting.

"Hey, I wanted to tell y'all Shelby's friend Mary since the sixth grade, I might add, is also a ΚΔΩ at UGA. She comes over a lot to visit with Shelby and I thought since we're shorthanded on help this weekend because of homecoming, maybe she could help us out?" JoJo suggested.

Shelby noticed all eyes were on her.

"She is my best friend, of course besides y'all. I think y'all will love her as much as I do. I think she'd be thrilled to help us out," Shelby said, as she waited for their responses.

Jenna spoke first. "I think it's a great idea."

Shelby watched as everyone agreed. "Then it's settled. If Mary wants to help, we'd be happy to have her. Why don't we all do the sleeping porch Saturday night and then we can get to know her?" Jenna asked.

"I'm in. Is everyone else?" Amy asked.

It seemed to Shelby that all of her friends were happy to have Mary's help. She was thrilled to have her sisters welcome her best friend. Now, all of her closest friends would truly be sisters. One happy family today and forever.

Shelby and JoJo rushed back to the dorm.

"I can't wait to call Mary," Shelby said excitedly.

"I know how much it means to you, Shelby, and I'm glad for you," JoJo said.

It was a little after nine p.m. when they returned to Tutwiler and Shelby ran to the lounge to call Mary.

After Shelby relayed the news, Mary wanted to know more about the coming weekend.

"So tell me a bit about them. I don't want to feel out of place when I meet them."

"Sure, so it's Amy Winslow. She is the president of ΚΔΩ. She's from Birmingham; well all of my friends are from Birmingham. They kind of grew up together. Their dads all knew each other and they went to the same church.

"Anyway, Amy Winslow is the granddaughter of Winslow Steel of Alabama. Her grandfather started it way back in the early nineteen hundreds. Her dad and granddad both graduated from Alabama," Shelby explained.

"Wow, so she's pretty rich then huh?" Mary interrupted.

"Yeah, but she's really nice, and you're going to like her," Shelby said confidently. "Then, there's Jenna Rowe. Her dad is a doctor and they live in Mountain Brook. I'm not sure exactly, but I think he's a heart doctor. He's some kind of bigwig at University Hospital in Birmingham. And then, Rachel Abernathy, her dad, and grandfather are big-time criminal lawyers. Someone said her granddad used to work for the mafia, but I don't know. None of their moms work and they are always down here in Tuscaloosa doing stuff with the girls. I met Rachel's mom a couple of times and she's real nice, too."

"Sounds scary to me," Mary confessed.

"Oh, no, Mary. Don't be, I promise you're going to love them," Shelby added.

"You know JoJo already, so, at least, you'll know someone else besides me. Anyway, the bake sale starts at eight a.m. why don't you come down Friday and spend the night with me?" Shelby asked.

"Okay, I can do that," Mary said. "I can't wait to meet your friends and hang out all weekend. It'll be groovy!"

Shelby couldn't have said it better.

~~~

The bake sale was a huge success. They raised more than twelve hundred dollars and Amy made sure Mary knew how much they appreciated her help. Shelby could see how happy it made Mary feel, even though she knew how scared she was earlier that morning when she first met everyone.

The afternoon was filled with football and the chaos from the win. They were tired and worn out from the day's activities when they finally arrived back at the house to a plethora of post-game food and treats from their house cook. After grabbing plates of food, they sat in the casual living room laughing and talking. It was like a slumber party. They needed pampering after such a busy and exhausting day.

"Hey, I have a fabulous idea. Let's do manicures and pedicures for each other," Shelby suggested.

Amy thought it was a great idea. "We'll go get our stuff," she said.

In a matter of minutes, Amy, Jenna, and Rachel all had their respective gadgets, files, polishes, remover, and cotton balls, ready to set into action.

"We don't have a beauty salon in our house at Georgia," Mary said sarcastically and they all laughed and shouted out,

"Girl, you have no idea," Jenna said as she held up several bottles of bright polish.

Before she knew it, Mary was sitting in the center of the room on a rug having her nails attended to by her sorority sisters. Shelby took care of Mary's hands, JoJo was on foot detail. Amy
~~~

and Rachel both brushed Mary's long, waist-length hair. Jenna, the beauty expert, as everyone in the house called her, did Mary's makeup for her.

Shelby motioned with her hand, "See how we welcome new sisters?"

"I ain't never leaving," Mary said, satiated.

~~~

The weekend turned out better than Shelby had anticipated. They had stayed up laughing and talking into the wee hours of Sunday morning much to the chagrin of other sisters who were actually trying to get their beauty sleep. Mary fit right into her family and it made Shelby happy. There was no greater joy than to have a group of friends as wonderful as hers and she felt blessed.

~~~

After months of a rigorous daily schedule, Shelby took a much-needed break and drove home for the weekend. Richard, of course, was disappointed because she had chosen to go to Valley instead of spending the last weekend before Thanksgiving with him in Athens.

"Richard, I really need a break. I want to visit with my parents for a couple of days," Shelby explained on the phone the evening before she left. "I'm beat and I think I just need to be lazy for a few of days," she told him.

"Well, okay then, if you insist," Richard said with a bit of disappointment in his voice.

Shelby sensed his discouragement. "Look, Richard, I've been to Athens for the last several weekends, dealing with classes all week, and then sorority sisters and house activities at night have just been overwhelming for me. I need this time to rest before finals start. So, I'm leaving in the morning and I'll be back on Sunday night. We'll get to spend time together over the holidays."

Shelby was not about to let Richard make her feel guilty for going home just one weekend. She was crazy about him and loved every minute she spent with him. He made her feel like a princess and gave her anything she wanted.

"I know, you're right. It's just that... I miss you," he said with a slight sadness in his tone. She could feel his disappointment and knew he was trying hard not to be upset. The fact that he loved her so made her heart beat extra fast.

"I miss you, too," she said, smiling into the phone as if he could see it.

"Maybe you need to lighten up on all that sorority stuff, Shelby, if it's as busy as you say it is," he told her.

"You know my sisters mean a lot to me. I'm not about to give them up. I'll be fine if I get some rest this weekend," she said sniffling. "Damn, I feel bad and the cold bug has made his way to visit me. I've gone through a half a box of Kleenex from sneezing all day and I've not had much sleep which I think is the culprit that has my immune system all whacked out," she said, feeling very annoyed.

"Shelby, you should hear yourself. You sound like some country bumpkin." He paused and then added, "So, I guess it's all decided?"

"Yeah, and don't worry, it's just for a couple of days and then we'll get to see each other again soon, I promise," she said in a comforting voice and wiped her nose again.

"Okay then. I love you," Richard said softly as they said their goodbyes.

~~~

"So how's it going dear?" Frances asked her. They were eating leftover spaghetti from the night before which happened to be Shelby's favorite meal.

"It's great, Mom, just real busy."

"How's Richard?" Frances asked.

"He's wonderful and I'm crazy about him," Shelby said as she wiped her mouth with a napkin.

Her mother smiled. "You know Shelby I'm glad you found Richard. I think he is perfect for you. He comes from a wonderful family and he will always take care of you. I believe God's blessed you with a great man, dear."

"You, think so, Mom?" Shelby asked as she glanced up from her plate.

"Yes, I do."

"Honestly, I wasn't sure I would ever fall in love again after I lost Jack," Shelby admitted.

"I know, I could tell he broke your heart," Frances said.

"He did. More than anyone could ever imagine," she said. She disappeared into the past memories and then cleared her throat. "Have you heard anything about him?" Shelby inquired.
~~~

Before Frances could respond, they were interrupted by the back door slamming behind her.

"Hey, Daddy," Shelby said as he walked by and kissed her on the head. She watched him as he rounded the table, bent over, and hugged and kissed her mom.

Shelby had always dreamed of marrying someone who would love her half as much as she knew her dad loved her mom. They were perfect for each other and it was what she wanted with Richard.

Joel was a mild-mannered man who was always soft-spoken and had a heart for others. He was the perfect husband and dad and Shelby knew how much he loved them and she recalled his sweet nature growing up.

"How are my two favorite ladies doing this fine evening?" he asked with a smile.

They both laughed. "Having a great time, as usual," Frances added.

"Well, don't let me interrupt the conversation. I could tell it must have been a good one when I walked in," he said kiddingly.

"We were just talking about Jack," Frances conceded.

"Oh. Have you heard from him, Shelby?" Joel asked.

"Not a thing, but I hope he's doing okay. I know he has to be enjoying Trevor," she said wistfully, knowing how much Jack always wanted to be a father someday. Someday was now. "He loves kids. He used to play with them after church, running around chasing them, as if he was one himself. You know, I used to tell him when we were in high school, that one day when we grow up and get married, I want to have four kids... oh, my goodness, he would just shake his head and laugh at that now," Shelby said with a bit of a chuckle.

"Gosh, dear, you probably ran him off with that notion," Frances said, as they all had a good laugh from it.

"We've seen how happy Richard makes you and that makes us happy and we only want what's best for you. We hope you know that," Joel said. "We think you made the right decision to let it be with Jack. Not that we don't like him, we had always hoped for someone like Richard though," Joel explained.

Knowing her mom and dad approved of Richard made her ecstatic about having him in her life.

~~~
~~~

After a few short minutes, they grabbed their glasses of tea and sat in the rocking chairs that lined the long, narrow front porch. “I see Jack around town a lot these days and he seems okay. I do recall he smiled a lot more back when y’all were together, though,” Joel pointed out as he swayed in his rocker. “I don’t see that in him much anymore,” he admitted.

Shelby turned to see the expression on her dad’s face, hoping to feel out his thoughts and learn more. “How so?”

“Yep, Ms. Pauline from church claims Denise is having some real hard times these days. She says Jack takes care of that boy of theirs most of the time,” Frances added.

This was all news to Shelby. Being so far away in Tuscaloosa and caught up in her own priorities, she hadn’t much kept up with the gossip around Valley. “Really, I wonder what’s wrong with Denise. Do you know?” Shelby asked her mother.

Frances clicked her tongue against her teeth and lifted her eyebrow. “Well, the word is she hurt her back about a year ago working down at the bowling alley and she had to take some pretty powerful pain pills to help her along,” her mom told her.

“Frances, we don’t know that to be true,” Joel interrupted.

“I know, Joel, but there have been several people around town saying the same thing,” Frances admitted. “Even going so far as to hinting that Denise has a problem taking too much of it and getting addicted to it.”

Shelby took a sip of her tea as she glanced across the street. Her heart was disturbed over the news. She knew her mom well enough to know Frances never believed in gossiping and was always careful not to spread news that wasn’t, in her opinion, true. She hoped, for Jack and Trevor’s sake, that what her mother was saying *wasn’t* so.

Shelby spent the rest of afternoon enjoying the cool breezes gently blowing across the porch of her parents’ home. They had excused themselves, leaving Shelby to herself. She thought a lot about Jack, wondering if she had only taken his call that day a few years ago... where would they be today? Even though her heart ached over his situation, she still found happiness in her life with Richard.

Chapter Eighteen

It was the worst Christmas Jack had ever been through. He didn't know what to do with Denise. He had thought for sure that the move would've helped matters. Instead, it only made everything worse.

She became more and more dependent on those damn pain pills. She would lie in bed all day and the church would have to call him at work because she hadn't picked Trevor up.

It was Christmas day and they had all gathered at his parents' home for their traditional family get-together. Everyone sat around the table and enjoyed dinner. Trevor was delighted with all the attention. Denise had placed his small plate on the highchair tray and handed him a spoon.

Jack watched Martha as she reached across the table, took Trevor's tiny hand, and helped him scoop up the food into his mouth. They all laughed when he spit out the mashed potatoes in bubbles. Jack noticed Denise seemed irritated when everyone else thought it was cute.

Suddenly, and without warning, Denise shouted, "Damn it, Trevor, stop that!" She reached over and slapped his hand. Her reaction startled everyone. Trevor began to cry hysterically. Jack saw the look in his mother's eyes and he knew what was coming next.

"Denise, he's just a baby. It's what they do," Martha shouted angrily and without hesitation. She reached for Trevor's hand and kissed it gently trying to get him to calm down. "There, there, little baby boy. It's okay."

"Denise, don't you ever slap him again," Jack burst out with a finger in her face.

"He's *my* baby and I'll do whatever I want. No one is going to tell me what I can and can't do," she sounded off loudly.

Jack stood up quickly and grabbed her by the hand. When she acted like she was going to slap Trevor again, he snapped back, "No hell you won't ever lay another hand on my son!"

Denise tried to pull back, but Jack's grip on her arm kept her seated. She twisted trying to break from him, but he held his ground as he glared into her eyes.

"Do you understand me?" Jack hollered in her face. "Now settle down, Trevor is a baby and getting angry at him is not going to do any good," he said as he slowly took a seat still holding tightly to Denise's arm.

"Yeah, it's always about Trevor, isn't it Jack?" Denise said.

"You're damn right it is. It'll always be about Trevor," he said. Jack had had about enough of her; she had been short and irritated for months now. It wasn't anything new. However, he wasn't about to let her take her frustration out on Trevor.

Jack noticed his mother as she threw in her two cents. "You have no right to treat him like that, Denise. You're a grown woman. You're supposed to love him and teach him things. Not slap him around. You need to be taught how to be a mother. Maybe someone needs to slap you around."

Denise slammed her hands down on top of the table as her eyes bore directly at Martha. "You bitch, you think you know everything." Denise shoved her plate across the table in her direction. "Go ahead. I know exactly what you're thinking. Admit it! I'm not Shelby. That's who you wanted for a daughter-in-law and mother to Trevor. Isn't it? Every time you look at me, I know you're wishing I was *her*," Denise said choking on her words.

"Denise, what has gotten into you? How could you say something as absurd as that?" Jack asked angrily as he let her arm go and slammed his fist on the table. "You sat here and slapped Trevor and now you're making it about Shelby?"

"So, now you're going to take up for her, too, aren't you, Jack?" she asked obviously hitting a nerve.

Jack grit his teeth together. "Don't you ever blame Shelby for anything in our marriage. She has never done anything to you, Denise. You could probably learn a few things from her," he said as he shot her a dirty look.

"I don't have to take this bullshit!" Denise stood up and shoved away from the table, turning over a glass of tea and spilling it into the casserole. She whizzed around and raced out of the room. Maw Hollis sat in silence during the whole incident in disbelief. Jack saw the pain in her eyes as she watched her granddaughter act this way.

Martha frowned at Jack across the dinner table. "I don't rightly believe I've ever spent a Christmas as terrible as this one."

There was silence around the room after the blow-up. Jack hung his head in shame and embarrassment. He just couldn't understand her blaming Shelby.

Suddenly, a loud crashing sound came from the other room. Jack and Sheriff Emerson sprung from their seats and ran to see what the commotion was about. As they turned the corner into the kitchen, there stood Denise with a butcher knife in her hand. She waved it at them and let out a blood-curdling scream. "Don't you come near me," she warned.

Sheriff Emerson pressed Jack behind him to hold him back. "Denise, you need to calm down," he said to her. Jack's heart beat wildly not knowing what to do.

Denise shook her head fiercely. "I'm so sick of y'all talking about me behind my back. You don't think I hear what you're saying?"

"Denise," Sheriff Emerson said softly. "Calm down, dear. Everything is okay. Please put the knife down."

"Nooo!" she hollered back and waved the blade in his direction.

Jack saw the devastated and terrified look in her eyes. What had happened to her to make her snap? It was like she was a stranger.

He stepped toward her. "Please, Denise. Please, honey, put the knife down," he begged.

She began to wave the knife at Jack now.

"What is wrong with you? Why are you acting like this?" he asked cautiously, trying to keep his emotions in check. He wanted to reach out, take her, and hold her in his arms.

"You don't know, Jack? You really are a dumbass," she snapped, with her eyes staring at nothing.

Once again, Sheriff Emerson tried to soothe her. He casually reached down, grabbed his radio from his waist holster, and quietly called for police backup.

Jack peered into Denise's eyes and he could see her blinking hard as if she were trying to gain her sight. Her eyes looked like those of a rabid animal.

Jack tried to stay strong as he begged her to give him the knife. He carefully stepped toward her. She stood still with the knife raised high in the air as if to attack anyone who came close to her.

"Denise, please tell me what's wrong, baby. What can I do to make it all better? Please let me help you," Jack pleaded with her.

"You don't love me do you, Jack?" she asked as she continued to stare in a daze.

"Of course, I love you," he pointed out quickly.

"No, you love Shelby. You told me that. You told me you hated me. Didn't you?"

"Denise, honey... that was a long time ago. It's in the past. We have Trevor now and I do love you. I want to help you. Please put the knife down and let's talk. Okay?"

"No!" she bellowed loudly.

"Honey, we're married and we have our family... you... Trevor... and me... Don't you remember? It's just us. Shelby is nowhere in our lives. She is marrying someone else now. Denise, baby, it's just us, I promise," Jack begged.

Denise's head started to jerk as if she were coming out of her trance. Jack continued to speak comfortingly to her. He took small, cautious steps toward her. She began to lower the knife when she started to realize where she was.

Suddenly, she fell to her knees and dropped the knife. "Oh, God, what have I done?" Jack leaped to grab her away from the knife as the sheriff kicked the blade from her reach. Jack fell to the floor next to her and held her tightly in his arms. She burst out into tears and bawled like a baby. "Oh, my God. Jack, please help me... please help me," she cried as her voice trailed off.

Everyone at the Christmas dinner had witnessed the terrifying scene. The police arrived shortly after she dropped the knife and they waited patiently for instructions from Sheriff Emerson.

Jack and Denise sat on the floor with his arms wrapped around her rocking her. He whispered to her over and over again how much he loved her and Trevor. "I'm going to get you some help, baby, and everything will be okay. I promise," he said with tears rolling down his cheeks; finally able to let them out.

Before the evening was finished, Sheriff Emerson had arranged for Denise to go to the hospital in Montgomery to be admitted to the psychiatric unit for a few days' worth of evaluation.

It was past midnight when they had arrived in the capital city and the hospital staff admitted Denise.

"Please go with me, I'm scared," Denise pleaded with Jack as they stood in the waiting room.

"Baby, I can't go with you. They won't let me," Jack said

sadly. His arms were wrapped tightly around her body, holding her close. “It will be okay. They are going to help you, honey. Remember, we’re getting you help. Trevor and I both need you to get well.”

He turned to one of the staff members. “Please let me walk her back to her room. I promise I won’t interfere,” Jack pleaded. The guy in the white jacket shook his head “no” and motioned it was time for them to go. Jack felt his heart crumble.

“Denise, I love you. Please don’t forget that,” he said looking into her eyes. He leaned down and kissed her delicately on the lips. She resisted when the staff tugged at her arms to get her to release the grip she had on Jack. Her cries tore him apart and he felt her fingernails as they dug into his arms like needles stuck in a pincushion in desperation to hold on as they pulled her away.

“Jack, please, I love you,” she cried out with both arms stretched in the air at him as they helped her to the opened door.

In a flash, the door closed behind them. The clanking sound rang out and his hands sailed to his ears in an attempt to drown out the noise of the lock. She was gone in an instant.

“Oh, God, what have I done?” he whimpered as he broke down. The faint sound of her voice crying out for him in the distance echoed in his ears. Jack stood alone in the open waiting room agonizing over his decision and prayed it was the right one.

He spent the next couple of days emotionally torn over his agreement to admit Denise. His mother was right... the holidays had been the worst he had ever experienced. All he wanted to do was get through them.

A few days later, Jack received his first call from the admitting physician.

“Mr. Emerson, this is Dr. Andrews, your wife’s doctor.”

“Dr. Andrews, how is Denise?” Jack asked impatiently.

“She’s doing about as good as can be expected. I had the opportunity to evaluate her and it is my opinion that not only does she need drug rehabilitation, but she could benefit from some psychological care at the same time.”

Jack was eager to hear more. “Okay,” Jack responded.

“She’s deeply depressed and along with the pills, well, I’m afraid in her case, it’s going to take some work to get her back to herself. I’m going to recommend that she be transferred to a rehabilitation center in Birmingham. They have a great facility that can address both her problems. I’m afraid if we keep her here, she won’t get the best possible care for her needs.”

"I understand," Jack said.

"I will arrange for a transport service to get her there," Dr. Andrews said.

"Why can't I take her?" Jack asked.

"I'm sorry, Mr. Emerson. Your wife is going through detoxification at this time and we will arrange for her to go early next week once she clears this hurdle."

"Do you know how long she will be there? Will I be able to visit?" Jack asked.

"Let's do this... she will be here for a few more days. I'll have the center contact you prior to her leaving and they will be able to fill you in on all the details. I highly recommend we don't try to hurry her through the program. It could be as long as ninety days," Dr. Andrews replied.

Jack was stunned by his response. "Can I visit her before she leaves?" he asked worried about her.

"It's probably not a good idea for you to see her now," the doctor reiterated. "The initial week of care is usually the worst for the patient and we ask the family to give us some time to get them through this period. I hope you can understand this is what's best for your wife."

Jack was hesitant to let her go, but he knew in his heart this was the only way for her to get the help she needed and so he agreed. "I have to do it for Trevor."

~~~

Mary was quick to fill Shelby in about the Christmas dinner incident with Denise on the following Thursday evening. They were silent on the way to the annual New Year's Eve party at Hank's uncle's farm. Shelby wondered how Mary knew about it?

"How did you find out about Denise?" Shelby asked curiously.

"My aunt is a nurse in Montgomery at the hospital where she was admitted. She said she first saw Jack in the waiting room and then she read the notes on Denise's chart."

"Wait... how does she know Jack if she lives in Montgomery?" she asked turning to look at Mary.

"She lives in Riverview, but works in Montgomery. I'm not sure how she knows him, though," Mary said finally.

"Oh, okay," Shelby, said as she paused for a brief moment before she confronted her again. "How in the hell does Jack do it?" she asked, as Mary drove.
~~~

"I don't know," Mary replied with sadness in her voice. "Jack has been through so much, and I don't know how he deals with all the crap that bitch dishes out. Denise is like a black widow spider and Jack got caught up in her web. Now, the only way he's going to get out of it is if she destroys him," Mary said angrily.

"Oh, Mary. I tried so damn hard to warn him about her," Shelby said bitterly. 'I didn't know much about her, but I had this gut feeling she was evil. You know the sensation that comes from deep down in the pit of your stomach," Shelby declared. "You need to listen to hunches like that."

"Apparently, the pit of your stomach was right," Mary quickly pointed out as she spoke harshly. "He needs to get the hell away from her crazy ass before she destroys him."

"Mary..."

"I'm serious," she continued. "Jack's married to a freaking fruitcake *and* he's had a baby with her. He works his ass off to take care of them. I get so pissed off every time I think how she manipulated him into having sex with her. I don't think I will ever figure out how she got him to do that. From what I hear, she's a psychotic, crazy woman," Mary said shaking her head in disbelief.

Shelby cringed at Mary's words about how Denise manipulated Jack into having sex. Mary obviously didn't have any idea about what actually happened, but she was right. Shelby had never spoken to anyone about the night she'd found Jack and Denise together. What Mary didn't know wouldn't hurt her, Shelby thought, as she breathed a sigh.

Little did Mary know.

"Well, serves her right to be in the nut house," Mary mumbled.

"I just feel so badly for Jack," Shelby said as she stared out the car window watching the trees passing by.

"I know what you mean," Mary said sympathetically.

It was no time before they arrived at the party. Everyone was excited to finally be together. It had been so long. Shelby was ecstatic to see all of her friends from high school; it felt like old times again.

They sat around the fire, hooting and hollering, laughing and sharing stories of all the crazy things they had gotten into over the years. The guys smoked cigarettes and, of course, everyone was a bit silly from the beer

Shelby gazed around the group and noticed Walter and

Sadie, as well as Hank and Wendy. "Dang," she thought, "I can't believe how happy they seem."

It wasn't long before Justin showed up. Mary had invited him. While Shelby wasn't keen on Justin, Mary couldn't tear herself away from the guy. She couldn't for the life of her figure out why. However, that was for Mary to decipher. Shelby gazed across the bonfire at them and she had to admit Mary seemed happy with him.

Shelby leaned her head back in her chair and thought about her sweet guy, Richard. She missed him and wished he had come to see her. She wasn't sure right at first if she was going to make the party when Mary called her.

Richard had hoped she wouldn't go without him when she called to invite him to come down. He couldn't and had to decline.

One thing for sure, Shelby wasn't going to have to worry about him not working or not taking care of her after they were married. Richard was such a workaholic, in a good way. She smiled thinking about spending her life with him. She assured him there was no one here he had to worry about, but he still preferred her to come to Athens instead.

She was glad she had made the decision to remain home, though. Besides, she was driving down to Columbus in the morning to spend New Year's Day with Richard and his family.

The night with her old friends brought back so many fun memories of the times they had all spent together. She recalled the many high school parties here on the farm. She felt somewhat displaced at times tonight when she thought about Jack. It didn't seem the same here without him.

She sat quietly in the lawn chair and looked fixedly into the flames. She reminisced of the last New Year's Eve she and Jack had spent together three years ago. Right here on the farm. She snuggled her scarf up around her neck, crossed her arms, and closed her eyes as she felt the warmth from the embers radiating out of the flames.

She could hear Jack's voice...

"Here we go, Tootie," he'd said as he held her tightly in his arms swaying to the music from the stereo of someone's car. Everyone began the countdown to midnight... 5... 4... 3... 2... 1... she could hear their shouts.... and in that very second, he leaned down and turned her face to his and kissed her. At first, it was firm and quick and then something happened and it turned into an intimately sweet kiss. "I love you, Tootie," he'd whispered to her. She could see his eyes sparkle as he gazed into hers. "I love you, too, Jack," she'd said back.

The memory made her stomach leap like a fish out of water. She could feel the sensation of his kiss all over again as if it were happening this very instant. She smiled and let out a small sigh.

Suddenly, she was spooked out of her thoughts. "Shelby, Shelby," Mary whispered as she shook her on the shoulder.

"Oh, I'm sorry, Mary," Shelby said with her eyes wide open and a grin on her face.

"No need to apologize. I know exactly what you were thinking about my friend," Mary said as she leaned down and hugged her best pal.

"Was it that obvious?" Shelby asked shyly looking up at Mary.

"Yep, it was, but let me tell you, Shelby..." Mary knelt to the ground beside her and spoke low. "You will always carry a piece of Jack in your heart, don't ever feel ashamed. The tragedy would be if you shoveled all the memories you two shared, scooped them up, and tossed them into some trash never to be thought about ever again. Always cherish the happy times, Shelby," Mary said to her. Shelby felt Mary's hand comforting her as she rubbed it across her shoulders.

"You're right. There were so many happy times," Shelby said and smiled at her friend.

"I know how much you love Richard. He's one kick-ass hunk of a man and you are going to have a wonderful life with him. That doesn't mean you have to forget Jack. Never feel bad about the love y'all once shared," Mary told her.

"Thank you, Mary. I needed to hear that," Shelby said feeling guilty.

~~~

It had been a long three months and it wore heavy on Jack's mind as he made the trip to Birmingham. Denise was being released from the clinic and he was feeling the jitters about seeing her. What was she going to be like? How was she going to react to seeing him... seeing Trevor?

The doctors had agreed to discharge her early in the spring. It had been a long row for her to hoe, but it appeared to Jack that she was ready to come home.

They had talked on the phone just about every night after he put Trevor down for the evening with the exception of the first few
~~~

weeks. In the beginning, Denise went through detox and they had not allowed Jack to have any communication with her. He had heard from friends about the nightmares people went through during the initial phases of rehab.

But, that was over and now she was coming home.

He was quite nervous since he had been by himself alone with Trevor for the last few months. He hoped Trevor was going to be as happy as he was to finally have their family together again. Folks had warned him not to be alarmed if Trevor didn't take kindly to her at first, but in time, he would warm up to her.

~~~

The months followed and Denise worked hard and managed to remain clean and straight. Jack was so proud of her though he knew it was a struggle every day for her. He had been warned that she could fall back into her old ways. She was fragile. A simple and innocent comment could set her back.

Almost a year had passed and he was optimistic, feeling certain she was now on the right track. She was staying home and being a mommy. He could tell she loved every minute of it.

"Jack, I'm scared about going to your parents' house for Christmas dinner. I keep having flashbacks to that awful day last year," she admitted to him.

Jack reached over and pulled her closer. "Baby, try not to stress over it. It's behind us and we want to forget about it, okay?"

"I know, I just need you to understand how I'm feeling," she told him.

"Let's not worry. Let's enjoy the day and being with family. You know I'll be there every minute with you," he said comforting her.

They all sat in silence around the dinner table Christmas evening at Jack's parents' home. Everyone was reserved, considering the memories of the previous year's incident.

Denise broke the silence while folks dug into their plates full of the traditional turkey and dressing meal. "I want y'all to know how truly sorry I am for what happened last year and how much I appreciate everyone's support through this terrible ordeal," she said in a soft tone of voice. "I don't ever want to go back there and I know with my family's support, I can do this." She turned to Jack and smiled. Then, she pressed her face into his chest as he reached over and pulled her close to him.
~~~

"We're going to always be here for you, baby," Jack said confidently. "Right?" he asked and scanned the room to see other people's reaction to her apology.

Jack cut his eyes at his mother, hoping she would follow with a heartfelt response when he noticed she was about to speak.

"Denise, we know it's been hard for you, dear. I want you to know how proud I am of you for the progress you've made this year. I can see it in Jack and Trevor both. They seem to laugh a lot more now they have the new Denise. You know, you can always count on us," Martha said as she looked toward Jack.

"We only want to see you happy and smiling," Sheriff Emerson noted.

Jack glanced at Maw Hollis, waiting to hear what she had to say. He noticed she wasn't as optimistic as his family. He quickly eyeballed her to make her aware it was her time to say something. Maw Hollis was not a real gracious type person and he knew it was going to be difficult for her to say anything nice. She had better come up with something quick and it had better be good, he thought.

"Yes, Jack's right. We're here for you," Maw said hesitantly as she turned away from his gaze.

"Thank you," Denise said interrupting Maw.

The noise rang out around the table and Jack was pleased. He noticed Maw's response was a little less than desirable. She sat across the table without uttering another word. Jack was puzzled and thought it was odd she didn't chime in with everyone else. After all, this was *her* granddaughter and she should be happy for her.

Jack continued to watch Maw's every move. What could she be thinking? It perplexed him and he couldn't help but stare across the table at her. She met his gaze and hurriedly turned away. Jack became annoyed with her and was determined to find out what was going on. Was she hiding something from him? If so, he wanted to know.

~~~

Finally, after four long years, the time Shelby had been waiting for was here. The University of Alabama Graduation 1978 was just one day away. Shelby sat in her dorm room wondering where the time had gone. Her parents would be driving up tomorrow for her special event. This would be her last night in Tuscaloosa and Mary was driving down from Athens for the
~~~

celebration since Georgia's graduation wasn't for another week.

They had planned to get together one last time with all of the sorority sisters for what they called their swearing ceremony. They were supposed to meet at the ΚΔΩ house at seven p.m. JoJo's sister, Sandra, had a swearing ceremony with her sisters back when she was at Alabama, so JoJo was the perfect one to put it all together for them.

Mary, JoJo, and Shelby left the dorm and met Amy, Rachel, and Jenna at the sorority house, greeting each other with hugs. She knew this would be her family for life.

Shelby was impressed that for once, JoJo was taking something seriously. It wasn't her nature, but she could tell this was important to her.

All six sisters sat with their knees bent and legs crossed Indian style. They held hands and formed a circle. JoJo lit a few candles and placed them around the room. It was still relatively early in the evening and the glow from the sun setting came through the windows.

JoJo cleared her throat as she began to speak. "This evening, we are going to take an oath among the six of us. We will always be sisters. We will pledge support for one another through good times and bad times. We will be there for each other no matter what or when. If any of us are ever in need we will drop whatever we are doing and come together as sisters to overcome challenges in our lives," JoJo explained. "Now, I'm going to ask each one to take the oath. All you have to do is say yes, and then I will move on to the next person. Once we have all taken the vows we will then raise our hands in the air," JoJo instructed them.

"Once we finish we will have pledged our lives as sisters forever. There will be nothing to tear us apart," JoJo said firmly.

Shelby watched as JoJo sucked in a deep breath and they all dropped their hands to the floor. They each shook their shoulders to relax.

"Do you pledge to be a sister of our group?" JoJo asked each girl around the circle. Each one said yes she would.

"Do you pledge to support your sisters during the good times and the bad times?"

"We will."

"Will you always be there for your sisters no matter what?"

One at a time, they responded they would.

"Will you help your sisters to overcome any challenges in their lives?"

They all agreed and said, "Yes."

"Okay, good. Now, let's raise our hands and repeat after me," JoJo said in a serious voice. "Forever!"

They threw their hands in the air and everyone shouted out "Forever" several times. Shelby felt goosebumps throughout her body as she gazed around the circle. These five sisters would be her family and it made her happy.

Little did she know how much she would need them.

Chapter Nineteen

It was a gorgeous day just two weeks before the wedding and Shelby was overwhelmed with all the work still left to do. She had just graduated from Alabama and was ready to begin her new job in Atlanta in the fall. With all the craziness—graduation down and soon the wedding—they would then rush off to Buckhead where she would start teaching kindergarten. She would work while Richard finished up law school in the spring of 1979. She was so excited and ready for the summer to come to a close.

Shelby sat at the kitchen table across from her mother. Frances had poured them a big glass of iced tea. Shelby grabbed a slice of lemon and squeezed it in hers.

"Mom, I can't believe I'm going to be married in just two weeks," Shelby said nervously. "I still have a million things to get done. It's been insane. All the bridal showers and teas that Mrs. Porter arranged for me have been mind-boggling and I don't think I can put anything else in my bedroom. It's overflowing now," she said as she smiled at her mom.

"I know, dear. Isn't it wonderful? You are so blessed to be marrying Richard. I know you will never have to do without. His family loves you and that warms my heart. I've prayed all your life that you would fall in love with someone who could give you everything you deserved. God has truly answered my prayers," Frances said tilting her head to the side with a smile on her face.

Shelby was absolutely taken by her mother. She was perfect.

"You know, I hope one day when Richard and I have a child, I will be just like you Mom," Shelby said softly.

"Thank you, dear. That makes me feel great and worth all the craziness of watching you grow up. You will be a wonderful mother," Frances replied. "Have you and Richard talked about having children?"

Shelby nodded. "Just a couple of times. He wants us to wait a bit and have some fun with just the two of us before we start planning a family. I don't want to wait too long. I'd have one tomorrow if I could," she said wistfully as she looked into her glass.

"I bet you would," Frances pointed out.

"It's good. It's really good, though," Shelby said, as she raised her glass, and finished off the last of her tea.

~~~

Richard led the way around the big fountain and along the flagstone path toward the beautiful country club entrance on Lake Oconee. Shelby trailed in awe at the opulence of the place, even though she had visited many times over the last year making all the plans for the wedding. Mrs. Porter had accompanied her each time to ensure every detail was completed to her liking.

Today was different, though. The nuptials were only three days away and then Shelby would be Mrs. Richard Porter. She grinned as the bellman greeted them.

"Good afternoon, Mr. Porter. We've been expecting you, sir," he said as he nodded. "Your accommodations are waiting. Mr. Willie here will escort you to your rooms."

Shelby observed the bellman as he graciously took a quick bow as she walked past. "Wow," she thought to herself, "I'm really grooving this."

She knew Richard was used to this kind of attention and noticed it never fazed him as it did her. Then again, the General was always sure to expect this type of behavior toward his family.

She and Richard roamed along the blossom-y path of rhododendrons in full bloom, as well as azaleas and budding roses. The path wound in and out of the dramatic scenery of trees through the meticulously groomed gardens. The birds sang sweetly in the background providing a serenade for their walk, the snorting noise of sneezing from a spooked squirrel scurrying into a nearby bush provided nature's percussion.

Shelby paused and glanced over the view across the grounds. The beauty of it all captivated her heart each time she visited. She dreamed many times of what it was going to feel like to walk through the gardens in her wedding dress and over the lush, grassy knoll laced with yellow rose petals and step into the
~~~

archway where the beautiful backdrop of Lake Oconee painted the horizon. She would look up at Richard. He would be standing there smiling at her. He would reach out and take her hand...

"Shelby," Richard called out.

Hearing his voice stirred her out of her daydream. Shaken from her thoughts, she stepped into the small bridal cottage as Mr. Willie unlocked the door and waved her in.

"Oh, Richard, it's beautiful," she said excitedly and noticed that her room was completely decorated with everything a bride could ever want.

Her wedding dress hung from the shutters of the window facing the lake. The veil was draped from a hook next to the mantle of the fireplace. The room was filled with yellow accents, her wedding colors. In the center of the room, a vast bouquet of long-stemmed yellow roses stood royally filled with spurts of baby's breath throughout. It made her gasp; much like a Cinderella story. There were pictures of Richard and her framed in white and placed around the cottage. Shelby squealed in delight as she danced around the suite taking in all the beauty.

"I hope everything is to your expectations, sir," Mr. Willie noted while searching for Richards's approval.

Shelby watched as he took out a bill from his front pocket and handed it to the gentlemen. "Yes, sir, I believe she is quite happy," Richard said as he nodded in the bellmen's direction.

She glanced across the room and saw Richard close the door.

"Well, you like it?" he asked.

"Ooh... my, I love it. Everything is so perfect," she admitted. Richard lifted her up and spun her around in his arms. "I love you, Shelby. You deserve this. I wanted everything to be perfect," he said as he leaned over and kissed her.

"I love you, too," Shelby said softly, between kisses.

Richard set her back to her feet. "Now, you settle in and I'm going to my room and rest for a bit before we go to dinner. Everyone will be here tomorrow and it's going to get really stressful. So, we need to rest while we can," Richard said.

"Okay," she said in agreement.

Richard closed the door behind him. Shelby walked over to the window enjoying the beautiful gardens. Tomorrow, everyone would be arriving and she couldn't wait to see them. Jenna had phoned her earlier at home to let her know she, Amy, and Rachel were coming on Friday. She was thrilled.

Just like they had promised to be there for each other always.

~~~

Chaos filled the bridal cottage as JoJo and Mary arrived in the early afternoon on the eve of the wedding.

"Oh, my God," Mary said amazed as they came through the door into the cottage.

"Are you freaking kidding me, Shelby? I just have to ask," JoJo said, wide-eyed. "Where the hell did you find this guy? I don't think I've ever seen anything like this even in my wildest dreams. This must have cost a fortune. You are one damn lucky lady."

Shelby squealed in delight as the three of them hugged and played around the room like little girls in a fantasy world.

"I don't know, JoJo. Sometimes I wonder myself. I don't know why he picked me. I'm just a simple girl from Valley, Alabama. I'm no Cinderella," she said as she laughed.

"You might not be right now, but come tomorrow you're going to be," Mary responded from across the room.

Shelby was the happiest she had ever been in her life. She had her two best friends and her family right here with her. She was marrying her Prince Charming tomorrow. Emotions began to overcome her as she lounged in her bed late into the evening.

She was so tired from all the preparations and just wanted to sleep. Tomorrow was her wedding day and she wanted everything to be perfect. She rolled over and gazed at the moon high in the sky. Her thoughts went to her heavenly friend, Gina.

"Hey, girl, I'm really getting married tomorrow. Can you believe it? I wish you were here with me, but I know in my heart you will be. I miss you," she whispered. Shelby closed her eyes and said a prayer.

"God, please watch over us. I know you have a plan for me and it's with Richard. Please bless our marriage as we prepare to take our vows. You know how much I love him and I'm so grateful you put him in my life. Please keep me safe. In Jesus' name, I pray. Amen," she said softly and pulled the satin sheet up to her face and smiled.

It was her beautiful dream coming true.

~~~

Shelby was awakened by a knock at the door. She squinted at the clock sitting on the nightstand next to her bed. It was one a.m. Who could it be? She reached for her silky sleep jacket from the end of the bed and threw it over her as she rushed to the door.

Peeking through the small peephole, she could barely make out the silhouette of a man that looked like Richard.

"Awww... he wants to see me before morning," she whispered as she unlocked the latch. She opened it and breathed out, "Richard."

The man shoved her to the floor. "Richard!" But, she couldn't make out his face. He grabbed her around the neck and lifted her up from the floor.

"You bitch," the voice said angrily as he began slapping her across the face.

The pain was horrendous and she could feel her heart beating out of her chest.

"Oh, God! Please help me," she begged.

"No one's going to help you now, you whore. You think you're going to get away with defying me? You're wrong," the man whispered angrily in her face.

Shelby closed her eyes tightly as he threw her against the wall. She felt her body go limp and then his hands seized her again before she hit the floor. He slammed her onto the sofa and began punching her in the face.

The pain was so intense that she almost didn't feel it; as if it were rising from her body through the terror flowing through her veins.

"Please stop, I'll do whatever you want," she cried out, pleading with the man. She could feel the warm blood pouring from her nose. Her right eye was swelling now and she could barely see out of it. She tried desperately to make out his face, but all she could do was lift her arms up over her head in defense as his fists continued to pound her neck and chest now.

He pulled her up from the sofa and made her stand up. She wobbled, weak and trembling from the agony. His voice deep and forceful, "Over my dead body, bitch."

She didn't know what was happening to her. Each blow to her body made her weaker and weaker. Then, she bellowed out in a bloodcurdling screech as she felt a final blow to her stomach that stole away her breath. The force of the punch made her hit the floor... everything went black.

She came to. Lying in a pool of blood, she remained motionless face down on the right side of her body in excruciating pain. Was he still here? She listened out and found that the room was now silent. She wasn't going to move for fear he was still around. She lay quietly and then, suddenly; she was startled by the sound of the door slamming open.

"Oh, God, Shelby," the voice shouted out in horror...

Shelby sat straight up in her bed. Sweat poured off her body. She grabbed her nightgown and quickly glanced around the room. The sun was shining through the small bridal cottage greeting her with the light of the new day

"Thank you, Jesus!" she gasped. "It was only a nightmare."

Shelby wiped the perspiration from her face and felt her body trembling from the dream. She hung her head in her hands as she tried to gain her composure. It had felt so *real.*

She sat motionless in her bed, trying to figure out what it was all about. She never had nightmares. Certainly nothing like this.

The man's words echoed in her mind. What did they mean? Why would she have this vision on her wedding day?

It was minutes later before Shelby had the strength to get out of the bed. She walked slowly into the bathroom where she was face to face with her image in the mirror.

"What does this mean?" she asked her reflection.

She flipped on the faucet and splashed her face with the cold water that rushed through her fingers. She softly patted her face dry with the thick bath towel.

An abrupt knock on the door startled her out of her thoughts. Still frightened from the nightmare, Shelby approached carefully and peeked through the hole. Relief cascaded over her. It was JoJo.

Shelby opened the door quickly and grabbed JoJo by the arm.

"Whoa, what's all this about?" JoJo asked in surprise.

Shelby held her friend tightly, so scared to let her go.

JoJo set her back and asked, "Shelby, what's wrong?"

"Oh, you can't imagine the nightmare I had," Shelby explained.

JoJo reached for her hand and walked her into the cottage as they sat together on the sofa. Shelby began to tell her about every detail of the nightmare, still troubled with fear from the dream. She could tell JoJo was upset, too.

"What do you think it means?" Shelby asked.

"It doesn't mean anything, Shelby," she said, almost fussing at her. "It's nothing more than a dream. Okay?" JoJo said comforting her.

"But... it was so real," Shelby argued.

"I know, but we all have nightmares sometimes. Nothing more. Now, try to forget about that crap. Today's your wedding day, Shelby!" JoJo exclaimed.

Shelby shot her friend a half-smile and tried to let it go. "I guess you're right," she admitted.

For the next few hours, Shelby couldn't abandon the images and memories of the nightmare. Pandemonium filled the cottage as the girls rushed around getting ready for the ceremony. Frances accompanied them and kept everything organized. Shelby loved that about her mom. She never got stressed over anything and always kept a smiling face no matter the circumstances. She only hoped she would be half the woman her mother was, she thought, watching Frances across the room.

Everyone had left the room with the exception of Shelby and her mom. It was only minutes before her walk down the aisle. Shelby stood in front of the floor-length mirror as she admired every detail of her exquisite gown. The sweetheart neckline was intricately embellished with a delicate rhinestone outline. The cap sleeves along with the bodice and long flowing train were draped with French lace. It was a perfect fit for her wedding.

Frances stepped over and trailed the back of her hand down Shelby's cheek. "You are beautiful and I love you more than you can ever imagine," her mother said in the sweetest voice. She hugged Shelby tightly and kissed her on the cheek. "You are the most gorgeous bride," she remarked.

"I love you, too, Mom," Shelby said as she beamed into her mom's eyes.

Shelby watched as Frances took her hands and held them in hers. Frances removed a small, white lace handkerchief from her purse and dabbed at the tears threatening to fall from Shelby's eyes. Shelby had given her the handkerchief the day before. She had a friend embroider Frances's initials on it along with a reference to her favorite Bible verse, 1 Corinthians 13: 4-8.

Neither Shelby nor Frances heard the knock on the door. "Shelby, it's time," Joel announced.

Frances gave Shelby one last hug and walked out the door. Shelby saw her dad grinning at her as she stepped toward her.

"You look absolutely stunning, dear," he said excitedly. "You ready?"

The room was silent as Shelby stood in front of the mirror one last time. Richard was waiting at the altar and she was ready to relinquish her heart and soul to the man she loved.

~~~

Jack sat quietly on the front porch of his parents' home. The Saturday newspaper laid on the edge of the table next to the chair. Sheriff Emerson emerged from his patrol car parked in the driveway and approached the front steps of the house. He walked over and sat down next to Jack. His father picked up the newspaper and began to read. Jack's heart throbbed painfully because he knew what was coming next.

"You doing okay, son?" Sheriff Emerson asked as he read the announcement.

"I'm okay, Dad," Jack replied hurtfully. "I guess I'm about as good as I could be."

"Today's the day, huh?" he asked.

Jack leaned forward in his rocker and rubbed his forehead confused and hurt by what was about to happen. "How is it that one, single incident in time can ruin your entire life?" he asked as he looked up and into his father's eyes.

"We can't question the things that happen in our lives," the sheriff responded quickly. Jack noticed his dad turn his head and look away.

"I know, but I have royally screwed up my life. I just don't understand how it could get any worse," Jack noted indecisively. "Denise is back in rehab again. I have to raise Trevor by myself, of course with help from you and mom. And, the girl I wanted to spend the rest of my life with is marrying someone else today," he said sadly. "It's just so hard."

They were interrupted by the sound from the radio calling for the sheriff to answer.

"Hang in there, son. Good things are going to happen for you one day," he said as he stood and walked away to answer the call.

"I am, Dad," Jack whispered softly.

Jack picked up the newspaper and softly said, "I love you, Shelby, with all my heart. I hope you have a wonderful life, sweetie." Then, he tossed the paper on the floor, he stood up and walked down the front porch steps.

~~~

"I love you, Shelby, with all my heart. I hope you have a wonderful life, sweetie."

Shelby smiled and turned to face her dad, "Well, I love you, too, Daddy, and I just know my life with Richard is going to be wonderful," she said curiously.

He frowned at her and then asked, "What do you mean, dear?"

"You said you loved me and I was telling you back," she said.

Joel scratched his head. "Darling, I do love you, but I didn't say anything," he responded.

"What do you mean? I heard you say you love me and you hope I have a wonderful life, sweetie," she said firmly.

"I promise I didn't say anything," he said with a puzzled tone of voice.

"Are you sure?" she asked.

"Yep," he said.

Shelby was confused by his admission. First, it was the nightmare, now she was hearing things. She closed her eyes briefly and shook the thoughts from her mind.

The wedding coordinator tapped the door lightly and stuck her head in. "It's time!"

Shelby took her dad's arm as they headed down the path to the grassy knoll. The wedding march began to play out over the speakers. Shelby trembled with excitement. With each step across the grass, her heart throbbed more and more, her eyes moved slowly from her friends, her mom, and her sorority sisters all converged at her wedding.

However, she couldn't tamp down the thoughts of Jack from suddenly racing through her mind. He was the one she had always dreamed of marrying. He was always the one who filled her heart with love. Yet, he had betrayed her and she had to erase him from her thoughts and focus on the person who was here before her. Loving her. Pledging himself to her only. She took a few more steps down the aisle. Jack was not at the altar, but Richard was.

She smiled as she shook the thoughts from her mind. "I'm marrying Richard. I love Richard," she said under her breath.

Everyone stood and smiled as she made her way to him at the front. Joel moved her hand and handed it over to Richard, just as the pastor asked, "Who does give this woman?"

"Her mother and I do," Joel said as he stepped away.

Shelby met Richard's eyes as she saw him gaze at her appreciatively and adoringly. "Yes, I'm marrying Richard," she said to herself.

Before she knew it, their "I dos" were exchanged, there was a gorgeous gold band on her finger, and Richard kissed her passionately before their friends, family, and God.

"Ladies and gentlemen," the minister said, "I present to you for the first time, Mr. and Mrs. Richard Porter."

Shelby was ecstatic as she and Richard, arm-in-arm, rushed down the aisle; she had finally married her prince charming. All the cheers and claps of encouragement from the crowd filled her ears as they passed each row of friends and family, and it filled her heart with joy.

Through all the celebration at the reception, she and Richard made their rounds from table to table.

"The wedding ceremony was absolutely wonderful, dear," the General said as he leaned down and kissed her on the cheek. Shelby had never felt comfortable around the General. She was always cautious and could never understand why she felt this way. He has always been very polite, but there was just something about him she couldn't put her finger on.

"Thank you, General, for everything. You made it perfect. I can't thank you and Mrs. Porter enough for all you have done to make today a dream come true," Shelby said happily.

"Good deal, my dear," he said as he turned and walked away.

The tables were dressed with low-lit candles among the towering displays of floral arrangements of enormous yellow roses filled with baby's breath and ribbon draping the tall glass vases. The guests all enjoyed the evening drinking, eating, and dancing to the wonderful music of the band. Shelby glanced around the huge white tent that was majestically sheltering the guests as the heat rose into the low nineties that afternoon.

Shelby saw Richard crossing the dance floor as he motioned for her to join him. She walked over slowly and met him hand-in-hand as the wedding director announced. "Mr. and Mrs. Richard Porter will take their first dance."

The music of Debby Boone's "*You Light Up My Life*" rang out as Richard took her into his arms. Their bodies swayed back and forth to the lyrics. She held him tightly and she could feel his gentle touch as she melted into his arms and relinquished her heart. All she could do was envision a wonderful life with Richard.

After their first dance, Richard excused himself and Shelby flew over to her sorority sisters' table where they were celebrating the beautiful event. Rachel raised a toast as Shelby approached them. "Here, here to Mrs. Richard Porter," they all chimed in as they lifted their drinks to clink together.

Shelby was elated as she sat down alongside Jenna and Mary.

"So, how does it feel to be all married up?" JoJo asked teasingly, leaning around the tall floral arrangement in the center of the table.

"I'm so thankful and it feels great!" Shelby exclaimed as she looked around at her best friends.

Amy burst into laughter. "I bet it does. You are the most gorgeous bride I've ever seen, Shelby," Amy said. "I hope to look half as good at my wedding as you do."

Shelby brushed off the compliment as she felt her cheeks heat up.

"I don't think anyone of us will ever be able to outdo a wedding like this," Rachel said.

"It was fabulous," Mary said with a grin on her face.

Shelby sat listening and watching her friends' laughter and chatter. Her life was a blessing and she couldn't be happier.

Later in the evening, after they had eaten, Shelby followed the low lights outlining the path to the cottages. She hadn't been able to find Richard and it was almost time to throw the bouquet and garter. As she approached the tiny cottage, she could hear voices through the open door.

It was the General and Richard. She quietly walked up to the crack in the door peeked in and began to listen. The General's voice seemed quite harsh and surprised her immensely when she heard him say.

"Look, Richard, I just forked out a quarter of million dollars for this gig. Shelby's a good woman and you better not screw it up. It's time you quit being a titty baby and be a man now," he said with his deep military command.

Shelby gasped at his words even as she quickly covered her mouth with her hand. She wished now that she hadn't been eavesdropping, but couldn't stop herself from listening to more. What had his father called him?

The General continued. "You better keep her happy or you know what will happen, don't you, son?" he asked starkly. She noticed the General was waving what looked like a large envelope in Richard's direction.

Shelby wondered what he meant by that, as well, but didn't dare move a muscle.

To Richard's credit, he spoke calmly, "Dad, I'm tired of you calling me names. I know what I am and I'm not a little sissy. I appreciate all that you've done for us, but trust me, I know how to keep her happy," Richard said angrily.

"You better because your life sits sealed in this package," the General said with a bit of anger as he threw the envelope down on the table.

When she heard a shuffling in the room, she figured it was Richard leaving the conversation. She picked up the hem of her wedding gown and rushed back to the reception so she wouldn't be discovered.

But...*what* was *that* all about?

Chapter Twenty

Like two peas in a pod, Trevor was the apple of Jack's eye. He adored his son and relished every minute they spent together. Now that he was four years old, Jack figured it was time to teach him how to fish. He grabbed up the gear and took off to the river with Trevor in tow. He suited him up in his life jacket and sat him safely in the boat as they rode off fishing for the first time.

That July afternoon, he taught Trevor to how to hook a worm, how to cast his pole, and how to reel in a fish. Jack smiled when he noticed how intent Trevor was about baiting his hook. There was no greater joy in his life than Trevor, even if his mother was the bane of Jack's existence.

Jack sat patiently waiting on Trevor as he tossed the fishing line out into the water. This was what Jack had dreamed about all of his life. Having a little boy and teaching him to fish. A true bond he knew they'd always share.

His thoughts somehow moved quickly to Shelby. He wondered what she was doing these days and if, now that she was married; she had any kids of her own. Losing her had been the toughest thing he had ever gone through, but his love for Trevor definitely replaced his broken heart. His mother said everything happened for a reason and he knew that was Trevor. Sitting here watching Trevor's every move just reminded Jack that he'd made the right decision.

Life had not been easy. Denise was in rehabilitation for the third time now. Her second bout was back in 1978 and now the most recent one happened in the summer of 1979. She struggled emotionally and mentally over her prescription drug abuse. She would be returning home soon after three months away in Birmingham again. Jack wasn't sure how he was going to fare this time. He kept reminding himself of his vows, *in sickness and in health*. He was just trying to make sense of it all.

Jack found out recently that Denise had come from a long line of alcoholics and drug addicts. It apparently ran rampant throughout her family, according to Maw Hollis.

Denise's dad had died at the age of thirty-eight from a drug overdose, which threw her mother into a spiral of emotional breakdowns over her loss. Then, she turned to alcohol. That was when Denise was removed from her home and sent to Valley to live with Maw Hollis. Denise had never spoken about her past much with Jack and he knew how much it hurt her when he tried to mention it.

Maw recently decided to tell Jack about the family history of emotional and mental incidents in order for him to understand Denise more and what all she was dealing with. He knew she had kept it from him and it made him angry at first. Now, he understood why she had done it and he had forgiven her for not telling him before they married. She was afraid he wouldn't have married her... and she was probably right looking back, he thought.

He knew he had to give Denise one more chance, but he had to deal with his own emotions concerning her addiction. At times, he felt like throwing in the towel, taking Trevor, and moving somewhere far away. However, he knew that would just be running from the problem. So, this time, he had made the decision to stick it out one last time despite everything that had happened in the past. He would be the man he needed to be. He was going to give his all to Denise, love her unconditionally, and do whatever it took to make their marriage right.

They had even spoken about having another child after she had returned from rehabilitation the last time. However, she had wanted to wait to see what happened. He thought having another baby would give her some sense of security. She wasn't so sure.

He thought about Trevor and Denise's relationship. He had not really bonded with her like other children had with their mothers. Jack was afraid Trevor would never get to know her like he should, so, for that reason alone, he had to give it one more go for Trevor's sake.

~~~

The year had flown by for Shelby and Richard after the wedding. Life was great. She loved being a teacher now. To walk
~~~

into the classroom and see those sweet, smiles warmed her heart. She kept herself busy planning her lessons and creating projects for the children. Living in their Atlanta apartment was wonderful and Shelby loved playing house, setting the place up with all of their wedding presents of dishes, silverware, cookware, trinkets, and decorations. There was only one more thing that would make her life perfect. A baby.

Richard had accepted a position at Glover, Rule, and Adams, PC in Atlanta. He had mentioned several times to her that they should try to find a home in the Martindale Brook community since she was already settled in at the elementary school there. Shelby was overwhelmed at the thought and couldn't wait to move into a home of their own.

Richard took the week off after graduation and they sat quietly on the love seat in their tiny apartment in the early summer of 1979. He held her feet in his hands and he rubbed them between his fingers.

"Richard?" Shelby asked. She saw him turn to face her. "Do you think we could consider having a baby after we move in the fall?" she asked.

"Hmm… we'll see," he said, continuing to massage her feet.

She adjusted a bit and pressed on. "You'll have been with the firm for about a year, and I'll have been at the elementary school for a couple of years. It would be perfect timing, don't you think?" she asked excitedly.

"I don't think we should rush into anything. I know how you are about organizing everything, but you know, sometimes babies just happen and you can't really plan them," Richard responded as he turned away nonchalantly and continued to watch a golf match on TV. Without facing her, he went on to mention, "Besides, you know Carl and his wife, Angie, from work, they have been trying for something like three years now and they haven't gotten pregnant yet. I don't want you to obsess over it as they do. It drives me crazy when that is all they talk about," he added as stared at the set.

Shelby could tell by his expression he wasn't interested in children right now. After all, he had told her in the past he wanted to wait a while. However, everything was perfect for them to start trying now. She'd have to bring him around to her way of thinking.

"I know, but it sure is a blast trying," she said and corralled him around the neck and threw her body onto his as she hugged him playfully.

"Shelby, come on. Stop! I'm watching golf," he said as he tugged her arms from his neck. Shelby was surprised at his reaction, but she wasn't about to let him turn her off. She wrestled with him and kept teasing. "Oh, come on. We can have fun while we try to have a baby," she said snickering.

She saw Richard's expression change as he cut his eyes at her in a sly way. "Okay, you're going to be in trouble if you don't stop, missy," he said as he reached over and tickled her ribs.

"You promise?" she asked with a grin on her face.

"You want a baby that badly, huh?" he asked, as he looked her in the eyes.

"Yes, I do, Richard, and if it doesn't happen this time, we'll just keep trying... right?" she said laughingly with a teasing tone to her voice.

He laughed and said, "Damn, Shelby... you always win. I'll tell you what; if you want a baby then let's do it. However, you have to promise you won't anguish over it if it doesn't happen right away like Carl and Angie," he said wide-eyed at her.

"I promise!" Shelby said almost in a squeal. "What are we waiting for?" She took Richard by the hand and led him down the hallway to their bedroom, leaving the golf match still boringly flashing on the screen.

~~~

Shelby and Richard's big move came shortly after the New Year's holiday, finally settling in their new home in Martindale Brook. It was everything Shelby had ever wanted and more. Richard had given her no budget and told her to just be prudent with the money. He was devoting all of his time at work since he was the new kid on the block, so to speak.

She kept herself busy, though, and Richard promised he would spend time with her whenever he could. He told her he would be handling some high-profile cases in the future per his boss, which meant his face was probably going to become familiar on TV at times. She was ecstatic at the news, and the thought of being married to a celebrity — that kind of made her famous, too.

It had been almost a year now and Shelby was getting worried since she had gone off the pill and she still wasn't pregnant. She wanted to talk to Richard about it, but recalled she had promised not to obsess over it. She decided she was going to give it another month and if she didn't get pregnant by then, they
~~~

were going to have to discuss their options and both get checked out by the doctor.

It was early afternoon in late March when Shelby got some disturbing news.

"Shelby, I just got a phone call from Mom," Richard said, somewhat out of breath. "It's the General. He's had a heart attack and they are flying him to Emory University as we speak. I'm leaving the office now. Do you want to want to meet me there?" he asked sadly.

"Oh no, honey. Yes, I'll be there as soon as I can get there," she replied.

"Okay, see you shortly," he said as the phone went dead.

Shelby had just gotten home from school, so she called the assistant principal to let her know what happened and that she wouldn't be in to work on Friday. She grabbed a few things and left for the hospital.

Richard arrived sooner than she did and was waiting in the emergency room.

"How is he?" she asked expectantly.

He shook his head. "No one has talked to me yet."

Shelby wrapped her arm around him and held tightly. "Where's your mom?"

"She's on her way and should be here in about an hour. They wouldn't let her fly with him, so she's driving up from Columbus now," he said with a worried look on his face.

"I'm so sorry, Richard. Are you okay?" Shelby asked as she watched him get up and pace the floor of the waiting room. He just nodded his head. It was at times like these that Shelby had always given Richard space. If he wanted to speak, he would. If not, then she waited until he was ready. It usually wasn't long before he would open up to her.

An hour later, Mrs. Porter came racing through the automatic doors of the Emergency Room and rushed over to them. "Richard, dear, have you heard anything? Have you seen him yet?"

"No. They know I'm here and said they would let us know something soon. It's all I know."

Shelby watched Mrs. Porter break down in Richard's arms. She could hear her sobs and her telling him she didn't know what she would do if he didn't make it.

"It was awful when he grabbed his chest and fell on the floor. I tried to help him up, but he wasn't responding," she said, choked up. "I called 911 and they were there in a flash."

"Mom, it's okay. Dad's where he needs to be and is going to be just fine," Richard, said confidently.

All Shelby could do was stand by and be supportive through this.

Within the hour, the doctor came into the waiting room, his face pale and long. "I'm sorry, we did everything we could, but he didn't make it," the doctor said apologetically.

Shelby watched as Mrs. Porter broke down, "No!" Richard stood holding his mother in his arms, emotionless. Shelby's heart went out to Mrs. Porter and she could tell Richard was shocked by the news. He and his mother stood quietly holding each other.

It had been a very long time since the last time Shelby had experienced death when Gina had died. Now, the General had made his heavenly appearance, as well.

Shelby sat quietly as she watched Richard and his mother as they took a seat across from her. Mrs. Porter hung her head as she wept. Richard had his arm around her shoulders trying to comfort her. Yet, Richard wasn't showing any emotions, which Shelby thought to be odd. The General had just *died*.

"Oh, Richard. I'm so sorry," Mrs. Porter said between sobs.

"Why Mom?" he asked.

"You know I did the best I could, but I was afraid of your dad and what he would do. I should have protected you, son, and I didn't, and you have to know how much I wanted to," she said sadly as she continued. "You're everything to me, but I didn't do what I should have. Please... you have to forgive me. I was always told you have to take care of your man, no matter what. I tried so hard," she said as she put her arms around Richard's waist.

"I know, Mom, but all of that is behind us now. You don't have to worry about it ever again," he said confidently as he took her head and gently laid it on his shoulder.

Shelby was stunned by Mrs. Porter's confusing words. What on earth were they talking about? She continued to watch as Richard held his mother and turned his head to look out the window of the waiting room.

~~~

The next few months were difficult for the Porters. Mrs. Porter couldn't bring herself to stay in her house alone now that the General was gone. She asked to come to stay with Richard and Shelby until she could get over the grief. Shelby spent a lot of time
~~~

with her consoling her. She often thought about the day in the ER when Mrs. Porter told Richard she was sorry for not standing up for him. Those words haunted her and she had wanted to talk to Richard about that day.

Richard, on the other hand, seemed a bit distant these last few months since the General died and had not wanted to talk much. He had cases he was putting together and found himself staying late most nights of the week preparing for court. Shelby was fine with that and she knew Mrs. Porter needed her right now anyway.

Shelby felt like Richard had not quite accepted the death of his dad. She had asked him on several occasions if he was okay and he would just mumble something at her. She worried about him and hoped it would pass soon. When he did come home early on a rare occasion, she noticed him being short with her, which she couldn't understand. He had never been like that to her before, so she figured it was his way of grieving.

"Shelby, dear, I've been here now for a few months and I love you both, but I think it's time for me to head back to Columbus," Mrs. Porter announced one day. "My sister, Anne, is coming in from California and she said she would stay with me as long as I needed her to," she said. "So, I'll be going home on Saturday."

Shelby could tell she was ready to be on her own again. "Mrs. Porter, if you think that's best and you're going to be okay," she said as she smiled at her.

Over the next month, Richard hardly ever got home from work before midnight and it was starting to wear on Shelby. She felt neglected and alone and just wanted to be with her husband.

"Hey, baby, do you think you can come home early this evening?" she asked him as she poured him a cup of coffee.

"I don't know, Shelby. I'll have to see what I can do," he said as he wrinkled up the paper and tossed it on the table. Shelby noticed he seemed a bit annoyed at her.

"Well, if you did... we could try having that baby we talked about," she said a bit cheerily. She winked at him in a teasing way.

"Shelby, you are a mess. Let me see what I can do," he said with a grin on his face. She knew right then she got him good. Richard had not smiled since his dad had passed away and it worried her even more.

"I tell you what, bring home your work, and put it in your office and then when we're finished, I promise to let you go back to your business," she suggested.

"I don't know how I could refuse a deal like that," he said, with a more witty tone of voice.

"You know, we've been trying for over a year now and I'm still not pregnant," she said waiting for a response. She was afraid of what he was going to say next, but she needed to know what he was thinking.

"Shelby, now you remember what I said about obsessing over this," he reminded her.

'I know, I promised, but I was just wondering if maybe something was going on with me, so I've made an appointment with Dr. Shields, my gynecologist, just to make sure everything is working correctly," she said shyly, not wanting to stir things up. "I hope that's okay with you?"

"I think that's all crazy, but if it makes you happy, then go for it," Richard said annoyed. She could tell he was getting impatient. "I don't understand why you women have to torment yourselves over having a baby. Like I've said before, if it happens, it happens," he said, seemingly angry.

"My appointment is in the morning. Dr. Shields said they could run a few tests and know if anything was wrong in just a couple of days," she told him.

"Well, don't get any ideas about me going to get checked out," he said as he snatched his coffee cup up and placed it in the sink. He turned and kissed her on the forehead. "I'll see you this evening," he said as he walked out of the kitchen.

Shelby sat alone at the table while she finished her coffee. He could be so irritating at times and he didn't have to act this way she thought after he left.

Shelby was hoping he would keep his promise and come home early. She smiled at the thought that tonight might just the beginning of a new life. She sure hoped so...

A few days later, Shelby got a phone call that made her feel a bit better.

"This is Dr. Shields. I just wanted to let you know all of your tests have come back and everything looks good."

"What a relief," she said. "Then, why can't I get pregnant?"

"Sometimes, when you really want to have a baby, you can stress too much over it if it doesn't happen right away. It inhibits nature from taking its course. You just need to relax and not get too tense about the process. But, if you need anything else, you can call me."

"Thank you, Dr. Shields," she said as she hung up the phone.

Shelby was thrilled and he was probably right, she had been restless, but only because she wanted a baby so bad. She wasn't going to worry about it anymore. When God wanted to bless her with a baby, then it would happen in his time.

Chapter Twenty-One

Jack sat on the park bench enjoying the Sunday afternoon weather in late May while Trevor kicked the soccer ball around the playground. Jack had read an article about how soccer was the newest fad in the sports arena and he wanted Trevor to learn how to play. Even though Valley had not warmed up to the idea of offering soccer yet, he knew if Trevor started now, when they did include it, he would be ready.

It had not been easy for Jack over the last five years having to raise his son literally by himself because of Denise's difficulties. She had been through three rehabilitation efforts and her weekly visits to the psychologist had put a strain on their relationship. Jack still prayed daily for her recovery. It was like living in their own world, just he and Trevor. Denise oftentimes segregated herself from the outside world, which left Jack with the entire household, child rearing, and financial responsibilities.

Jack saw Trevor running toward him as he kicked the ball in his direction. "Daddy, come play with me," Trevor laughed. Jack could see the smile on his face as he got closer.

He got up from the bench and raced out to kick the ball away from Trevor. He could hear the giggles coming from his boy and it thrilled him to pieces. Jack was madly in love with his little fella.

"Hey Trevor, try to get the ball from me now," Jack called back at him. He kicked the ball in Trevor's direction. Trevor ran for it and stole the ball from him. Squeals of delight came out of his mouth. Jack grabbed him up into his arms and swung him around in circles and then they tumbled to the ground and burst into laughter. Jack glanced down at his son lying on his back in the grass and Trevor's eyes met his.

"Son, you make me the happiest daddy in the whole wide world, you know that?" Jack said, with a big smile on his face.

"Daddy, I love you and you make me happy, too," Trevor said. Jack tickled him and blew on his tummy making pooting sounds, which set off Trevor's high pitched laughter.

"Stop it, Daddy," he shouted, laughing fiercely. Trevor tried to pull away from Jack's grip, but he held on to him tightly as they wrestled and rolled around in the grass.

The hours flew by after a playful afternoon at the park.

"Come on, buddy, let's get on to the house. It's getting late and we need to check on Mom and get you fed and bathed before bedtime," Jack explained in a tender voice.

"Oh man, I'm not ready," Trevor said intensely as he picked up the ball and took Jack by the hand holding his head down to show his displeasure at having to leave.

"It's okay. We'll come back tomorrow afternoon if the weather is good... after I get off work. How about that, does that work for you?" Jack asked. "Maybe we can get Mommy to come with us the next time," he added.

"Yeah, if she feels like it. Daddy, why doesn't Mommy like me?" Trevor asked disappointedly with his head still down.

Jack gasped at Trevor's words. He was speechless and it felt like a wrecking ball had struck him in the chest and had literally taken his breath away. *Oh no, he can't think that way,* Jack thought in horror.

"Son, Mommy loves you. Why would you say that?" Jack asked even though he already knew the answer.

"Because, Daddy. She's never happy and doesn't do anything with us. She's always asleep. You do everything. It's always just you and me," Trevor responded.

"I know it's hard for you to understand right now, but Mommy is sick. She goes to the doctor every week. He's trying to help her get well." Jack choked on his words as he tried desperately to cover and make excuses for Denise's behavior.

"Yeah, but when is she going to get better?" he asked, dropping his shoulders and looking up at Jack with sadness in his eyes as they walked to the car.

"Real soon, we hope, son," Jack said sympathetically.

Silence filled the car on the drive home. Jack was nauseated from hearing Trevor's question as he played their conversation over and over in his mind. His son's struggle and confusion were painful and sickening.

How was he going to get Trevor through this? How was he going to get Denise to see what was happening and how she was affecting him? How was he going to get through it himself? Trevor was his whole world and deserved so much more than a mother who ignored him. He was heartbroken.

Later, after dinner, Jack shooed his son to his room. “Trevor, it’s bedtime. Are you ready? Come on and I’ll tuck you in,” Jack said in a persuasive voice.

“Aww... Daddy, do I have to?”

“Yep, now go give Mommy a hug and goodnight kiss and tell her you love her,” Jack said firmly. He watched Trevor dance over to Denise, who was sitting in the recliner watching TV. He hugged and kissed her and Jack was relieved to see Denise returned his “I love you.” However, he wasn’t convinced; her words felt empty, at least, to him. Trevor came bouncing across the room and grabbed Jack by the hand and off to his room they went. He jumped into his bed, grabbed the sheet, and pulled it up over his body. Jack sat down beside him and quietly watched Trevor’s every move.

“Trevor, you are my heart and soul, and you mean everything in the world to me. I love you more than life itself. You know how much that is?” Jack asked as he looked down at him.

“No, Daddy how much?”

“A lot more than this,” he said with both his arms stretched out to his side as far as he could get them. “Like, to the moon and back,” Jack said as he pointed to the window where the moon shone through the glass. He watched as Trevor turned and peered into the sky.

“That’s a long way, Daddy,” he said in a soft whisper.

“Yes, it is, Trevor, and don’t ever forget it. You promise?”

“I promise, and I love you to the moon and back, too,” he replied with a sweet softness to his voice.

Jack bent over, kissed him on the forehead, and gave him a big hug before he stood and walked to the door. He reached up and flipped the light switch off. The room was dark except for the turtle night-light glowing against the wall.

He walked into the living room and said his goodnight to Denise as she sat staring at the TV. He leaned down and kissed her on the head.

“You coming to bed?” he asked.

“Maybe in a while,” she responded.

Jack felt anger building up. “Look, Denise, we need to talk,” he said firmly.

“About what?” she asked and turned away from the TV to look him in the eyes.

Jack forcefully blew out a deep breath and explained, "Trevor doesn't think you love him."

"What? That's crazy! He knows I love him," she snapped.

"No, you don't understand. He really doesn't believe you love him. He told me so this afternoon," Jack said annoyed. "He said it's because you never do anything with us."

"Oh, that's just kid talk," she said brushing it off.

"Stop it," Jack said in a threatening way. "Look, I know you're having a hard time, but Denise, you got to get out of this funk you're in. I can only do so much. He needs a real mother..."

"Oh, like maybe Shelby?" she interrupted in a forceful tone.

Jack was shocked at her response. He swung around in disbelief of what he had just heard. "You have no right to say such a thing. Shelby has been out of my life for years now, thanks to you," he said sharply and then suddenly he realized what he had said and his words trailed off. He cupped his mouth ashamed of what he had just blurted out. "I'm so sorry, Denise. I didn't mean that," he said apologetically. He could see her eyes filled with hatred as she glared across the room at him. He wondered how she could really hate Shelby that much.

"Jack, you just need to be honest with yourself and me. Let's face it. You will never have Shelby out of your life. Everyone thinks I'm fragile and they are always sidestepping me for fear I might go off the deep end again. The thing is, I'm not as sick as everyone thinks I am. I hear what's said and I know you love me because of Trevor. You will never love me like you love Shelby and you need to admit it," she said frowning at him.

Jack was stunned to hear her words. She was different, unlike her usual self. She spoke more like the Denise he used to know. He was speechless and didn't know how to respond. Was she right?

"Denise, I will admit Shelby was my first love. You and I both know that. She's happily married to someone else now and that is all behind us," he said trying to persuade her. "Why can't you just let it go?"

"Why can't you just admit it?" she hollered out at him. "You will never convince me you don't love her." He watched her as she stood from the recliner and slammed the pillow down on the floor. "I'm not the one with the problems, Jack. You love Shelby and that's your issue," she snapped at him as she stomped out of the room. She left him sitting speechless on the sofa.

He couldn't believe in his wildest imagination that she was blaming him for all of her problems. Where did she get these ideas? He knew in his heart that he had tried everything to make her happy. Now she was blaming him?

~~~

The alarm blared across the room and shook Jack from a deep sleep. He reached over and turned it off. He rolled over to see Denise with her back to him.

It had been a long night and he had tossed and turned most of it after the incident with her. The last time he recalled looking at the clock it was three thirty a.m. He was tired and five a.m. came too early.

In no time at all Jack was showered and shaved. Trevor was dressed and fed, and they were in the car on their way to drop him off at daycare. This had been their morning routine for the last three years. Today was no different. Trevor was a bit fussy getting ready and somewhat whiny. Jack hoped he had not heard the commotion from the night before, but his optimism was demolished when Trevor turned to Jack as they drove away from the house.

"Daddy, who is Shelby?" he asked with a puzzled look in his eyes. Jack's heart sank to his stomach. "I heard Mommy say you love Shelby."

Jack cleared his throat as he searched for the right words. "Ahem, there was a girl I used to like when I was about ten years old and I really liked her a lot when we were in school. Her name was Shelby. Then, I met your mommy when she moved here to live with Maw Maw.

"Maw Maw Hollis?" Trevor asked.

"Yep, that's right," Jack, said as he nodded at him. "Anyway, your mommy and I got married right after high school and we had you. Shelby went off to college and married someone else," he said as he tried to keep the conversation light. "Mommy and I had you and you stole our hearts and we fell madly in love with you," Jack said lightly, hoping this would be the end of it.

However, Trevor's curiosity about the lady named Shelby was sticking with him. Jack was in a pickle and he knew it. "Daddy, do you think Shelby would love me?" he asked.

Another knife pierced Jack's heart. *Oh my God, how do such huge questions come from such a tiny brain?*
~~~

"Son, why do you ask that? You don't know Shelby," he asked a bit puzzled.

"Okay, so Dad, it goes like this. If you love Shelby and she loves me then she would have to love you too, right?" he asked excitedly with his hands waving in the air as if he was trying to get Jack to understand.

"It's not that simple, son," Jack struggled for an answer to his outrageous and inquisitive mood all of a sudden. "What are you trying to say, Trevor?" Jack asked hesitantly.

"You see if you love Shelby... and I love Shelby... and she loves us, then maybe we could be a family. Mommy is always so sad and I don't think she likes you or me. 'Cause you know how she is. Grammy always says you should love your family. So, since we don't love each other, maybe we could have a different family and that way we could be happy," he said decisively.

His heart ached as he heard Trevor's reasoning. It was horrifying to hear such painful words coming out of the mouth of a five-year-old child. God knows, even as young as they are kid's sense when something is not right.

Jack was once again dumbfounded as they pulled into the church parking lot. "Well, buddy, you got me. I don't know what to say," Jack said admittedly.

Trevor smiled and said, "You don't have to say anything, Daddy. Just think about it okay?"

Jack watched him open the car door and leap out. "Wait, Trevor, would that make you happy?" he asked.

"Yep, I just want us to be happy," Trevor, said.

"I love you, Trevor, with all my heart," Jack said as he gently touched his son's chest with his fist.

Before slamming the door, Trevor shouted back, "I love you, too, Daddy... with all my heart."

Jack saw him motioning to his chest with his fist and then a big smile appeared on his face. It melted his heart. Jack blew him a kiss and sat quietly as he watched his little man, the one who understood more about happiness and life than he himself did. Trevor disappeared into the building.

"My heart and soul..." Jack whispered.

Chapter Twenty-Two

Jack pulled into the parking lot at the mill. He couldn't avoid Denise and Trevor's words as they played out in his mind. Was Denise right? Was he still madly in love with Shelby? And what about what Trevor said? Was it over the edge to even imagine the possibility of him, Shelby, and Trevor being a family? He wondered...

The rest of the morning sped by and it was time for lunch. Jack joined everyone else at the picnic tables out back by the river. He listened as they chatted about a lot of different things, but mostly he noticed their laughter. His mind began to wander; Trevor's words weighed heavy on his heart and he knew it was time to do something to make things better for them. He had actually known this for a while now, but had denied it. The conversation with his son finally made him realize it was time. Trevor was right that they all needed to be happy.

The whistle blew signaling lunch was over, and Jack joined the crowd as they headed back to the spinning room. There was a lot on his mind and decisions he knew he had to make.

It was late afternoon and Jack had been working on one of the spinners most of the day. He crawled up under the machine to tighten one of the gears when he heard heavy footsteps approaching. At first, he didn't pay much attention, and then, he heard the voice of a man.

"Jack?" the deep voice asked.

Jack twisted around from underneath the spinner, looked up, and saw one of the sheriff's deputies staring down at him.

"Yeah?" Jack said hesitantly.

"I need to talk to you," he said.

Jack crawled out from under the spinner wiping his hands on a towel as he stood up. "What's going on?" Jack asked the deputy. He had seen this gentleman a couple of times with his dad, but he really didn't know him. Jack sensed something wasn't right. His mind raced quickly when he saw the deputy's face.

"Is something wrong? Is my dad—" Jack asked as he watched the deputy's eyes.

"Look, Jack. There's been an accident and I need you to come with me to the hospital," said the deputy.

"Accident? Who?" Jack quickly asked. "Is it my dad? Is he okay?"

The deputy shifted his weight between his feet. "Your dad's fine."

Jack's mind raced again wondering who, but he never expected the words that came next.

"It's your son, Trevor. Your dad is with him at the hospital and they sent me here to pick you up," he said delicately.

"Oh, my God! Is he all right? What happened?" Jack hollered as he cupped his mouth with his hand. He could hear everyone's sighs in the background. "Let's go."

Jack heard the deputy's words as he exhaled shakily as if trying to keep from panicking. Thoughts of Trevor raced through his mind. He fell from a tree and broke his arm... or he scraped his knee jumping off the swing at daycare... or tripped or... his mind clouded with hundreds of thoughts. Whatever it was, he would be there shortly and he could hold Trevor in his arms and make everything all better.

It was no time when they were in the squad car with the lights and siren blaring. Once again, Jack asked, "Is Trevor okay? What happened?"

"I'm not sure, Jack. I was on a call about ten miles up Highway 29 when they called me on the radio and said there had been an accident and for me to pick you up and get you to the hospital as quick as I could. Man, that's all I know," said the deputy.

Jack began to pray silently. *"Please God, whatever it is, please let Trevor be okay. Please?"*

Within minutes, they were racing through the doors of the Emergency Room at Lanier Memorial Hospital. The place was crawling with police officers. Jack thought it was odd, but then again it was Sheriff Emerson's grandson who was hurt.

"Dad," Jack yelled across the room as he rushed over to his parents sitting in the corner.

"What's wrong? What has happened to Trevor?" Jack asked.

"Jack, you need to sit down, son," Sheriff Emerson said as he pointed to the chair next to his mother. Sobbing uncontrollably, she reached for Jack's hand.

"Please tell me what happened, please Dad... tell me Trevor's okay?" Jack pleaded.

"We don't know anything about his condition right this minute. We're waiting to hear. But, Jack," his dad said as his voice began to crack. "Trevor was hit by a car," Sheriff Emerson said trying to be strong.

"Noooo!" Jack's voice echoed throughout the room. He fell to the chair, numb from the news. "He's going to be all right, isn't he?" he asked pleading up at his father. Jack watched his dad's expression and knew it was bad. "No. He's going to be fine. I know it," Jack said forcefully. "He has to be. Tell me what happened."

"We don't know exactly, but from what the witnesses said. Trevor was playing in the yard with his soccer ball and it rolled out into the highway. He ran after it and was hit by a car."

A gunshot to his chest wouldn't have hurt this badly. "Where was Denise?" Jack asked, nodding his head.

"From what I can tell, she was in the house. The deputies went to the door and knocked several times before she answered. They said she looked like she had been asleep. They asked her where Trevor was and she didn't know. They also said she was lethargic because of the way she responded to their questions."

Instinctively, Jack's fists balled at his side. "So, she was out of it as usual," he bellowed loudly. "Denise was asleep while Trevor was playing in the yard with no supervision. Oh, my God, how could she do this?" he asked angrily. Then, he stood up and demanded, "Where is she now?"

"She's in the waiting room around the corner," his dad said as he waved his hand in the direction of the area.

Jack scrambled over and threw open the door of the small room. He could see Denise sitting emotionless in a daze swaying from side to side. She had been crying because her eyes were bloodshot, but he wasn't so sure it was from the tears.

"What the hell have you done, Denise?" Jack shouted out in a rage. "What happened to Trevor?" He reached down, grabbed her shoulders, and shook her, trying to get her attention. She just sat unresponsively.

Jack felt his dad's hand on his shoulder. "Come on out and leave her alone, son," Sheriff Emerson said. His dad pulled him away and he fought back.

"No, Dad. This is all her fault. Trevor is hurt and she's to blame," Jack snapped. Sheriff Emerson embraced him tightly in his arms as Jack tried to pull away. His dad's grip was firm. Finally, Jack gave in and left the room.

It felt like hours had passed when the nurse came to ask them to come back and have a seat in the room all to themselves. She told them the doctor would be in shortly and to let her know if they needed anything.

"Is Trevor okay?" Jack asked with fear in his eyes.

"Dr. Worthington is with him and he'll be in to let you know something," the nurse said as she left the room.

Jack paced the floor as his parents sat quietly in the corner. He noticed his dad had left a few times returning without saying a word.

Another hour passed and Jack sat silently praying for Trevor. The door opened and a tall young man entered the room.

"Mr. Emerson," he asked as he looked around the room. Jack sprang from the chair and ran over to the doctor.

"Yes, how's Trevor? Is he okay? Tell me he's going to be fine, right?" Jack said as he nodded his head yes and watched the doctor's eyes waiting for a response.

"Mr. Emerson, Trevor's injuries were extensive. He had severe trauma to the head along with some internal bleeding. Please know that we did everything we could to save him, but he just couldn't hold on. I'm so sorry," the doctor said as he shook his head.

"No, please tell me he's okay, please," Jack, pleaded as he fell to the floor on his knees with his arms stretched out and begged the doctor.

"Again, I'm sorry," the doctor said. "It's never easy. Especially when it's a child."

"Oh, God no! Please don't take him from me! Please, he's all I have left, Lord," Jack cried out with his arms reaching into the air as he begged.

Jack clenched his chest as if he were having a heart attack. He was exploding on the inside. "It can't be true... no... no... no..." he yelped out fiercely as his body trembled. He shook his head and his eyes widened in horror. "Trevor is not gone. I won't believe my son is gone..." he kept repeating over and over.

Sheriff Emerson knelt down next to him as Jack rocked crying uncontrollably. Jack looked up into his father's eyes. "Dad, please tell me this is just a nightmare. Trevor can't leave me, Dad," he shouted out in horror. His bloodcurdling cries echoed throughout the waiting room as everyone quietly witnessed the heart-wrenching incident.

Jack felt like the gates of hell had opened and had begun to suck him in, devouring his body and soul as he struggled to pull himself out of the darkness.

Moments later, he hung his head in his hands and wept. How could this happen to his precious Trevor? What was he going to do without him?

"No!" Jack cried out. "Trevor! I love you son! Please don't leave me!"

~~~

Shelby had just walked in the door from playing tennis at the country club when the phone rang.

"Hey, Mom. How are you?" Shelby asked, surprised to hear from her.

"Shelby, you need to sit down. Something bad has happened," Frances said hesitantly.

Panic kicked in and she asked, "Mom, is Dad okay?"

"Yes, dear, he's fine. It's not him. I wasn't sure if I should call or not, but I knew you would want to know."

Trembling, Shelby listened carefully. "What is it, Mom?"

"Jack's son, Trevor, died today in an accident. He was hit by a car outside of his house," she said. Shelby could hear the crackling of her mother's voice. "Oh, Mom, no," Shelby cried out. Her knees weakened as she sank into the chair next to the kitchen table with her hand over her pounding heart. She felt her lungs gasping for air as she tried to catch her breath. She couldn't believe what she had just heard.

"Oh, Shelby, my heart is broken and I feel so sad for Jack. You know he's been through so much and now this. Sweetie, I just don't know what he is going to do without Trevor," Frances said choking on her words.

"Mom, I have to go," she said shocked over the news and trying to gather her thoughts. She hung up the phone and sat quietly at the kitchen table. Tears filled her eyes and flowed down her cheeks. She was numb. Why did this have to happen?

"Jack, I'm so sorry," Shelby whispered.

The phone rang again and startled her out of her thoughts. "Hey, baby," Richard, said when she answered the phone.

"Hey, honey," Shelby, replied, trying to disguise her shaky voice.
~~~

"I'm sorry, but it looks like I'm going to have to stay late every night this week. They just handed me a case that's going to trial on Monday and someone dropped the ball," Richard explained. "I know you wanted to go out with the gang on Thursday night, but it doesn't look like I'm going to get to. I'm sorry," he said.

Shelby tried to quickly gain her composure from the terrible news. "It's okay, honey, I understand. It's no big deal and we can do it some other time anyway," she responded. Shelby's thoughts immediately rushed to Jack. Maybe she should go home.

"You know what? It's been a couple of months since I've been to Mom and Dad's. If it's good with you, I think I'll go to Valley for a few days," Shelby struggled with her words trying to smooth over her emotions.

"You know what? I think that is a great idea. Go down and have a few days of rest and relaxation and tell your parents I send my love," Richard said supportively. She wasn't sure she should say anything to Richard just yet about Trevor.

"I think I'll throw some clothes in a bag and head down this afternoon. You going to be okay while I'm gone?" Shelby asked.

Richard laughed. "I'm a big boy and I will be just fine. You have a good time and I'll see you when you get back."

She wasn't sure a "good time" was possible, but she had to go where she knew she had to be. Thank heavens Richard was so supportive of her. "Love you," she said and hung up.

It was only a few short hours later when Shelby pulled into her parents' driveway. Her mother greeted her at the kitchen door. She hugged Shelby as they stood in the doorway.

"Mom, I had to come," Shelby admitted sadly.

"I know you did," Frances replied.

"Do you think it was terrible of me to leave Richard and come?" Shelby asked.

"No, dear, you love Richard and he's your husband. Jack was, is, and will always be your friend and when our friends and family hurt, so do we. It's good that you came. Are you going to the funeral?" Frances asked.

"I don't know yet, I'm not sure if can do it," Shelby told her. "I just keep thinking about the day we buried Gina. You know the General just passed away, and now Trevor. It's different when a child dies, Mom," she said.

"I know. Just think about it," Frances whispered. "The funeral isn't until Friday, so give yourself a couple of days to decide. Your dad and I feel like we need to be there, so we are going and you can sit with us if you want," Frances told her.

"We'll see," Shelby said as she brushed a hair away from her face.

~~~

The next few days were the darkest of Jack's life. He sat and watched the news reports blasted all over national television. The early investigation found that a congressman from Atlanta had struck Trevor. It appeared there might have been alcohol involved in the accident, one news station reported. Jack stood up, walked over, and turned the television off. He had heard enough of it now. He went to the window and stared at the field across from his parent's home.

In a few short hours, he would be burying Trevor. He would have to say goodbye to the only thing that mattered in his life. He didn't know how he was going to be able to do it. Jack had not seen Denise since that day in the emergency room. It made him sick to his stomach to even think about her. He knew in his heart it was her fault. He couldn't understand why God had taken Trevor from him. What had he done to deserve all the heartbreak?

There was a knock at the door. It was his dad.

"Are you ready to go to the church, son?"

"Not really," Jack said sarcastically.

"Maw Hollis called. She said the doctors have Denise sedated and they don't think it would be good for her to go to the funeral," his dad said sadly. "They're worried she might be suicidal."

"I don't care. I don't want her there, not anywhere around Trevor," Jack snapped back.

"Son, try not to be bitter. I'm sure she's hurting, too."

"Not nearly as much as I'm hurting, I can promise you of that. Besides, she's got the pills to ease her pain. I don't have anything," Jack said angrily.

Jack cast a sideways glance at his dad standing in the door of the bedroom. "Dad, that woman has ruined my life. First, she took Shelby from me and now Trevor, the only two things in my life that I ever adored and loved with all my heart and Denise has destroyed them both. I don't ever want to see her again. She can rot in hell for all I care," Jack spurted out.

"I understand," Sheriff Emerson said as he motioned for Jack to follow. "Let's go do what we have to do."
~~~

~~~

The church was filled to capacity as Jack glanced around the sanctuary. All these people had come to give their condolences and he appreciated each and every one of their kindnesses.

The ceremony was short and sweet and he was afraid he wouldn't make it through without breaking down emotionally. The pianist played "*Amazing Grace*" tenderly as everyone filed out of the church.

Jack looked around, hoping to see the one person who could have brightened this otherwise devastating tragedy, but she wasn't there. Did she even know? Did she even care?

He held back the tears as they raised the diminutive casket and rolled it down the aisle to the hearse. He reached out and touched the coffin, his friends stopped long enough for Jack to have a few seconds with Trevor.

Jack closed his eyes as he mumbled, "Trevor, she would have loved you with all of her heart, but most importantly, she would have wanted me to tell you, how much she loves you," he said thinking about Trevor's last words...

~~~

Shelby stood at a distance watching as everyone crowded around the tent covering the family in the cemetery. She wept and her body trembled from the sight of Jack's broken heart. It was unbearable. She caught herself just short of a panic attack, trying desperately to hold back her emotions.

She anguished now over never having the opportunity to have met Trevor. "Why had I not met him?" she cried. She had thought about Trevor so many times, fantasizing that he had been her and Jack's son. She had never told anyone how she felt and now it was like burying her own child.

Jack sat on the front row at the gravesite as they lowered Trevor into the ground. He couldn't hold back any longer.

"Trevor, I love you," Jack bellowed out.

There was silence in the crowd for several minutes. He sat with his head bowed and kept thinking, he didn't know what to do... he was lost... heartbroken and terrified of how he was going to make it. First, it was Shelby and now Trevor, he wasn't sure he could live without them anymore.

After he had gathered his thoughts and wiped his tears, Jack stood up and looked over the crowd of people now chatting among themselves. He was numb and indifferent now, and he just wanted to get away. It was all too much for him.

He caught a glimpse of a woman off in the distance standing all alone near a headstone. She was dressed in black, wearing dark sunglasses, and appeared to be wrenched in agony. She seemed faintly familiar to him, but he was so caught up in his own grief that he turned away.

When suddenly... he looked back.

He noticed that she saw him and then, she began moving away. His heart sang out in hopes that it was *...her*

Shelby had come to him in his darkest hour.

He rushed toward her making his way through the crowd. His heart called out to hers, *please don't go.*

He raced down the hill of the cemetery toward her when she hurried into her car and sped away. Jack ran to catch her, but there was only dust and gravel from the drive left and he couldn't make out who she was.

He knew in his heart that it was Shelby. It had to be.

A rush of adrenaline raced through his bloodstream and his heart filled with excitement. She came. There was no doubt in his mind it was her and he could feel her love even from a distance... as he stood watching the car disappear.

He returned to the graveside and thanked everyone for coming as the crowd began to dissipate.

He addressed his parents, "I need some time to myself. Excuse me, please."

All he could think about was Shelby. She had come to him and he needed to see her. He wanted her to know how Trevor felt. Knowing his Tootie, she would be ecstatic once she found out what Trevor had said just hours before he died.

Maybe if she knew, things could be different and he was not about to let her get away. Not now. He needed her more than ever and he would do whatever it took to see her.

And he knew where to find her...

To be continued...

About the Author

Recently retired, traveling, and enjoying life, Katherine Kobey hung up her career after over thirty years in the health care industry as a corporate executive to pursue her lifelong love of the literary arts.

She is an avid reader and writer of short stories and poems. Now, as a first-time novelist, she contributes her achievement to the many women who have shared their personal experiences from the heart. The emotional transformation of their stories to words has been the inspiration for her literary work.

Katherine believes as music is to the ears, so is writing to the heart.

When she is not traveling, she spends her time in Birmingham, Alabama, with her family.

To learn more about Katherine Kobey, visit her online at:

Facebook: www.facebook.com/katherinekobey
Website: www.katherinekobey.com
Email: Katherine@katherinekobey.com

Preview of Part Two

After a breakfast of coffee and a muffin on Monday morning, Shelby sat down and opened her address book. She had to call all her sorority sisters and invite them to the honorary dinner. The firm had reserved the head table for Richard and her, along with eight seats for their special guests. Richard assured her he had plenty of friends who would be there and she could invite whomever she wanted to join them at their table.

"Hi Mary, it's Shelby."

"Hey, Shelby," Mary said in an eager voice. "I heard about Richard's news."

"Well, I can't talk but for a minute. Are you busy this Saturday?"

"Hmm... no, I don't think I have anything on the calendar. Why?" she asked.

"Richard's law firm is having a recognition dinner Saturday evening at the Ritz Carlton downtown Atlanta and we have a table for ten and I was hoping you and all the girls could come join us," she explained.

"Wow, heck yes I would love to come. What time?"

Shelby could hear the excitement in Mary's voice and she was thrilled.

"It's at seven p.m.," Shelby added.

"Great, I will be there," Mary, whooped with joy.

"Mary, thank you. I hope you know it means a lot to me to have my best friend there with me," she said.

"I wouldn't miss it for the world," Mary replied.

"Let me run, I have to call everyone else. I'll see you on Saturday then. Love you, Mary," she said meaningfully.

"Love you too, Shelby," Mary replied. Shelby heard the click on the other end as she hung the phone up.

The morning passed quickly. Shelby had five of her sisters committed to the dinner and was waiting for Rachel to return her call. She was hopeful they would all be there with her.

Shelby felt queasy as she stood up. "Ugh…" she whimpered and rubbed her stomach. Come to think about it, she hadn't felt good now for a few weeks. She sat back down for a few minutes as she tried to shake the sick feeling. She couldn't understand why she felt so bad. What would make her feel this way? She'd been so nauseated lately.

"Oh, my, God," she squealed as a thought popped into her mind. "Could it be? Could I really be pregnant?" she said out loud. She took in a deep breath. It would explain why she has been so tired and sick every day.

"I can't believe it. I'm pregnant," she whispered over and over. "Please, God, let me be pregnant," she pleaded with tears of joy filling her eyes. Shelby was so overcome with the thought of it that she had to find out quickly.

After lunch, she picked up the phone and called her Ob/Gyn, Dr. Shields' office.

"This is Shelby Porter. I think I might be pregnant and was wondering what I need to do to find out for sure," she asked giddily.

"Hold on and let me get Dr. Shields' nurse," the receptionist said.

Shelby waited anxiously for the nurse to answer. "This is Dr. Shields' nurse. So, Mrs. Porter, you think you're pregnant?"

"Oh, Lord, I sure hope so. We've been trying for over a year now. I was there a few months back to make sure everything was okay with me. Dr. Shields told me to stop obsessing so much over it and let it happen. I made the commitment not to worry about it and now I think it's happened. Just like he said it would," Shelby said as she rambled on.

"It's wonderful news, Mrs. Porter. Why don't you come by this afternoon and we can run a urinalysis on you and see what it shows? It usually takes about twenty-four hours and we will have the results," she explained.

"Great, I'll be by shortly," Shelby, said in anticipation of what this would mean.

Shelby hung up the phone and within the hour, she had stopped by Dr. Shields' office and left a specimen for them to test. She was beyond thrilled at the thought of a baby raced through her mind. Richard was going to be ecstatic, as well. How was she going to surprise him? One thing was certain; she knew she had to do something big when she told him.

Shelby spent most of the afternoon hoping and praying she was pregnant and making plans for sharing the big news.

"I know," she said talking to herself. "I'll announce it Saturday night at the dinner." After all, they had asked her to give a short speech and she'd work it in. This would be big and he would love it. She took in a deep breath. "I know I am... I have to be," she whispered.

The next morning, Shelby sat nervously awaiting the phone call from the doctor's office. She paced the floor all morning and she hadn't heard from her. "If they don't call soon, I'm going to call them," Shelby said impatiently. She had spent most of the night tossing and turning thinking about the baby. The phone rang out and Shelby's heart skipped a beat, as it scared her out of her thoughts. She darted across the room and grabbed the receiver off the wall.

"Hello," Shelby said eagerly.

"Mrs. Porter, this is Dr. Shields' office. I wanted to let you know you were right. You're pregnant!" she said cheerfully.

"Oh, my gosh," Shelby said as her voice began to crack. "Thank you,"

"We're going to make you an appointment and I'll give you a call back in a couple of days," the receptionist told her.

Shelby was speechless as she hung up the phone. She tilted her head down to see her flat stomach and she rubbed it in a circular motion. Tears of joy filled her eyes as they crept slowly down her cheeks. She couldn't believe it. She was going to have a baby.

57097266R00130

Made in the USA
Columbia, SC
05 May 2019